THORNTON BROTHERS

BOOK FOUR

Torn

SABRE ROSE

For more information about the author visit:
www.sabreroseauthor.com

ISBN: 171865541X
ISBN-13: 978-1718655416

1

TYLER

The whiskey wasn't doing its job. It was supposed to dull my mind, blur the memory that thudded through my head, but instead, it only served to make it more vivid.

Lauren kissed him.

His hands were twisted in her hair.

His mouth was on hers.

Her mouth was on his.

I had walked into the bar to find her after her mother had uttered those words. I didn't follow immediately. She said she needed to be alone.

Alone.

So I wasn't expecting to find her sitting across the bar from him, smiling, laughing, touching. I didn't expect to see her lean across and tenderly tuck his hair behind his ear.

At first I was confused. A little hurt, but mainly confused. But I was prepared to give her the benefit of the doubt. Then, as I walked towards them, he leaned forward, wrapped his arm around her waist and pulled her close, crushing those foul lips against hers.

She didn't pull away.

In the second it took me to reach them, rage flooded my veins. Rage that left Gabe with a black eye, split skin over his cheekbone and a fat lip. Rage that had words flying viciously from my mouth. Rage that left Lauren crying in the middle of the foyer.

Afterwards, I sat at the bar and drank, wanting to forget everything I had just seen. But it didn't work. With each sip, each swallow, each burn as it slid down my throat, the memory flashed through my mind. One drink, two, three, and still it was there as clear as the moment I witnessed it.

I should have known it would happen. It was what I deserved from the way I took her from him. I guess I was naïve to think she would be different with me. But still I wanted her. Still, part of me ached to run to her. But now was not the time. I didn't know what to say.

As I sat at the bar, swirling the contents of my next drink, staring at it as though it might hold the answers to a question I wasn't sure of, slurred singing drifted from the lobby. My watch told me it was midnight. I had no idea how long I'd been sitting there. Hours? Minutes? The voice in the lobby was low and drunk, and one that I recognised, although I don't think I'd ever heard Hamish Thornton sing before. My father wasn't one usually easily led to joviality. I guess we had that in common.

Pulling myself from the seat, I was surprised to find myself swaying. Although I didn't feel drunk, the effects of the alcohol must have been working in some ways more than others.

Dad was dancing to unheard music under the chandelier in the lobby. The same chandelier that Lauren had cried under only hours before.

"Tyler!" He smiled when he saw me. A drunken grin, to be sure, but still a grin. Another novelty for the usually sombre leader of Thornton Industries. "You and Gabe get your shit sorted out?" he asked loud enough for the girl at reception to scowl.

"You look like you should be in bed," I replied.

Dad twirled under the lights. "Can you feel it?" he asked.

It was a strange sight. Hamish Thornton, so tall, so severe, dancing with his arms held wide as though he was trying to catch the particles of light that dripped from above.

"Feel what?" I was in no mood to indulge him so my words were short and sharp.

"The freedom," he said. "The peace. The quiet. The aloneness."

I wasn't sure if he was talking about me or him. He hadn't been witness to the fight between Gabe and me, or the display between Lauren and me afterwards, but I certainly wasn't enjoying the aloneness. Especially not with the images that burned into my brain.

"Where's Billie?" I asked.

"Shhhh," Hamish hissed, holding his finger in front of his mouth. "I said I'd do it right, this time." He slumped to the floor, tugging at the knot of his tie. "I said I'd be there for the kid because I wasn't there for you boys."

Apparently drunk Hamish was confessional Hamish.

"Maybe that's why you all hate each other so much. Well, you and Gabe, anyway. Maybe it's not that bitch's fault, after all. You didn't get the attention you needed from your Dad so you've got to create it somewhere else." He gave up on undoing the knot of his tie and simply tugged it until there was enough space for him to pull it over his head and toss it away. "Anyway," he continued, "I told Billie we'd do it together." He took a deep breath and rolled his eyes. "To me, that meant coming home in time for dinner, maybe bathing the kid at night or reading it a story or something. I even thought I'd change the odd diaper or two. Do you know I never changed one single diaper with you boys? Not one. Not with you. Not with Jake." He listed us off using his fingers. "Not with Clark. Not with Gabe. But Billie has different ideas. To her, doing it together literally means doing everything together."

He struggled to pull himself off the floor, coming close to me and waving his finger in my face.

Apparently drunk Hamish was dramatic Hamish.

"Every time he wakes at night, she drags me in there with her to feed him. Every single time. We don't take turns. Nope. Every single fucking time. But it's not the baby that's getting to me. It's her." He stuck his finger in my chest. "I'm so sick of the sight of her. I just want some peace. I love the woman, I do, and she's a wildcat in the bedroom, but—"

Enough. "Please stop talking." The sound of his voice was irritating, but hearing about his marital woes with Billie was too much. Frankly put, I didn't give a fuck. I had my own shit to deal with.

"I'm just sharing my life with my son. Just because I'm putting in the hard yards with this kid, doesn't make me any less proud of you, Tyler. You're the rock of this family. You hold it together. The hard worker. The dutiful son." Hamish paused. "Apart from when you are kicking the shit out of your brother. You really shouldn't do that, you know." Hamish swayed on his feet, the pallor of his skin quickly fading. "I need fresh air," he said, swallowing. "I need to clear my head."

He stumbled towards the entrance and staggered outside. It occurred to me that I should follow, make sure he was okay, but he was a grown man. I wasn't my father's keeper.

Turning back to the bar, I sat in the same seat and signalled to the bartender to bring over the bottle of whiskey. Clearly it wasn't working because I simply had not consumed enough. And there was a solution to that problem.

But the universe conspired against me.

"Tyler, we need to talk."

"Fuck off," I growled over my drink, not looking behind me. I knew that if I turned and saw his face, my fist would end up pressed against it.

"It wasn't her," he said.

"Fuck off," I repeated. "If you care for your physical wellbeing, I would advise turning and walking out of here."

I wanted to hurt him. I wanted him to be in as much pain as I was, and because I couldn't cause that sort of emotional pain, I was willing to substitute it with physical.

Gabe's hand dug into my shoulder. The same swell of rage from earlier came rushing through me but I swallowed it back, hissing at him through my teeth. "I'm warning you, Gable. Get your fucking hand off me."

"You don't deserve her, you know. It felt good to kiss her again. Right." He leaned close enough so I could feel his breath on my neck. "Familiar," he whispered.

That was it. I was going to knock his fucking block off. But before I had the chance, the sound of shattering glass blasted through from the lobby. Gabe and I locked eyes briefly, confusion and surprise passing between us before we both sprinted towards the noise.

There was a car under the chandelier. The glass walls of the entrance to the casino were shattered, and a dazed and confused Hamish opened the door of the car, looking as surprised as the rest of us to find himself in the middle of the lobby. A trickle of blood ran down his forehead and dripped over his eyelashes. He reached up and touched it gingerly.

Gabe ran over, taking Dad's hand away from the wound and peering into his eyes. "Are you okay?"

Hamish looked around the foyer, up at the chandelier, over at the elevator doors and then eventually at me. "What happened?" he asked.

When the police arrived, he swung his arms violently, telling the 'pigs' to get their dirty hands off him. In the end, the only way to restrain him was with handcuffs.

Apparently drunk Hamish was aggressive Hamish.

The police led him away, curse words falling out of his mouth quicker than I thought his drunken state was capable of, and cameras flashing as the media invited to the casino opening gathered to get the scoop on the antics of the head of Thornton Industries.

After sending someone to find Billie and calling the family lawyer, I found my seat at the bar again and resumed drinking. I didn't have the headspace to deal with this. Thoughts of Lauren consumed everything.

Thinking felt like wading through sand. Thoughts were there. Memories were there. But they were dimly lit at the back of my mind and I struggled to bring them to the fore.

* * *

Trying to sit up, I slumped back against the pillow when my head pounded with pain. Stupid whiskey. I drank too much last night. The pounding in my head and the foul taste in my mouth were testament to that. Rolling over, I reached for Lauren only to find her side of the bed empty.

Ignoring the parts of my body that were screaming for me to stay still, I attempted pulling myself up to a sitting position again.

The lights were on. The curtains framing the windows were open. I was fully dressed and lying on top of the bed, rather than in it.

It took a while for the fog to clear and my brain to start working at its usual speed, and when it did the memories of the night before came flooding back with a vengeance. Dad being marched in handcuffs to the waiting patrol car. Flying fists and drops of blood. Gabe's mouth on Lauren's. Her tears as I yelled at her in front of the crowd of people.

Fumbling through my pockets, I pulled my cell phone out, checking the screen for notifications. There were none from Lauren. No missed calls. No texts pleading for forgiveness. For all I knew she could be with him right now. Lying in his arms. The image of his hands roaming over her skin pierced my head. I needed to stop those thoughts before they drove me straight back to the bar.

I called Sadie. "What room are you in?"

"Tyler?" her voice was soaked in confusion. "What time is it?"

"What room?"

"602, grumpy arse."

I hung up and strode to her room, purposely trying to think of anything and everything that didn't remind me of Lauren. Sadie answered after the third knock, bleary-eyed and dressed only in her underwear. "What's so urgent that you had to wake me at 7am on a Sunday morning?" she asked, rubbing the sleep from her eyes.

A wave of nausea washed over me and I pushed past her and ran into the bathroom in time to empty the contents of my stomach into the toilet bowl. Sadie stood behind me, arms crossed and frowning.

"Regretting those drinks last night, huh?" she said.

Wiping my mouth, I sat back against the bathroom wall and looked up at her. "Where is she?" I couldn't help it. Tears welled in my eyes and I cursed them under my breath.

Empathy softening her stance, Sadie collapsed to the floor beside me and I rested my head on her shoulder. "Did you two not work things out last night?"

I rolled my head off her shoulder and leaned against the bathroom tiles. "What's there to sort out? She kissed Gabe."

"You don't really believe that do you?"

"I saw it, Sades. It's a little hard to deny it happened."

"But you believe she kissed him back? You believe she wanted it?"

"It sure didn't look like she was complaining."

Taking me by surprise, Sadie grabbed my face between her hands and pushed her lips against mine, kissing me firmly and aggressively, before pulling away and looking at me, eyebrows raised, my face still squished between her hands.

"What the fuck did you do that for?"

She shrugged and grinned wickedly. "You didn't appear to be complaining."

"I also didn't encourage it."

"Nor did you pull away," Sadie replied, letting my face go and wiping the back of her hand across her mouth. "That was gross. Your breath smells of vomit."

"That's stupid. It's different."

"Different how?"

"How? It was Gabe."

"So if she had 'kissed'," she put air quotes around the word, "someone other than Gabe, you'd be fine?"

"That's not the point and you know it. I stole her from Gabe. There was always the chance she'd change her mind."

Sadie pulled herself up from the floor and stood staring down at me, hands on hips and scowling. "You're being stupid. Lauren loves you and you know it.

"Thanks for your support," I mumbled, reaching across to flush the toilet bowl and getting to my feet. Another wave of nausea washed over me, but I pushed it aside.

"You should find her and apologise."

"What for?"

"For not giving her the chance to explain. For yelling and embarrassing her in front of all those people. For not believing her."

"Cheers for the advice. I'll think about it," I replied sulkily.

* * *

Dad was released after spending the night sobering up in a cell. They charged him with drunken and disorderly conduct, assaulting a police officer and drunk driving. At the minimum, he'd end up losing his license and doing community service. At the most severe, he could serve time. The lawyer assured us that was a highly unlikely scenario, given his standing in the community and his lack of a criminal record. Other than one other DUI, he was clean.

I threw myself into work. I knew I should call her but I didn't know what to say. I couldn't get the image of them kissing out of my head no matter what I tried to drown it with.

Three days passed before Gabe sauntered into my office. Sadie, working out the final days of her notice, skipped in after him, apologetic that he had passed without her warning me. I waved, dismissing her, but she raised her eyebrows, questioning me before closing the door behind her when I gave a firm nod.

Gabe looked foolish in a suit; a child playing dress up. His hair was tied back in a ponytail, but it only served to make him look younger. Stupider. The cut on his lip had healed a little, and the bruising around his eyes had a tinge of yellow.

He stood with his arms crossed over his chest, but the tapping of his foot gave away his nerves. "We need to talk."

I didn't look up. I continued to stare at the screen, one that blurred with black and white numbers because I had been staring at them so long, trying not to think of Lauren.

"Tyler?" Gabe stepped forward. I caught the movement in the corner of my eye but still refused to look up. "Tyler?" he said again, this time more forcefully.

"What do you want, Gable?" I lowered the lid of my laptop. Using his full name would annoy him. It was something our father did.

"We need to talk," he said again, this time pulling back the chair and sitting down. Memories of when Lauren sat in that exact position flashed across my mind but I pushed them aside. Thoughts like that wouldn't help anyone. I spent enough time dreaming of her at night, I didn't need her image haunting me during the day as well.

"Well, talk," I ordered.

"Look." He sat forward, hands clasped together between his knees. "I'm sorry about Lauren. I don't know what—"

"Don't speak about her," I ordered. I couldn't stand for her name to be on his lips. I didn't want him talking about her, thinking about her. I didn't want him having anything to do with her.

"I just wanted to explain that—"

"There is nothing to explain."

"You've talked to her?"

I shuffled some papers on my desk. "No." I picked up a pen and started flicking the tip, leaning back in my chair, and crossing one ankle over my knee in an attempt to appear relaxed. "Have you?"

"Well," Gabe shifted uncomfortably, "I called her to make sure she was okay."

My teeth clenched until my jaw ached. "And she answered?"

"You've hurt her, Tyler."

"I've hurt her?" Anger started to course through my veins again. I took a deep breath and swallowed. "What do you want, Gable?"

He looked at me a while longer, as if weighing up his options and then leaned back in the chair, his hands behind his head. "Dad was the one who was going to show me the ropes. He had begun, in fact, you know, before. But now that he's unavailable—"

"He'll be back soon."

"He's being sent on a thirty-day rehab and anger management course," Gabe replied.

I didn't know that, but I wasn't about to let him know. "And your point is?"

"I'm left a little uncertain of my role within the company."

"And you would like me to do what, exactly?" I looked up at him openly this time, meeting his eye and glaring with as much hatred as I could muster.

"Help," he said. "I'm not sure what to do. Dad had only just started with the—"

I lifted the lid of my laptop and turned my attention back to the screen. "See Sadie on your way out. She'll tell you someone that will be able to help."

"But don't you think with all that's going on, the media fishing for more stories, we should at least pretend to have a unified front, for the sake of the family, the company?"

"I would hardly call a local online gossip rag the media. And as for a unified front?" I said, the anger causing my cheeks to flush. "You kissed my girl, how unified was that?"

"After you stole her from me."

"I never once kissed her while she was with you. Well," I smirked, "not that I initiated, anyway."

The muscles in Gabe's jaw bulged back and forth as he gritted his teeth together. "I'm trying here, Tyler. I'm trying to—"

Slamming the lid of my laptop down, I stood and leaned over the desk. "I don't care what you're trying to do you little piece of shit. Go grow up somewhere else. Right now, I can't stand the sight of you so please fucking leave before I give you matching black eyes."

Gabe rose from his seat without a word and walked out the door, leaving me to draw in a ragged breath at his departure.

Sadie walked in as soon as he left.

"I suppose you heard all that?"

"You suppose right." She crossed her arms and glared at me in the way only Sadie could.

"And you think I shouldn't have reacted the way I did?"

"I think it's time you went to see Lauren."

"She told me to leave her alone. I'm a man of my word."

"You're stupid, that's what you are. You've been trying to hide it but I can smell the alcohol on your clothing in the morning. I can see the lack of sleep in the dark patches under your eyes. I see the mounds of leftover food. You need to go sort this."

I sat back down in my chair. "And what do I say? What can I say?"

"The truth."

"Which is?"

"Tell her you were wrong. Tell her you've been lost without her. Tell her everything and anything that's on your mind. But most of all, listen."

"And if that doesn't work?"

"Well, at least you would have tried. It's been three days. She's had time to think, now it's time for you to go and see her before you lose her completely."

2

LAUREN

My room was chaos. Clothing I hadn't worn in years littered the floor. Empty plates streaked with food stains sat on the bedside cabinet and the curtains were drawn, letting little light into the small room. Morgan sat on the end of my bed as I hid under the covers. Only the occasional tap of her fingers told me she was casually scrolling through the news feed on her phone.

Pulling the covers down, she turned the phone around and a frozen frame of Tyler, complete with split lip, was shoved in my face. "Was it sexy?"

"Sexy?" I repeated, pushing the phone away.

"Having them fight over you? Like, literally fight. Physically. With punches and split lips and black eyes and blood." She said the word blood like some sort of starved vampire.

I groaned and snuggled deeper down in the bed, still keeping the covers firmly at eye level. "Go away."

Morgan adjusted herself on the edge of the bed, hooking one ankle under her knee and making no move to leave. "I know I shouldn't, but I think I'd like it if two men fought over me. Alistair's never had to fight for me. I'm not sure if he would. He would probably want to work things out in some pathetic talk or something. That man's got no backbone."

I sighed deeply but it was lost in the bed covers. "Not when it proves that the one you actually love doesn't trust you."

"True," she replied absently, turning her attention back to the phone. "You should see the comments. Some people are certain the fight was over a girl. They're even claiming they know who the girl is. Did you make new friends I'm unaware of?" Morgan shoved the rise of my hips, causing the bed to wobble. "Others say it was because Tyler was jealous Gabe got some promotion at work."

I threw the covers off and got out of bed. "Fine," I huffed. "I'll get up. And you shouldn't be reading that stupid gossip column. It's just people with nothing better to do."

"About time," Morgan muttered.

For the past four days, I had holed myself up in my childhood bedroom, hiding from the world, binging on peanut M&Ms— surprisingly supplied by my mother—and watching daytime television on the smallest TV screen in the world, although Mother assured me that it was perfectly fine. I think she dug it out of storage. I needed to be back in the city soon for a meeting, but going back to the city meant facing Tyler and I wasn't sure I was ready for that.

Crossing my arms, I glared at Morgan. "For the record, Gabe didn't receive any promotion. He just got a similar position."

"I take it by your delightful mood today he still hasn't called?"

I didn't reply and dragged an old suitcase out of my wardrobe. "Help me pack."

Morgan looked up from her perch on the bed, shook her head and then scooted further back to prop herself against the wall. She flashed the screen in my direction again, this time showing an image of Gabe. "I think you should invite him over for a visit. I'd be more than happy to comfort the poor boy."

"For fuck's sake, Morgan, you're married."

Morgan chewed on her bottom lip, attempting to contain a grin. "Did you just swear?"

"And what if I did?"

She shrugged, the grin still barely hidden. "Nothing. I won't say another word." She turned her attention back to her cell phone again, scrolling through photo after photo of that dreadful night. "Nothing like a good old scandal to arouse interest, is there? Half these people would have never even heard of Thornton Industries before this and now they're all over it like hungry wolves. Suddenly it matters how many properties they own, what cars they drive, how much money was donated to charity. A week ago they didn't give a crap."

Dragging clothes from the closet, I threw them into the faded and slightly torn case. The clothes were dated. Badly. And most of them wouldn't fit me anymore. I was a little more curvaceous in my thirties than I was in my teens.

"I do have to admit that Alistair and I potentially had the best sex we've ever had after your little scene, though."

I froze in the middle of pulling a denim jacket out of the closet. "Excuse me?"

"It got me a little hot and bothered, all that drama at the table, the way Tyler spoke to Mum when she called you barren, the fight between him and Gabe. I literally jumped him when we got back to the room."

Covering my ears with my hands, I shook my head. "Please make it stop."

"He was into it too. He was a lot more aggressive than normal. I liked it. Usually he just sort of climbs on top and does his thing while I moan and make noises that I know will make him finish sooner."

I started humming to cover the sound of her voice, but she stood and walked over, pulling a dress out of the closet, before leaning close. "Oh Alistair," she moaned. "Oh yes, just like that. Yes, yes, yes," she imitated climaxing. "Fuck me, Alistair!" She laughed at my expression. "Oh, my dear little sister. How easy it is to shock you, but I bet you have stories of your own, don't you?"

"Can we please change the subject?"

"You're no fun, you know that?"

"So you keep telling me."

Morgan examined the dress in her hands. "Please tell me you're not set to repel men by wearing this, are you?"

I ripped the material from her. "Don't you have somewhere else to be?"

"But then who would help you with this very important task of packing clothing that you haven't worn in years? And nor should you," she muttered. "Did you really use to dress like this? I seriously wonder what Derek saw in you."

"It's for charity."

"Charity?" Morgan picked out another dress and held it against her body. "I'm not sure charity would want this."

"Well, they can cut it up and use it as rags, for all I care. It's not about the clothing."

Tossing the dress to join the others on the floor, Morgan resumed her position on the bed. "What is it about then?"

"I'm cleaning. I'm sorting. I'm organising. I'm creating a fresh start."

"Wouldn't that entail chucking out the clothes you actually wear?"

"They aren't here. And even if they were, it's not like I can afford a new wardrobe. Just consider this symbolic."

Morgan tilted her head to the side. "Of?"

"Of creating a fresh start, you idiot." I threw a shoe, which she dodged and it hit the wall, leaving a black smudge.

"Mum's going to tell you off," she mocked in a tell-tale voice.

"I'm creating a new me. One that doesn't need a man. Especially a man that doesn't trust me. And especially a man with the name Thornton."

"So you're going back to Derek then?"

I threw the other shoe, but again she swerved away from it and it hit the wall.

"That's two marks now. Mum's going to be so pissed. She may even ground you." Morgan picked up one of the shoes and turned it over in her hands, examining it as though it were a foreign object she was tasked to identify. "Will you move back to your old house?"

"No," I said firmly. I had already tossed the question around my head over the last few days. "It's rented out for another eight months yet, they are good tenants, and my business is in the city."

"With Tyler's assistant?"

"She's leaving the company."

Morgan rolled her eyes. "Good timing." The shoe was thrown into the air and landed neatly in the suitcase. "Hey," Morgan said, clearly pleased. "Did you see that? I've still got it." She mimicked throwing a netball into a hoop. "So where are you going to live?"

"I'm not sure yet."

"Off to a good start then."

"Morgan, please," I groaned. "I'm dealing with this. I'm going to get everything sorted." I pulled myself up straight and set my shoulders. "I'm going to concentrate on my business and let life take me where it wills."

"Really taking charge there, huh?"

At my cold glare, Morgan held up her hands. "Okay, I get it. I'll stop."

"Good."

"Good," she repeated. She was silent for a while, turning her attention back to her phone, before putting it down and sighing. "I know I said I'd stop but are you really going to let this one little fight break you up?"

My shoulders slumped. "It wasn't this one little fight. He can't get over the fact that I was with Gabe and there's nothing I can do about that."

"But he knew that when you started dating."

"Yep. He knew it. I knew it. But with Gabe moving to the city and working within the same company, things were just going to get harder not easier."

"So you decided you're better off without either of them."

"Exactly," I agreed, though there was little conviction to my words. The truth was, I didn't know what I wanted. I wanted Tyler, but I also wanted Tyler to trust me. His actions so far proved he didn't. And the fact that he hadn't even bothered to call. Mind you, I hadn't either. We were stuck in some strange communication standoff, both of us waiting for the other to make the first move. And I'd been tempted. I'd typed out messages, brought up his contact details and stared at the numbers until they blurred together, but I never pressed the button.

"Even though you adore him?"

Her words hit me hard and a rush of tears welled. I sat on the bed beside her and stared out at the mess I had created. "Even though I adore him," I repeated.

Morgan opened her arms and I fell into them, leaning against her shoulder as she squeezed me tightly. "You're going to be okay."

"I'm going to be okay," I said robotically.

"No," Morgan corrected. "You're going to be fucking wonderful."

I laughed and pushed away from her. "Careful, or you'll take the title of black sheep of the family away from me."

Morgan patted my cheek. "Oh my dear sweet sister, how naïve you are. I married my high school sweetheart, who I never had pre-marital sex with and gave birth to a beautiful daughter, providing a grandchild. I'm still married. I live close to my parents and I work as a part-time music teacher. You, on the other hand, got pregnant before marriage, lost the baby, got dumped, started a relationship with a man ten years your junior and then dumped him for his older brother. No matter what I do, I could never take that title from you."

"Cheers for the support."

"Anytime, sister dearest. Anytime."

3

LAUREN

Having given up on my new start in life beginning with the cleaning of my childhood bedroom, I closed the door to the mess and made my way down the hall, following Morgan. I hadn't bothered to get dressed and was wearing shorty-pyjamas that came from the late nineties. I hadn't washed my hair since I arrived, and had barely washed my face. In fact, I think I may have had the colours of peanut M&Ms smudged across my chin.

But when I walked into the kitchen I didn't think of any of that, because, when I rounded that corner, I found Tyler sitting at the kitchen table next to my mother with one of the family photo albums open.

"Tyler!" Morgan exclaimed, turning to look at me with wide eyes. "What a surprise to see you here." Her hand snuck across the table and slapped the photo album shut. "Too far, Mum," she muttered and shook her head, clasping the album under her arm. "No one should have to see those."

I was stuck in the doorway, transfixed by the sight of him. Dressed in a dark t-shirt and jeans, he sat at the table, looking as beautiful as I'd ever seen him. My heart lurched. His dark hair hung loosely over his forehead instead of being swept back like he wore at work. And it was slightly damp. Flashes of Tyler in the shower, the water streaming over his naked body as he ran his hands through his hair, came to the fore of my mind. My heart began to race.

Tyler locked eyes with me. "Lauren." Just the sound of my name on his lips had me fighting the urge to run to him, wrap my arms around his neck and kiss him like there was no tomorrow.

"Lauren," my mother's harsh tone cut through my thoughts. "Aren't you at least going to say hello? Tyler's come all this way to see you."

"Hi." My hand waved of its own accord. A tiny, pathetic wave. Cursed hand. Clearing my throat, I attempted to regain my composure, although I wasn't sure it was possible dressed in pyjamas that were clearly too small for me.

"You could have at least got dressed," Mother muttered as if reading my thoughts.

I tugged the hem of the shorts down a little. "I would have if I had known we had visitors," I replied, taking the seat opposite Tyler. His eyes stuck on me like glue. I met them briefly but had to look away when my chest began to ache from the intensity of his gaze. He was searching my expression, trying to gain a sense of my thoughts. I didn't want him to see, so I set my eyes on the table and slid part of the newspaper over so I would at least have something to look at.

Mother whipped the paper away. "Don't be so rude, Lauren. This man has come all this way to see you, the least you can do is be polite." The more she treated me like a child, the more I wanted to act like one, although I did resist the urge to give her the finger behind her back.

"It wasn't far," Tyler said to Mother, though I could still feel the heat of his gaze on me. "Could we perhaps go somewhere and have a conversation?"

My mind screamed. Conflicting thoughts battled for dominance. Yes. More than anything yes. Take me away. Give me privacy so I can lose myself in you. No. Stay away. I can't be near you. I can't inhale your scent, I can't get close and not want you to touch me.

"Well, away you go," Mother flicked a tea-towel in my direction. "All he's asking for is a conversation."

Tyler removed his gaze, but only to throw a withering glance Mother's way. "Please?" he said, though the word was ripped from his throat like it was torture for him to use it.

Without answering, I rose from the table and Tyler followed. We walked down the hallway and I opened the door to my small bedroom. "Sorry," I said waving my hand over the mess. "I'm in the middle of something."

Tyler blinked when he entered, his eyes adjusting to the dim light. "In the middle of a hurricane perhaps?" he asked.

I pushed some clothing off the bed and indicated for him to sit. The only problem was it left nowhere for me to sit except next to him, so I awkwardly folded my arms across my chest and leaned against the wall. He looked out of place perched on the edge of my single bed, staring at the posters and photos that covered my walls, faded and worn with age. After a few moments of silence, he leaned forward, resting his elbows on his knees and looked at me.

And there were those eyes again.

The ones I didn't want to meet because I was afraid of the response they would elicit. I was afraid my body would betray my mind. I was afraid my mind would betray my body.

"How have you been?" he asked.

"Wonderful," I replied. I didn't mean to take such a sarcastic tone, but I was guarding myself. It slipped out unintentionally. "You?" I asked, slightly softer.

"Not so wonderful."

I slunk down the wall until I was sitting on the ground, my knees tucked to my chest. "Is your dad okay? I saw him on the news."

Tyler laughed nervously. "He's off to rehab." He twisted his hands hanging between his legs. "Come home."

"Is that a question or an order?"

"Of course it's a question," he replied, making no attempt to hide his annoyance.

I looked over at him, pushing away the tears that had sprung to my eyes. "You yelled at me in front of all those people. You called me a liar. You said we were a mistake."

"You kissed him!" Tyler yelled. He took in a deep breath, shoulders visibly rising and falling. "You kissed him," he repeated this time more calmly.

"I did not kiss him, Tyler. He kissed me. There is a difference."

"It didn't look that way from where I was standing."

"Well, that's what happened but I can't make you believe it. That choice is yours."

I turned to face him, straightening my slouched position against the wall. "It's something we can't escape, Tyler. I was with Gabe before I was with you. It's always going to be there. I knew it before we started dating but I just ignored it because I wanted you. I needed you."

With his head hung low, he peered up at me through dark strands. "And now you don't?"

"I—" My voice caught in my throat. "I think it would be best if I didn't."

"That's not the same thing." He shuffled closer, encouraged by my lack of conviction. "You still want me, Lauren, and I still want you. You have been all I can think about. Every day at work I've tried to push you out of my mind by dealing with the shit-storm Dad's arrest caused, but I haven't been able to do it. You're there. All the time. Every second, every moment of the day. And at night... at night it is way worse. I'm drinking more than I've ever drunk just to try and drown your memory. Not because I want to forget, but because I can't function knowing that you won't be there waiting for me in bed, sleeping with your hair all in a mess over your face, your body twisted in the sheets."

By this stage, he had moved closer and taken my hands in his. My skin burned under his touch. His thumbs traced circles over the soft pads of my flesh, causing ripples of longing that tingled through my body.

It took all my strength, but I pulled my hands away and stood, gaining some distance between us. "But you don't trust me?"

"I don't trust him," Tyler corrected, also getting to his feet. "I'm not sure what you want me to say. I can't stand the thought of you being around him. I don't want you to have anything to do with him."

"You can't ask that of me. He's your brother."

"I can't lie. I can't change the way I feel. I saw you kiss him, Lauren."

Stepping across the gap that existed between us, Tyler tilted my chin, lifting my gaze to meet his, looking deep into my eyes. Anger and temptation fought within. The temptation to melt into him. Say I was sorry for an offence I wasn't guilty of just to feel his arms around me. Agree to avoid Gabe just to keep him happy.

And anger that he would demand that of me.

Then he kissed me.

Despite its startling beginning, it was gentle, almost as though it were a question. He deepened the kiss when he felt my lips respond to his and pulled me close, pressing my body against the firm lines of his, melding my flesh to fit his, reminding me of the way we felt. My hands lifted to thread through his hair as desire and emotion overwhelmed me. There were so many things wrapped up in that kiss, but I think the reason it lingered with me was because we both knew it was a kiss goodbye.

Tyler broke away first, pressing his forehead to mine, his hands still wrapped in my hair and mine in his. "I loved you, Lauren Greer," he said, his voice breaking over my name.

Tears threatened but I pushed them away with sheer determination and lifted my chin, even though it wobbled.

Loved. He said loved, as in the past.

And then he was gone.

4

LAUREN

Stuffed into Mother's small car, the trip back to the city was painful. Mother lectured me, scolding me for letting another good man go. She was certain I was going to go back to 'that young man.' But seeing Gabe was furthest from my mind. Despite him calling a significant amount of times, I had only talked to him once, after Morgan—fed up with me ignoring his calls—answered for me.

So when my cell phone rang, I was grateful that it was Sadie's name that filled the screen. Grateful it wasn't Gabe. Grateful the call would shut Mother up for a blissful few moments.

"Hey," I answered, letting relief flood my voice.

"You okay? You sound like I've just rescued you from falling into a volcano or something."

I glanced over at Mother and replied, "Close enough."

"Anyway," she said, "I hear you're looking for a new place to live."

"News travels fast."

"He's just worried about you."

"I'm fine," I said forcefully.

"No place to live, no place to work, but you're fine."

"I'll sort it." I just didn't know how or when.

"Well," she said with a big sigh. "The thing is, I've got an extra room at my place."

"I suppose this was Tyler's suggestion."

"As I said, he's worried about you. But it wasn't exactly his idea, he simply advised me of your situation and I have a spare room. It was a team effort. But anyway, it doesn't matter who came up with the idea, it matters if you'd be keen."

I let silence prevail for a few seconds. Living with Sadie would solve the problem, but it would do little to keep me away from Tyler. And with my emotions tossing between pissed off and missing him, I didn't think I could trust myself to be around him. Ironic. Not only did Tyler not trust me, I didn't trust myself. The only difference was who we didn't trust me to be around.

Sadie took my silence as hesitation. "It's not as though you've got other offers, and Tyler's already promised that he will not darken our door. Unless you invite him to."

"I'll think about it."

Sadie sighed again. "What's there to think about? Come on, Lauren. It would just be the two of us. I'm finishing up working in a few days and then we can concentrate on our business. You've remembered we have that meeting at Haven's Rest, haven't you?"

"It's a hard one to forget." It was to be our first attempt at producing a marketing campaign.

"I've come up with a name by the way."

"A name for what?" I asked.

"Our company."

I waited but she didn't continue. "Which is?" I finally asked.

"Okay, give it a minute before you respond."

"Okay," I agreed cautiously.

"Slag."

"Slag?" I repeated, my voice rising.

Mother glared at me from the driver's seat. "That's not a very nice word, Lauren."

"I told you to give it a minute," Sadie said.

"Why Slag?"

"Because it means to talk about someone, or something, you know, like marketing. Getting the word out there."

"But it means talking about someone in an insulting way, not a positive way, and it generally is in reference to women."

"But that's what makes it so great. We're women. We can claim the word, turn it into whatever we want. You've got to admit that people will remember it."

"They will," I agreed. "I'm still not sure if that's a good thing."

"We'll talk about it more when you arrive. Tyler's already organised for all your stuff to be shipped to my place."

"He has?" My voice broke.

"Oh, I'm sure he just wanted to make it easier for you. Though Smudge is still back at the loft, slinking around like someone stole his milk. I tried picking him up to bring him here but I think he hates me."

"He hates everyone," I replied.

"So it's sorted then. I'll see you when you get here."

* * *

Mother didn't want to travel home in the dark, so she simply dropped me at Sadie's and drove away, leaving me clutching a small bag and staring at the house that would become my home. Wedged between two other houses, it looked small and out of place amongst the more opulent homes on the street. The white paint was faded, some of the wooden planks were damp with rot, and one of the windows had a giant crack splitting through the middle. A broken concrete path and uneven steps led up to the entrance.

Taking a deep breath, I dragged my bag up the crooked stairs and knocked on the door.

"It's open," Sadie shouted.

Pushing with my shoulder, the door creaked as it swung open. Sadie stood dressed in yoga pants and a baggy sweatshirt. She had a tea towel slung over her shoulder, reminding me of Peta.

"You made it," she said, walking over and wrapping her arms around me, squeezing tightly. "Welcome to your new home." Sadie swept her arm around the space. "It's not much, and nothing like you're used to, but it's warm." She led me down the narrow hallway, stepping over piles of magazines stacked against the walls. "It may come as a bit of a surprise, but I'm a bit of a slob at home." She flashed me a grin. "Sorry."

She wasn't wrong. I secretly wondered if she had hoarding tendencies. There were piles of stuff everywhere. Clothing either ready to go into the wash or waiting to be folded, crowded one of the doorways.

Everywhere I looked there was clutter. It contradicted everything I thought I knew about her. The Sadie I knew was clean, organised to a fault, and groomed to perfection. Her office space was spotless and nothing was out of place. Clearly her personal life was a little different.

"This," Sadie said, fighting with the door opposite her bedroom before it swung open, "is your room. Tyler's already dropped your things around and set up your bed and stuff."

"My bed?" I entered the room and sure enough a double bed had been erected against the far wall, complete with bedding. "I didn't have a bed at Tyler's place."

Sadie waved her hand, dismissing my comment. "Yeah, but Tyler said your stuff was rented out along with your house and I didn't have a spare. I've got the receipt if you want to change it."

I shook my head. "It will be fine."

Sadie strode across the room and opened the wardrobe. "I've hung most of your clothes but there's still another couple of boxes over there for you to unpack." Clapping her hands together, Sadie grinned. "It's going to be so good having you here. I didn't like it when Saxton moved away. I hated living with my brother but I've hated living alone more."

Picking my way through the maze of boxes, I sat on the edge of the bed, suddenly feeling worn.

Sadie sat beside me. "It's going to be good, you'll see." She patted my knee before standing. "You get everything sorted and I'm going to cook us tea. Correction, I'm going to attempt to cook us tea. I'm not that good at it. Last time I tried to cook pasta it caught on fire. No shit. Might have been something to do with the lack of water, but hey, a girl has got to start somewhere, right?"

Sadie shut the door behind her, the base crunching over the uneven wooden floor. I sat and looked around the room. It was small and smelled a little funny, but it was mine. With a renewed determination, I got off the bed and started to unpack the boxes strewn over the floor. I didn't remember having this much when I moved into Tyler's, but apparently I had collected a lot over the months we lived together.

Once my clothes were unpacked, my books stacked neatly in two piles on either side of the bed to act as nightstands, a rug thrown over the cold wooden floors and my shoes in a line under the window, I flopped onto the bed and opened my laptop. It took a few seconds to whirl into life and then I somewhat hesitantly opened Facebook. The first notification I noticed was a message from Peta. I felt bad about not updating her with what was going on with my life, but the truth was I just didn't feel like discussing it with anyone, even if she was my best friend. Her message was all capitals, screaming her displeasure.

I TAKE IT YOU'VE LOST YOUR PHONE?

And that was the entirety of the message. Reaching across to my handbag, I tugged my phone out and plugged it in to charge. After a few minutes of scrolling through my newsfeed on my laptop, ignoring where people had tagged me in the comments of posts relating to the Thornton's, and trying not to stare at the photos of Tyler for too long, my phone flicked into life. I dialled Peta and spent half an hour explaining the last few days of my life. As soon as I hung up, a screaming beep sounded through the house. I opened the bedroom door to find Sadie in the hallway, flapping a tea towel in the direction of a smoke alarm.

"Shut up!" she yelled. "I haven't even started cooking yet, you idiotic thing!"

"Everything okay out here?"

Sadie looked at me sheepishly. "How do you feel about takeaways?"

* * *

Food devoured and wine consumed, Sadie and I sat on the couch in the lounge, staring at the television. The wine had dulled me a little and warmth crept up my insides. The house didn't seem as cluttered as when I had first arrived, but I wasn't sure if it was because I had grown accustomed to it, or if Sadie had had a clean-up. On the way to collect dinner, we had stopped by Tyler's loft and collected Smudge who was now sitting on the back of the couch, staring out the window with wide eyes and flat ears.

Walking into the loft was strange. Even though Sadie had told me that Tyler wouldn't be home, it didn't stop my heart from racing as we rode the elevator and the door rolled open. Part of me hoped I would walk out and find Tyler on the couch, dressed like he usually was when he was done for the day; shirtless, grey sweatpants, and black glasses sitting across his nose.

He wasn't.

Smudge hadn't been difficult to find. He was stretched out in his usual sun-drenched spot. When we left, I put my key on the kitchen bench, my heart constricting a little at the thought that I wouldn't get to use it again.

But it was what I wanted.

"So," Sadie said, stretching out on the couch beside me, her feet planted in my lap. "You haven't said what you think of the name yet."

"Slag?" I replied, taking a sip of wine to cover my smirk.

"Still not winning you over?"

"It's clever, I guess."

"You guess? Have you got a better idea?"

"We could play with our names?"

Sadie rolled her eyes, swirling the red wine around the glass tumbler. "What an original concept. Sadie Anderson & Lauren Greer. Or maybe just Anderson Greer."

"Who says your name will go first?"

"Fine. But Greer Anderson doesn't have the same ring." Sadie lifted her brows, eyes sparkling. "Sadie, Lauren, Anderson, Greer, get it?"

"Get what?" I replied.

"Our initials. They literally spell Slag. See?" she said, just as a knock sounded at the door. "It's meant to be."

Sadie fought with the front door before it finally groaned open. "Oh," she said. "It's you. What do you want?"

"Is Lauren here?"

At the sound of my name, I poked my head around the corner to look down the hallway. The person waiting at the door was hidden by Sadie leaning against the doorframe, arms crossed.

"For you, no," Sadie said, her voice dripping with disdain.

Gabe pushed Sadie aside and strode up the hallway. I quickly ducked back to the couch and managed to throw my feet up and start scrolling through my phone as he walked into the lounge. Wearing baggy jeans and a tight fitting t-shirt, he walked towards me and my heart lurched a little as he dumped himself on the couch.

"Hey you," he said.

"Hey," I replied.

"Finally got that phone fixed, huh?"

"Peta said the same thing."

"So it's not just me you're ignoring."

"I wasn't ignoring anyone. I just needed a few days to myself. And I did answer."

"Once," he corrected.

Sadie came back into the room, grabbed the wine bottle from the bench and sauntered back over to take a seat. "Feel free not to make yourself at home." She threw a daggered look Gabe's way.

"I'm just here to check on Lauren," Gabe replied, narrowing his eyes and glaring at Sadie.

"Well, as you can see, she's fine." She took a large gulp from her wine glass then promptly replaced the liquid she had just consumed.

"She is also right here and can speak for herself," I added.

"If Tyler's not allowed to come over, I don't see why he should be."

"I never said Tyler's not allowed over."

"Tyler's not allowed over?" Gabe repeated. "So things are really all over for you two?" There was a fragment of hope in his tone.

"Yes," I said at the same time as Sadie said, "Temporarily."

"I'm sorry." Gabe lowered his head, toying with a thread from a tear in his jeans. "I shouldn't have kissed you."

"Damn straight," Sadie spat out.

"I just couldn't resist, you know. I just had to try."

"I just had to try," Sadie echoed, mocking Gabe. "She was with Tyler. You should have had more respect."

"Like he did when I was with her?"

"That was different," Sadie said.

"Different how?"

"Enough," I cried, putting up my hands. "I know you're sorry, Gabe, and I forgive you. But it still doesn't change anything. Tyler doesn't trust me. So how about we just change the subject. How's work? I honestly never thought I'd see the day that you worked for your father. Not after the way you used to go on about him."

Gabe chuckled. "Me neither. Though now, I don't technically work for him. He had to take a step back to attend rehab."

"How's all that going?"

Gabe shrugged. "Not sure. He's just gone in and there's no contact allowed. Not that it really worries me. Before Jake came home it had been a while since I'd spent time with any of them."

Sadie let out a scoff.

"What?" Gabe asked bluntly.

"A while since you'd spent any time with them? You mean, because you drunk yourself into a stupor and then ran away overseas and gallivanted around the place on Tyler's money."

"Family money. Not Tyler's," Gabe corrected.

"You seriously believe that? After Hamish kicked you out of the house, you then think he turned around and funded your 'soul-searching' mission overseas? Come on, Gabe, open your eyes. That money came from Tyler and you know it."

"I didn't know it and I don't know it," Gabe threw back. "Either way, it's not like they couldn't afford it."

"You ungrateful little shit." Sadie got to her feet. "I'll be in my room if you need me," she said to me, and then to Gabe, "with my door open."

"It smells funny in here, Sades," Gabe yelled after her. "You didn't try cooking again, did you?"

Sadie gave him the middle finger before slamming her bedroom door shut.

"I guess she forgot about leaving her door open," Gabe said.

Immediately Sadie's bedroom door creaked open a fraction. "Perhaps I should tell Tyler about this little visit."

"Go ahead," I yelled back. "I'm not doing anything wrong."

The door closed.

"I'm not sure what she thinks I'm going to do," Gabe muttered.

"Try and kiss me again?" I offered.

A red flush blushed over his cheeks. "Look, I am sorry. I never meant to cause problems for you and Tyler. I had no idea he'd react that way."

"Yes, you did."

Gabe smiled sheepishly. "Okay, maybe I did. But I never meant to hurt you, I swear."

Silence hung between us. Gabe toyed with the thread hanging off his jeans a little more. I stared at the images that flashed across the television screen, looking but not really seeing any of them.

"I suppose you've been keeping up to date with all that stuff about you guys splashed over social media?" I said finally.

Gabe groaned and tilted his head back against the couch, slouching further down in his seat. "Where do they come up with that shit? I even saw one article that had a quote by a supposed ex-girlfriend of Jake's, commenting about his time in the army. He never had a girlfriend while he was in the army. The whole thing was a bunch of shit but it didn't stop people from posting it online. It's just a crock. These people didn't give a shit who I was a while ago, and now they're scrolling through all my photos and writing false articles all because of Hamish. The man's an arsehole."

"An arsehole you want to work for."

"Because of you, Lauren. I did it for you."

"I never asked you to. I never wanted you to."

"It was the only thing I could think of that might win you back. Showing you that I was more than a twenty-something loser."

"I never thought of you as a loser, Gabe."

"Can you tell me what I did wrong then? What made you turn to Tyler instead of me?"

"Gabe, it's been too long—"

"I'd do anything, Lauren, anything to get you back."

"Being with someone isn't what I want at the moment."

Gabe looked up at me through the thick blond hair overhanging his eyes and smiled. "I'm going to change your mind."

5

LAUREN

"So?" Sadie asked as we looked around one of the newly revamped rooms of Haven's Rest. "What are your initial thoughts?"

I chewed on my bottom lip. "That these rooms look just like every other hotel room I've ever been in."

Sadie rolled her eyes. "Those sorts of comments are not helpful. Now put that camera up to your eye and tell me what you see."

I did as she asked, but it served little purpose to change what I saw. The bed was still a bed. The wardrobe still a wardrobe. The bathroom still a bathroom. Sure, it had all been updated to modern lines and dull colours, but basically, it was a room like all others. It was there to serve a purpose and little more. It was to be whatever the person needed it to be.

Sadie walked over to the bed and danced her hands through the air theatrically as if attempting to grasp an idea. "Nope." She shook her head. "Still nothing." Flopping to the bed, she lay on her back and stared at the ceiling. "I'm beat. My mind is blank. These rooms could be anything, anywhere. There is nothing to make them stand out."

I lifted the camera and snapped a shot of the immaculately dressed and perfectly groomed Sadie lying on the bed, blonde hair spilling over the covers. We had lived together for over three weeks now, and I felt like I was only just getting to know her. Sadie was a contradiction and an enigma. At work she was everything organised and controlled. At home she was everything but.

Moving to take another photo, I hoped inspiration might strike if I caught the correct angle. "Maybe that's what we need to concentrate on."

"What? I literally said nothing." Sadie sighed.

"On the fact that the rooms could be anything, anywhere. Behind closed doors they could be anything you wanted."

Sadie sat up, eyes shining. "Like how it could be an outdoorsy family getaway for some and a fuck-pad for others!" she exclaimed.

I frowned. "Not exactly what I was thinking, but close enough." I took another shot of the light hitting the small jewel-studded lampshade in the bathroom.

"I can see it now." Sadie stood and paced the room, talking almost more with her hands than her voice. "We could have it set up as friends gathering for a drink before a night on the town. A group of girls sipping wine, scattered makeup in the bathroom, clothes spread on the floor."

"Not everyone lives like you, Sadie. Have you noticed that there is actually a floor in my room?"

Ignoring my comment, Sadie stood with her fingers clutching her chin. "Only one problem with all this."

"What?"

"Models. Considering our budget is somewhat limited at the moment, getting enough models for the initial concept will cost us more than I'd like. We could consider using people we know, just for that concept shoot, but it usually shows in the finished product."

"Remember you said that my images show humanity without using humans? Why don't we do that here? Have everything you just talked about, but with the people gone. Like they simply vanished. Poof."

I walked over and grabbed a couple of wine glasses out of the cupboard. "Half-finished glasses, maybe a spill of wine. Clothing tossed over the bed, makeup scattered by the mirror. Shoes toppled onto their sides at the edge of the bed."

Sadie picked up one of the glasses, placing her lips on the edge, feigning taking a sip. "Smudged lipstick on the glass." She clapped her hands together. "Oh, this is perfect. The slogan could be, 'Behind closed doors our rooms are whatever you want them to be,' or something like that anyway."

She looked around the room as both of us imagined the different scenarios. The scattered roses, chocolates, champagne on ice and messed sheets. The tennis rackets, gym shoes and sweaty clothing piled in a corner. The wet footprints from the occupant recently returned from the pool.

"I think we're onto something here."

Sadie's phone rang and she brought it to her ear. "Hello? Oh, hey," she said, her voice softening. She angled her body slightly away from me, a sure sign it was Tyler on the other end of the line. "Of course I don't mind. I'll call over in a bit. It's going great." Her eyes slid to mine. "She's fine. Good. Good. Yep, I'll tell her. See you in a bit." She hung up.

"Tell me what?"

Sadie screwed up her nose. "You know that function we're going to tonight?"

I sighed. "Tyler is going to be there."

Sadie had insisted we attend a fundraiser for networking purposes. I hated the thought of networking but Sadie insisted it was important for a new business.

"He just wanted me to let you know."

"Mission accomplished. I know."

"And you're still going?"

"It's not like I'm trying to avoid him, Sadie. Our paths are going to cross from time to time."

"So you're not annoyed?"

"It's a fundraiser. He has as much of a right to go as I do," I replied.

Sadie looked at me sceptically, head tilted to the side.

"It's fine," I repeated with more determination than I felt.

The last few weeks had been difficult. I missed Tyler. A lot. I fell to sleep thinking of him and each night my dreams were a jumbled mess of dark hair, strong hands, soft lips and fervent kisses. Lately though, the dark hair began to blur with blond, and brown eyes blended with blue. My memories had begun to blend together in a terrible nightmare of trying to keep everyone happy and ending up miserable.

Dressing for the fundraiser that night took me longer than I had ever taken to get ready for an event. Despite being annoyed with Tyler, I still wanted him to look at me and want me. It was cruel, I know, but I still longed for the feel of his eyes on me, his hands on my flesh, his mouth on my lips.

In the end, I went for a simple black dress, one that flowed to the floor but had a single split up my legs and a deep-cut exposed back. I accented it with a simple diamond necklace that Tyler had given me and a pair of black heels. Sadie helped me straighten my hair so it hung down either side of my face, almost reaching my waist. She never said anything, but the smirk across her face told me she was having a difficult time keeping her mouth shut. She knew what I was doing.

It was a small gathering, just a few people who had exclusive invites. I was only there because I was Sadie's plus one. She was only invited because she knew Tyler Thornton. We were there for our business, to mingle and market. Despite my initial hesitation, and after talking to a number of people, I had to admit that Sadie's suggestion of our company name was a perfect way to break the ice when talking to potential clients. It was also something that was sure to stick in their memories. Sadie had printed business cards, her name on one side and mine on the reverse. People chuckled when Sadie handed them out, immediately commenting on the name.

An hour into the event and I still hadn't spotted Tyler. I was beginning to wonder if he had decided to skip it altogether. Feeling the need for some fresh air, I left the room and headed outdoors, plucking my phone from my bag in an attempt to ward off anyone looking for conversation.

But it was out there that I spotted Tyler. He was talking to a group of people, a glass of whiskey in his hands, and dressed impeccably in a black suit. His eyes met mine as I crossed the path. My heart fluttered merely at the sight of him.

"Excuse me," I heard him mutter to the group of people he was with.

I felt him fall into step behind me. Of course, I couldn't see him, but I knew it was him. My body sensed him. I felt his presence as keenly as if he had gripped me from behind.

"Lauren," he said. I would never grow sick of the way he said my name. It was a command and a question. A plea and an accusation.

I turned and met his gaze, doing my best to mask my attraction and bring my defiance to the fore. He invaded every defence I had, assaulting me merely by his proximity.

Dark eyes locked on mine and he smiled. "Lauren," he said again, tipping an invisible hat.

The world faded as my attraction to Tyler flooded my senses and drowned my resistance. His voice reminded me of when he'd growl my name. One whiff of his scent and I was there, pressed against his naked body, my head resting on his chest, one leg splayed across him.

I was transfixed, trapped by his eyes.

"Tyler." His name came out as a gasp.

"It's good to see you. I hope you're well?"

I struggled to regain my composure, feeling the heat creep up my cheeks as visions of us entwined in the bedsheets came unwantedly to my mind.

He seemed to know what he did to me, how my body responded to him despite my attempt to ignore it. He stepped closer, invading my space.

I scanned my surroundings as though looking for someone, mustering what indifference towards Tyler I could. "I expected you to have a date," I replied, lifting my chin a little.

"I don't play games, Lauren. You know that. I would have brought a date had I wanted the company of another woman. I don't."

His eyes bore into mine, trapping me in his gaze until Sadie stepped beside us.

"You definitely need one of these." She pressed a business card into Tyler's hand.

Moving his eyes away from mine, they dropped to the card. "Slag?" he questioned.

"Sadie's idea," I was quick to say.

"Clever," Tyler replied. His eyes only flicked to the card briefly, otherwise, they remained stuck on me.

I swallowed, my heart thumping in my chest. His eyes lowered to my throat. I wanted to reach out and touch him. I wanted to bring his fingers to my mouth and taste him.

"How is the family?" I asked, wishing he would leave at the same time as desperately hoping he wouldn't.

"As well as can be expected. Billie isn't impressed you haven't been to see her yet."

"I—I—" I stammered, unsure what to say. It had never entered my mind to go and visit Billie. With my life no longer tied to either of the brothers, I'd assumed my friendship with Billie would finish.

"You may be able to get rid of me, but don't think for one minute it will be as easy to get rid of Billie. I'm afraid she's claimed you for life."

"I should really go visit her."

Tyler's phone beeped and he slipped it from his pocket, excusing himself by taking a step away.

Sadie leaned in close. "You cannot tell me you don't have feelings for that man. The way you're looking at him doesn't lie."

"I never said I didn't have feelings," I hissed back. "I said he didn't trust me."

"He didn't trust—" Sadie started, then held up her hands. We'd had this conversation many times before and usually Sadie was unapologetic. Tyler was her boy, as she put it. She hated seeing him hurt and that's exactly what he was according to her. Hurt and lonely.

Tyler stepped back, cleared his throat and caught my hand by the wrist, sending shock waves of excited tingles through my limbs.

"Can I speak to you for a moment?" At my look of panic, he added, "It's not about us. Not really."

I followed him to a secluded corner of the garden. His eyes roamed over my body appreciatively, making me want to throw my dress to the floor and wrap my body around his at the same time as wishing I had more layers. His eyes lingered on the split showing my leg just a little longer than necessary.

I cleared my throat, hoping that somehow it would dislodge the knot of need stuck there. "You wanted to talk to me?" I repeated, hoping my voice didn't betray the conflicting thoughts racing through my mind.

"Have you looked online lately?"

The flesh where his fingers had encircled my wrist still burned. I wanted to lift it to my nose and inhale the scent of him. I took a step back and shook my head. The stories of the Thornton men had died as quickly as they had surfaced. They were merely a flash in the gossip pan.

He cleared his throat again, visibly nervous. "Another story has come out," he said. Tyler tilted his head from side to side as though tossing up options. "It involves you."

"Me?" I repeated.

"And me."

I knew the time would come where I could possibly be known as Tyler's partner by the media. We had been together at the casino's opening night, the media were there. To be perfectly honest I was surprised it had taken this long for them to figure it out, though I was grateful it had. The last thing I had wanted was to be splashed over social media like Tyler, Jake and Gabe had been. Even Billie didn't escape the ridicule, people commenting on everything from her age, to her outfits, to her choice to leave the baby to attend the opening night.

Tyler's features twisted into discomfort. "And Gabe."

The colour fell from my face.

"And the fight at the casino," he added

"Show me," I ordered.

Tyler handed over his phone. I ignored that my image was still the background, and clicked on the icon he indicated, opening a link from his newsfeed.

The first image was a picture someone had pulled from my profile with the heading, 'Is this woman the reason for the fight between the Thornton Brothers?' And it wasn't the most flattering image they had to choose from. It was one taken of Peta and me, arms wrapped around each other while out for a few drinks, only Peta had been cropped out and my eyes were glazed and red.

I quickly skimmed the article which claimed a 'source' close to me said that I had dated both the eldest and youngest of the Thornton Brothers, and, in fact, there was a time when the 'source' was sure I was dating both at the same time. They went on to describe me as a nice girl, though nothing special, in fact, the source had difficulty explaining why two such men would want me. But they did go on to explain how I was left devastated after my fiancée left me at the altar for another woman.

Sickness lodged itself in my throat. I exited the article and started to scroll through the comments.

'I don't get what all the fuss is over,' the first one read. 'FFS how is this news?' was the second comment, with another person replying, 'It's a gossip site, you twat.' Another comment simply said, "Eww. Siblings. That woman needs to get some morals."

I scrolled down until I reached the final comment. It simply read, "She's a bit chubby, isn't she?" with a response of, "I wouldn't kick her out of bed."

"Who wrote this?" I asked, trying not to let the tightness in my throat slip into my voice. The article was posted on a blog which only identified the author as E. Blaire.

"I've got no idea but I intend on finding out." Tyler stepped closer and I resisted the urge to lean into him and inhale his scent. His hand drifted in the space between us, the threads of his neck flexing as he worked his jaw back and forth. Dark eyes skimmed over my body before coming back to rest on my eyes. They were filled with lust and desire and it gave me the strength to straighten my shoulders and lift my chin.

"Thank you for telling me."

Tyler snorted. "That's all I get? Thank you for telling me?" He stepped closer again, his mouth dangerously close to mine.

"Did you expect more?"

"Lauren," he growled and the heat of his breath brushed against my skin.

I closed my eyes as the memories of all the times he had said my name like that crashed over me. Steeling myself, I forced my eyes back open and smiled. "I should be getting back to Sadie. We've got networking to do." Turning on my heel, I walked away.

"Lauren," he called again, but I gritted my teeth, resisting the urge to turn back, and walked into the room, losing myself in the crowd of people.

* * *

Seeing him again addled my brain.

I was intoxicated by him.

Drunk on the memory of him.

If I had been strong, I wouldn't have spent the evening flicking through the photos I took of him. I wouldn't have let my mind wander back to that day in his office and my bold and brazen behaviour. My body wouldn't have quivered and trembled at the memory of later that night.

But I was not strong.

* * *

The next evening, I sat on the couch with Sadie, reading and rereading the article over and over, looking for hints of who had spilt my secrets. I stared at the images of me. None of them flattering. All of them true. They had managed to pick me out from the group of people gathered around the two brothers as they fought on the floor of the bar. The image perfectly reflected the look of horror on my face.

"Ignore it," Sadie said, digging a spoon into a tub of ice-cream.

"All very well for you to say. It's not your face splashed across the media."

"I would hardly call one little article 'the media'." Sadie rolled her eyes and sucked on the tip of the spoon before tilting it towards me. "Want some?"

I shook my head as someone pounded on the door.

Sadie lifted her brows. "I'm telling Tyler if it's Gabe."

"It's not Gabe," I said, pulling myself up from the couch.

"It could be," she replied.

"It's not."

I pulled the door open to be greeted by Billie. "You are here," she said in a tone that implied I'd been ignoring her.

"Hey, Billie." I opened the door wider and ushered her in.

"Don't you 'hey' me," she replied, heels clipping over the wooden floor. She stopped halfway down the narrow space, peering into the bedrooms and shaking her head before continuing to walk into the lounge.

"I expected more of you, Lauren Greer." Billie plonked herself down into a spare chair. "Here I am, basically a widow, and you haven't even come to check how I'm doing? What if I was an inconsolable mess? What if I needed help with Oliver? I was counting on you in my testosterone-filled world, and you let me down."

Sadie whistled as I sat back beside her. "Not good, L," she said, having chosen to adopt the nickname my sister used. She shook her head. "Not good."

"I'm sorry," I offered, more of a question than a true apology. It had honestly never occurred to me to visit Billie. I was certain that I would be on the outs with both her and Hamish after having messed—Hamish's word, not mine—with both men.

"No need to be sorry. I've come up with a way you can make it up to me."

"You have?"

Billie rolled her eyes dramatically. "Do you actually have anything to add to this conversation or are you just going to sit there and offer pithy comments and terse replies?"

Sadie elbowed me. "Yeah, L. Is that all you're going to do?"

Without waiting for a reply, Billie adjusted the way her shirt bunched over her breasts and sighed. "You know that Hamish's time at the resort is coming to an end next weekend."

"Resort?" I questioned and Sadie elbowed me again. "I do," I said more firmly, even though I didn't know. Hamish Thornton's schedule was not on my mind. Ever.

"You do," Billie confirmed. "Well, the entire family is to attend a weekend at this lodge. An adventure therapy weekend."

"Adventure therapy?" I repeated.

"It's where you complete various adventure-themed tasks as a group in order to bring you closer and help work through any issues," she said, as though reading off the back of a brochure.

"Sounds delightful." I still wasn't sure what this had to do with me, but I was beginning to suspect. Billie wanted me to babysit Oliver, and I couldn't think of anything I'd like less. I needed to distance myself from the Thornton family, not become the youngest son's babysitter.

"Hillis said it will be good for the family," Billie said firmly.

"Hillis?" Sadie asked and it was my turn to elbow her. We didn't need to encourage Billie by requesting details.

"My therapist. I needed one after all the shit I've been through. He's the one that runs these weekends and he said it would be perfect for our situation. So we leave at six o'clock on Friday evening. Be ready."

I looked at her questioningly. "Ready to…?"

She frowned. Well, attempted to, anyway. Her eyebrows bunched but the skin around them did nothing of the sort. "To come, of course. Hillis thinks it's important that you are there since you are so involved in our current family issues."

I shook my head before I even started to answer. "I'm not going."

"Yes, you are," Billie shot back.

"No," I replied firmly. "I am not."

"You owe me," Billie attempted to raise her overly manicured brows.

"I owe you?"

Sadie could barely contain her grin. "Come on now, L. She's got a point. You clearly owe the woman."

"What fucking point?" I said, struggling to keep my annoyance at bay.

Billie threw her hands into the air. "You just answered your own question."

Getting to her feet, Billie walked towards the hallway, as I looked over at Sadie who just grinned back at me stupidly.

"I told the sitter I'd be home hours ago. Remember," she threw over her shoulder, "we'll be here six o'clock Friday to pick you up." She shut the door behind her.

"What just happened?" I asked, turning to Sadie.

Sadie dipped the spoon into the ice-cream and sucked the contents off loudly. "You heard the woman. You're going on an adventure therapy weekend with the Thorntons. I almost wish I was going too, just to see how uncomfortable it's going to be." Her eyes twinkled. "You're going to have so much fun!"

6

LAUREN

Squished beside Billie, I rested my head against the glass and stared out the window at the blurred scenery, asking myself how I ended up here. Billie obviously hadn't told any of the others that I'd be coming on this awful trip, judging from the looks of surprise when I climbed into the van. No one said anything, though. They looked about as happy as I was about my inclusion.

Since Hamish sat in the front seat beside the therapist/driver, I had the option of sitting between Gabe and Tyler, or climb over Jake and Billie to sit next to the window. The choice was simple.

Hillis, Billie's therapist, looked nothing like I imagined a therapist. Instead, he reminded me of the outdoor instructors we had on school camps. Dressed in cargo pants, a light t-shirt and a cap, he chatted from the driver's seat, intentionally or unintentionally unaware of the discomfort surrounding him. His jokes met silence from everyone apart from Billie and Hamish who were going overboard in an attempt to find him funny.

Hamish appeared different after his time spent in rehab. More open, more interested in Billie but at the same time, less sure of himself.

The drive took about an hour and a half and only Billie, Hamish and Hillis spoke. Finally pulling up in a gravelled carpark, the van stopped and I was grateful to stretch my legs, doing my best to avoid both Tyler's and Gabe's gaze.

"Welcome to Camp Hillis." The therapist smiled broadly. "Yes, I named the camp after myself. No, it isn't really called Camp Hillis. That only happens when I'm running the show." He paused, waiting for the laughter that Billie and Hamish gave. Taking off his cap, Hillis called us to form a circle around him. "First, the rules. No cell phones."

"Excuse me?" Tyler spluttered.

"You're excused." Hillis grinned, shoving his cap towards Tyler. "Cell phone." When Tyler refused, Hillis rolled his eyes. "There is no reception, and no data available out here anyway."

"Then there is no reason for me to hand my phone in," Tyler growled.

"For fuck's sake Tyler, it's just a phone." Gabe pulled his from his pocket and placed it in the bowl of the cap.

"Thank you," Hillis said exaggeratedly. He shoved the cap in Tyler's direction again but Tyler shook his head. The rest of us put our phones into the cap. All except Jake. He didn't bring one. In fact, I wasn't even sure if he owned one.

"Now, as I suspect Billie would have explained to you, this weekend is to help you all with your relationships and dependency on alcohol and drugs as coping mechanisms. I'm looking at you, Gabe." Hillis gave him a stern glare as Gabe smiled innocently and held up his hands. "And also to help you re-connect as human beings."

Leaning closer to me, Gabe whispered, "Just shoot me now."

"So," Hillis continued. "Back to the rules. There is to be no drinking, no drugs, and no communication with the outside world. During your time here you will refrain from any conversation which brings tension or attention to the relationship issues you are currently facing. Nothing between fathers and sons. Husbands and wives. Girlfriend and boyfriends. Exes." He looked pointedly at me. "And nothing between brothers. If a conversation does come up, you are to stop it immediately. This weekend is to develop relationships first and deal with issues at a later date."

"Doesn't that kind of defeat the therapy part of this weekend?" Gabe whispered.

I took a step away.

"You will be eating together, completing activities together and even sleeping together."

Gabe looked over and wiggled his eyebrows. "I don't have any objection to that."

"So if everyone would gather their gear and follow me, I will show you the accommodation quarters."

What I expected was a dorm room with single beds evenly lined against the wall. What we got was an empty room with mattresses and pillows laid in a circle, heads together, with handwritten name cards resting on each pillow.

"Go ahead, place your bag on the mattress with your name. This will be your bed for the first night here. Each sleeping arrangement has been made from understanding the family dynamics and placing people where they would benefit from the most growth."

I wandered around the circle, looking for my name. Sure enough, there I was, wedged between Tyler and Gabe. Gabe looked at me and shrugged, a smirk stuck on his face. Tyler didn't look at me and instead, threw his pack onto the mattress. Dressed in jeans and a t-shirt, he looked nothing like the calm and controlled businessman he usually came across as. His t-shirt was tight, emphasising the sculptured swells of the body beneath it. Despite telling myself not to, my eyes kept slipping to him, reminding me of all the times I had lifted his shirt over his head, exposing the chiselled chest below. Of all the times I had pressed my lips to his chest. Of all the times I had run my tongue over his flesh.

"Isn't this exciting?" Billie chirped, interrupting my thoughts. "It will be like we're all kids again, sleeping on the floor during a sleepover. I haven't done that in years!" She clapped her hands together.

"See?" Hillis said. "Billie's got the right attitude. The only way you are going to get something out of the weekend is if you put the effort in with the right attitude. Billie and Hamish have that attitude and since the rest of you agreed to come along, I suggest you start by adjusting yours to follow suit."

"There is some debate on the agreeing part," I muttered.

"I don't even know why I'm here," Jake said, throwing his bag to the floor and then flopping onto the mattress. "I don't have issues with anyone."

"But you do have issues," Gabe teased.

"None that can be solved by singing around a campfire."

Hillis looked over at Billie sharply. "I told you not to tell them any of the activities."

"I didn't!" Billie exclaimed, her eyes growing wide.

"Shit," Jake cursed. "We're seriously going to sing songs around a campfire?"

"Is there a local taxi service available?" Tyler asked.

"Of course not," Hillis replied impatiently, taking Tyler's question more seriously than intended. "Now that the surprise has been ruined, if you would all meet me outside for our first night, we will be cooking sausages for dinner over the campfire."

Billie frowned. "I don't eat meat."

"Since when?" Hamish asked.

"Since I decided not to," Billie replied, somewhat aggressively. "Most likely when I was left alone while you were in rehab from drunk driving your car into the front of the casino."

"Lead the way," Jake said to Hillis, rubbing his hands together. "Let's get this over and done with."

Of all the things I imagined myself doing with the Thornton family, sitting around a campfire eating half-cooked sausages off a stick was not one of them. Billie and Hillis led the conversation, talking about frivolous things that no one else was interested in since topics of any depth were strictly off limits. Hillis told us of the activities we could expect over the weekend. First on the agenda for the next day was rock climbing. Apparently, trust issues would be dealt with during this exercise as we would be responsible for belaying each other as we climbed. A nauseated knot began to twist in my stomach. Although I had never had a problem with heights before, the thought of dangling from a rope wasn't appealing. After the rock climbing was complete, we would eat lunch and then head off on a silent trek to a campsite where we would spend the night in tents under the stars. I failed to see how any of this would help, but Hillis assured us that he had completed many of these activity therapy weekends with many families, and they always ended with a positive outcome. What he considered a positive outcome was never discussed.

After we ate black and pink sausages, Hillis got out his guitar, but after two failed attempts to get everyone to join in, he excused us for the rest of the evening with a resigned, but not defeated look on his face. On our tour of the facilities earlier, we had been shown a heated rock pool in a man-made cave just down a grassy hill. Making sure everyone else was occupied, I slipped on my bathing suit and headed down the path with a towel securely wrapped around me.

I needed to be alone.

I needed for Billie's voice not to be sounding in my ear, Gabe's eyes not to follow my every move, and for Tyler's avoidance to stop playing over and over in my mind. He had not uttered one word to me, and although I had caught his eye a couple of times, he looked away quickly as if determined to show me he didn't care if I was here or not.

Steam floated out from the cave to greet me. I had to duck my head, but once I was inside, the cave opened up into a small room with seating around the water's edge so you could sit with just your feet dipped in or submerge yourself completely. Lights recessed into the ceiling reflected on the water. Unwrapping the towel, I sunk into the liquid warmth, sighing when I lowered to my shoulders, letting my head fall back on the edge of the pool. It was exhausting just being around these people. Hamish mainly avoided me, but a small frown appeared in the lines between his brows anytime he was confronted with my presence. Gabe vied for my attention. Jake didn't care. Billie's voice had reached a level of shrillness unheard before in her efforts to convince herself this was a good idea, and Tyler's refusal to even look at me affected me more than I cared to admit.

With steam coating my lungs and heat caressing my body, I was in a state halfway between awake and asleep when I heard a throat clear.

"I didn't think anyone was here."

Tyler stood at the entrance to the cave, a towel wrapped around his waist, the rest of him unclothed. I swallowed the wave of desire that overwhelmed me at his appearance and nodded.

"Don't let me stop you," I said, impressed with the lack of emotion placed in my tone.

Tyler removed the towel, folding it into a neat pile before stepping into the water. He submerged himself next to me, only a swirl of water between us, and rested his head against the edge. "Do you think we're actually allowed to talk in here?"

I laughed, tension melting from me when he spoke with no malice in his voice. "I'd say it depends on the topic of conversation but maybe we should run it by Hillis just to make sure."

Tyler lifted his arms and stretched them along the pool, his fingertips resting just by my shoulder. "I'm surprised you agreed to come."

"I wasn't really given a choice."

"Me neither," Tyler agreed. "That Billie, huh? She's rather skilled at getting her own way."

"I'm blaming the baby." Sitting up, I fanned my hands over the surface of the water, acutely aware of how close Tyler's body was to mine. If I just let my foot float a little to the left, I would touch him. While staring down at my skin, made so pale by the water and the lights, Tyler shifted, the water swirling around his body as he moved closer. Putting his arms back on the edge of the pool, one of them reached behind my shoulders, skimming the air between us but not touching.

His eyes were closed, his head leaning back, his face tilted to the light. Shadows danced in the hollows of his features, shielding his expression. It would have been so easy to reach across and touch him. So easy to ignite the feelings that jolted between us like lightning. Although the state of our relationship had changed, my feelings for him hadn't. The need to touch him, the need to have him touch me was as strong as it had ever been. As if sensing my eyes on him, Tyler opened his and my heart raced as his gaze fell from my eyes to my lips. His eyes darkened with desire and he moved towards me, his body about to trap mine when Gabe sauntered in.

7

LAUREN

"I'm not interrupting anything, am I?" Gabe teased as Tyler quickly moved away from me.

Disappointment crept across my chest. Disappointment and annoyance. I shouldn't be so easily swayed by seeing Tyler shirtless. Placing his foot between us, Gabe sunk into the water, wrapping his arms around us both, grinning stupidly until Tyler stood, water streaming down his body, and climbed out.

"Don't leave on my account," Gabe called after him. But Tyler didn't reply. Instead, only wet footprints were left behind. "That guy has zero chill," Gabe said, his arm still wrapped around my shoulder. "I hope you two weren't talking about your relationship. It's against the rules. I, on the other hand, would never defy the rules by talking. Besides, there are things other than talking which I'd far rather engage you in."

Physically lifting Gabe's arm away, I sighed. "Why do you have to taunt him like that?"

"Like what?" Gabe appeared genuinely confused. "You were mine first, Lauren. That makes him the bad guy, not me." Gabe locked his hands behind his head, eyes sparkling. "Now you're not with either of us, and I don't know about Tyler, but I'd like the chance to change your mind."

I remained silent beside him, my mind still stuck on Tyler and the desire to run after him.

"I know you still have feelings for me, Lauren," Gabe said.

"I'm not having this conversation again." I stood, ready to leave Gabe alone in the pool, but Gabe stood too, his eyes travelling over my body now that it was exposed and out of the water. "I miss you. I miss us." He reached out, just the tip of his finger trailing over my arm, following a drip of water. "I miss the way you feel under—"

"Gabe, please," I said, stopping him before he said words he couldn't take back. Words I didn't want to hear. "You're making—" But I was interrupted by Jake ducking low to enter the cave. He held up his hands when Gabe scowled in his direction.

"Tyler told me I had to."

"And since when do you listen to Tyler?"

Jake shrugged, his back pressed to the walls of the man-made cave, shoulders hunched and looking entirely out of place. "Since I had nothing better to do." He looked over, watching as I wrapped a towel around my shoulders. "You alright?"

"Of course I'm alright," I replied, a little more annoyance in my voice than I intended. "I'm fine."

"Fine," Jake repeated, eyebrows lifting.

"See?" Gabe said. "She's fine." Gabe leaned over the edge of the pool. "We were actually just going to partake in some forbidden activities before you so rudely interrupted us." He held up a clear plastic bag, the green leafed contents leaving nothing to the imagination. "Care to join?"

Jake looked over at me. "Don't leave on my account."

"I was leaving anyway."

"Oh, come on, Mrs Robinson," Gabe said, a grin covering his face at the use of the old nickname. "Break free. Have a little fun. Or did being with Tyler all that time make you forget how?"

Jake pulled himself from the wall. "You don't have to ask me twice. Lauren?" he asked once he was waist deep, the water creating a dark line across the shirt covering his stomach. "You can't tell me that the offer doesn't tempt you?" Jake lowered himself so he was sitting in the water, stretching his arms out along the edge of the pool like both his brothers before him. "I won't tell Tyler."

"I don't care if you tell Tyler, it's just that…" I let my words trail off. It was just that I didn't want to be alone with Gabe? That despite not being with Tyler, I was still letting him influence my choices? I let my towel drop to the floor. "Move over," I said to Jake, choosing to sit next to him rather than Gabe.

The state of blissful contentment that took over a few minutes later was exactly what I needed. I forgot about Tyler's body so close to mine. I forgot about his scowl when Gabe entered the cave. I let go of why I was there and simply enjoyed being there. Although Gabe tried to slide around the side of the pool to sit beside me, Jake made a game of blocking him, insisting that he had promised Tyler to cock-block Gabe with each attempt. Thankfully, probably due to a previously inhaled substance, Gabe found this funny and it wasn't until the swirling steam of the room convinced us it was difficult to breathe, that we left.

The cold night air bit into my skin and I wrapped the towel tighter around my shoulders, falling behind the two brothers as they climbed the narrow steps back up the hill to the house.

Tyler sat outside, staring at the blank phone in his hands. He caught my hand as I passed, his fingers wrapping gently around my wrist. A breath caught in my throat at the sensation that bolted through my body, freezing me in place just as it had done every time before.

"Did he touch you?" Tyler's voice was rough.

"Tut, tut, tut," Hillis's voice called out the window. "That sounds suspiciously like a conversation involving some issues."

Gabe's grin stuck out like a light bulb behind him.

"Time for bed people, and remember, although I will not be sharing in the same intimate circle as you, I will still be listening to every word spoken during the night. In order for you to gain the most from this experience, you must adhere to the rules."

Tyler's grip on my wrist dropped, but his eyes still scanned my face, searching for any clue of my response in my expression. I let my gaze fall to the ground. I didn't owe him an explanation. After silently waiting, Tyler sighed and walked towards the house, letting me fall into step behind him.

Gabe and Jake stood in the kitchen, a cupboard open behind them and a bag of marshmallows on the table. Jake's fist dove into the bag and returned with a handful of sticky sweetness, popping them one at a time into his mouth. He chewed and swallowed under Tyler's glare, and then offered him the bag. "How many?" he asked.

"How many what?" Tyler replied, grumpily.

"How many can you fit in your mouth?"

"Challenge accepted!" Gabe yelled, grabbing for the bag. "How many of these things do we have? I'll go first. One," he counted. The numbers grew more mumbled as he shoved marshmallow after marshmallow in his mouth.

Jake lifted a single brow in Tyler's direction, the signature move of the Thornton men.

"Not in the mood," Tyler replied to his unspoken question.

"Are you ever?" Gabe garbled, a marshmallow popping out of his mouth. "That doesn't count!" he half yelled, half mumbled, shoving the offending sweet back in.

Tyler walked out of the room, throwing me a look over his shoulder I couldn't decipher as Gabe continued to shove more marshmallows into his mouth until saliva began to fall. He spat the marshmallows into the sink. "Seven. Fuck, I thought I would do better than that."

Jake looked at the sticky mess. "I can do more."

"Like hell, you can." Gabe turned to me. "You going to try?"

"What the fuck?" The curse word sounded funny on Hillis' lips. Unnatural. Briefly, I wondered if it was what I sounded like when I swore. "Well, there goes tomorrow night's campfire activity."

Gabe did his best to look guilty, but he ended up simply laughing. "Sorry, man, I didn't know you were saving them for something."

Hillis snatched the bag out of Jake's hand. "Everything on this trip is planned for the best outcome. I do not appreciate you messing with things."

"I'm sorry," Jake offered, plucking marshmallows out of his mouth. "I didn't realise these little guys meant so much to you."

"It's not the marshmallows." Hillis let out a frustrated sigh that was much too serious, and I had to swallow the splutter of laughter that threatened. "It's the fact that you have zero respect for the work I do. Your father has just spent thirty days in rehab, attempting to put his life back together, and you boys come along and act as though this is all a joke. How do you think that makes him feel after all the hard work he's put in?" Hillis stood, arms planted firmly on his hips, his glare altering between Gabe and Jake.

"Shit," Gabe said. "I didn't realise Dad's life was that bad. I mean, from all the overseas trips, the fancy houses, the company and all, I figured he had his shit sorted. Thank goodness you're here to correct me."

Jake snorted and a marshmallow shot out of his mouth, landing on the indignant face of Hillis. Jake froze, waiting for Hillis' reaction before bursting into laughter. "I'm sorry. I didn't mean to mallow your face." He swiped at the offending marshmallow, but it stuck to Hillis' skin.

"Bed. Now," Hillis stated calmly, despite the puff of pink stuck to his cheek. He pulled it off, leaving a sticky residue in its wake.

After changing in the bathroom, I padded across the wooden floor and tucked my clothing inside my pack, ready to be worn again the next day. Supplies were strictly limited. Billie watched me from across the room, her wide-eyed expression following my movements in the dim light.

"It's good," she said to no one in particular. "This is good. This is good," she repeated, tossing and turning. "I am comfortable in my surroundings. I am happy and at peace with myself."

"I am shit at talking under my breath," Gabe added, mocking her tone.

Laying down on my mattress with my head turned towards Gabe, his teeth shone at me through his grin. "Hey, Mrs Robinson," he whispered.

I turned over, only to be met by Tyler's gaze. It had always amazed me how much he could say without opening his mouth, and as I lay there, eyes locked on his in the semi-darkness, his intention was clear and the familiar feeling of arousal began to warm my insides. Feeling the heat creep into my cheeks, I snuggled down into my sleeping bag, tucked my head under the covers and shielded myself from exposing the thoughts racing through my head.

8

LAUREN

I didn't know I had a fear of heights until I attempted rock climbing. It had never struck me before. Not when witnessing Peta leap off the edge of a bridge with nothing more than a bungee cord tied to her feet. Not when looking out the window of a high-rise building. Not when climbing the scaffolding of the casino. Not when leaning over the edge of the railing while Tyler held me in place and did—well, did things I didn't want to think about in my present state, but after taking those first few steps up the rock wall, even with Tyler being the one gripping the rope that held me, I found myself frozen.

"You can do it," Hillis said firmly, as if, somehow, his tone could overrule my fear. "Just lift your hand up and a little to the right and you will find the next grip."

I shook my head, my heart beating out of my chest, and then stopped as soon as I realised the movement made me even more unstable. "I don't want to do this anymore," I said.

"I've got you," Tyler called out gently. "You just have to trust me."

Even in my frightened state, the irony of his statement still amused me.

"Don't look down," Billie yelled from the safety of the ground. "Look up. Look at Jake."

I attempted to do as she said and lifted my head. The rock stretched before me in what seemed like an endless slope of vertical grey. Jake waved from the top, crunching down on an apple, his hair piled in a loose bun on the top of his head.

"Come on, Lauren. It's easy," Jake called out, his words muffled by apple.

"Easy for you to say," I yelled back, and then gripped tighter to the rock as a wave of vertigo washed over. I closed my eyes and started to breathe deeply. There was simply nothing I could do. I was stuck a mere six feet off the ground.

Jake had made it look simple. While Hillis was taking us through the safety precautions, listing the equipment we would need, the steps we would follow, Jake had approached the cliff and began to hoist himself from point to point, at times only hanging by his fingertips.

Hillis had yelled at him to come down, but Jake had merely laughed and scaled his way to the top, pulling himself over the ledge and looking back down at us as we worked ourselves into the harnesses.

"I've probably done more rock climbing in one day than you've done in your life," he called back down to Hillis.

"There are procedures in place for a reason," Hillis called back, his usually ruddy cheeks turning an even brighter shade of red.

"Okay," Jake called out in reply. "I'll just be up here waiting while you enforce them."

Hillis picked me first. I had thought the look of sheer terror on my face might persuade him to choose someone else, but no such luck.

I gripped the rock with my entire body, well, that's what it felt like, anyway. I hovered as close to the cliff as possible, trying not to think about the tenuous placement of my fingers or the fragile holds of my feet. Technically, I knew if I fell, Tyler's rope would hold me in place. There was no way he would ever let me fall to the ground, but that didn't stop my brain from imagining every possible scenario of how that rope would fail. When what strength I had left began to fade, I couldn't help the tears that slipped out. Despite telling myself otherwise, I was quite literally frozen with fear. Risking a glance down, I met Tyler's eyes and mouthed out the word help.

"I need someone to take this," Tyler said, looking to the rest of his family.

"You are Lauren's assigned support. To give your position to someone else would be to—"

"Oh shut the fuck up," Tyler growled. "Just take my fucking place so I can go help her."

Hillis' face turned beet red but he didn't back down. "Lauren needs to learn how to deal with this situation herself and control her fear. This is exactly what I was talking about in therapy through adventure. It forces us to—"

"Help!" I wailed. I was doing a terrible job at controlling my fear. Rather than dissipating, it was increasing. My heart jumped sporadically inside my chest. My hands were sweaty and sticky and I was certain I was going to lose my grip at any moment.

"I've got this," Gabe said. I felt—rather than watched—him take the few steps below me until his body encased mine, forming a wall, shielding me from both the height and the fall. "It's okay," he whispered in my ear. "I've got you. We're going to do this together."

"I can't." My voice trembled. My foot slipped, but Gabe reached out and grabbed my thigh, giving me something to lean against.

"One step at a time and we can do this."

"I can lower her back down to the ground if she just leans into the rope," Tyler shouted from below.

Gabe's hand slid down the back of my thigh. "We're going to start with this leg first, okay?"

I nodded, comforted by the security of his body, and lowered myself cautiously, ready to freeze again at the slightest scare. Gabe stayed with me, whispering words of encouragement, and allowing me to lean on him for support until, after what seemed like an eternity, my feet reached solid ground.

Billie clapped me on the back. "You did it!" she said excitedly as I dropped to my knees, wanting to be as close to the safety of the ground as possible.

"She did not do it," Hillis corrected. "She came back down. The purpose of the activity was to…" Hillis' voice faded to nothing as Tyler approached, anger clearly flashing over his expression.

"Enjoyed that, did you?"

"Excuse me?" I asked, my hand over my heart as the pounding slowly subsided.

"Is that why you came? To mock me?"

"Excuse me?" I stuttered again, not quite believing the words that came out of his mouth.

"You heard me. Was that display purely to piss me off?"

I shook my head, my thoughts scattered and not comprehending. In my mind, part of me was still stuck on that cliff. "I never—"

"Well, mission accomplished, Lauren. I'm officially fucked off."

Tyler jerked the remainder of the rope through the carabiner and let it fall to the ground. The muscles of his body were strained, the threads of his neck tight.

Bending down beside me, Gabe rested his arm across my shoulders. "And how fare thee now, sweet damsel?"

Instead of answering, I watched the set of Tyler's shoulders as he strode away, shrugging off Gabe's affection.

"What's pissed him off now?" Gabe asked.

I shook my head, unable and unwilling to answer.

* * *

After lunch, our next scheduled activity was the silent trek to the campsite we were to stay at for the night. At first, the thought of a silent trek worried me. It seemed awkward and stupid, walking for hours without talking, but after Tyler's recent outburst over my supposed behaviour, the silence was welcome, despite being punctuated by Billie's heavy sighs.

Billie's positivity for the weekend had dramatically dropped over the past few hours. It started with her complaining how uncomfortable her mattress was and cumulated in her refusal to even attempt rock climbing. The image of me pressed against the wall, harness digging into my butt, sweat dripping from my ghostly-pale forehead, may have had something to do with it. And then the realisation that tonight would be spent on the ground with nothing to shield us but a roll of thin foam and our sleeping bags, was almost too much for Billie. When she thought of an adventure weekend, roughing it in tents had never occurred to her. I'm not sure what exactly she thought we would do, but I imagined it was more along the lines of a spa weekend, despite their lack of adventure.

Once the trek was completed, the tents erected, and campfire lit all under the cover of silence, Hillis announced that we were now free to talk, as long as the topics didn't include any of the issues we were currently facing.

No one said a word.

We sat around the fire as the sun fell over the ocean, listening to waves crashing against the rocks. Our tents were placed in a wide circle around the fire, two to each, apart from me. I got to spend the night alone. And after the day I had, I couldn't think of anything better than climbing into my sleeping bag and closing myself off to the world. How I longed for my little bedroom back at Sadie's house. The one where I didn't have to watch Tyler glare at me across the flames, or Gabe wink in my direction every time he made a crude joke. Part of me was waiting for Hamish to call the whole thing off, declare it was a stupid idea, something, anything, to get us all out of there. But either from the rehab therapy or the lack of alcohol in his system, Hamish remained silent, content to let the weekend play out as it willed. He never once commented on the ability of his sons, other than to compliment them, but he did studiously avoid me and made sure he was never placed in a position where he actually had to acknowledge my presence.

Once the sun had set and the ocean was left dark and foreboding, I zipped open the small entrance to my tent and crawled inside without bothering to remove any clothing other than my boots. It was cold and I shivered inside the padding of my sleeping bag, silently begging warmth to creep into my bones.

As the fire crackled and shadows danced over the walls of my tent, I wondered how on earth I had ended up here and why I didn't put my foot down when Billie insisted I come. Maybe there was a part of me still not willing to give up my relationship with the

Thornton family. Maybe I was addicted to the drama, to the roller coaster of emotions I experienced whenever I was around them. With these thoughts floating through my head, the voices around the fire finally faded into oblivion.

I woke in the wee hours of the morning. The fire still crackled and shadows still danced across the walls of my tent. I strained to listen for voices, but nothing greeted me other than the waves on the beach. Unzipping the bottom of my sleeping bag to free my feet, I leaned over and opened the tent. Embers glowed in the darkness and flames licked the sky. I wanted to fall back asleep, ignore the thoughts that told me I needed to put the fire out, but the images of my tent bursting into flames while I slept wouldn't leave. Pleased to be out of the enclosed space, I stretched when I exited the tent and shuffled over to the fire, keeping my sleeping bag firmly tucked around my chin. The night had only got colder since I had gone to bed and my breath came out in white puffs. A figure was hunched by the fire, sitting on a log and poking the embers with a stick. Sparks flew into the air like tiny fireflies.

Tyler looked up as I approached. "Can't sleep?" he asked, his anger from before seemingly gone.

"I thought the fire had been left unattended." I moved opposite him and sat as close as I could to the fire without my sleeping bag melting in the heat.

The stars were out in force. I had never seen so many. They dotted the sky as though I were sitting under a blanket littered with pinpricked holes which allowed the light through.

"Can I ask you something?"

I tensed, dreading the question that I thought would come, and nodded.

"Has your mother always been like that?"

I laughed with relief, pleased that his annoyance at me was short lived. "Like what?"

"A bitch," Tyler offered.

Picking up a discarded stick, I poked the embers like Tyler had done before, sending a spray of sparks into the night. "Pretty much," I replied. "Why do you think I was so keen to move out of home?" I dug the stick into the ash. "I know she means well, but it's a brand of caring most people don't appreciate."

"It's good she cares," Tyler said. He sat up straighter on the log, adjusting his feet so they lay out in front of him. "I wish my mother was a little more like her."

When I looked at him questioningly, he amended his statement. "Okay, maybe not. But, as you said, she does care even if she has a strange way of showing it."

"How long has it been since you've seen her? Maybe she's changed."

"I doubt it." Tyler stared at the fire and the flames danced across his eyes. "I'm thinking of going to see her, actually. I just wish I didn't have to do it alone."

I swallowed the lump in my throat at his silent accusation. "What about Jake?"

Tyler shrugged. "True."

The wind picked up and blew smoke in my direction. I moved across the grass, finding a better place to sit. With Tyler's gaze directed at the fire, I was able to study him and a surge of nostalgic sadness crept into my chest. An outdoors Tyler was not one I had seen before. He looked at home under the stars. I was used to seeing him with glasses perched over his nose and a laptop on his knee which often jiggled with impatience. Out here he looked at peace.

"You look at home out here," I said, voicing my thoughts.

Tyler broke the stick in his hands and tossed it on the fire. "Dad used to take us camping every year when we were younger. It was the only time we actually got to spend with him. No business calls taking his attention away. No wife." He chuckled. "It was men only on those trips, even though we were only boys."

"And you all got along?"

"It was only Jake and me. By the time Clark and Gabe were old enough to go, the trips had stopped."

"It would have been nice if you all had got to share that. Maybe you could all start now."

Tyler grunted. "I can't see that happening."

"I hate that I've been the one to do that."

"We had our problems long before you came along, Lauren." Again his eyes locked on mine and the reflection of the flames licked over them. "Can I ask you another question?"

"Go ahead."

"Did he try anything?"

The familiar tightness in my chest returned. Fear. Guilt. I wasn't sure exactly what it was. "Who?" I feigned ignorance.

Tyler didn't answer, just lifted that one brow.

Adjusting the sleeping bag around my shoulders once again, I picked up the stick I had left stabbed into the ash. The bottom was black and white, burnt to a char. "It's really none of your business anymore, Tyler," I replied, hoping to avoid the conversation.

"It will always be my business. I can't even describe what it felt like watching him help you down from that rock today."

"You might not be able to describe your feelings but you still managed to make them known," I muttered. Then, taking a deep breath, I added, "I guess that's why, despite my initial hesitation, this weekend has been good for me. It has reminded me why we don't work. There would always be this thing between us."

"There was no need for him to touch you the way he did, no reason for you to allow it."

"Allow it?" I repeated, my voice growing louder. "I was petrified, Tyler. I was quite literally stuck to that wall with no way to make my limbs move. If Gabe hadn't helped, I'd probably still be there."

"I should have been the one to help you."

"You were. You held the rope. You needed to trust me, Tyler. Regardless of what Gabe chooses to do, it's me you need to trust."

Getting to his feet, Tyler began to pace around the fire, stopping and turning in the opposite direction each time he reached the space where I blocked his path. "I don't know how to do that. I don't know how to stop feeling what I feel when he's anywhere near you. My blood boils. It's like a red haze passes over me and all these things I don't even mean start to spill out of my mouth, usually hurting the person who means the most to me."

"I can't be with you and feel guilty every time I see or talk to Gabe. It's not as though he's simply some ex who I can avoid. He's your brother, Tyler. If I'm with you, our paths are going to cross. I can't just ignore or avoid him."

Tyler stopped pacing, running his hands through his hair and expelling a frustrated sigh. "I know. I know. I just don't know how to stop it. How do you stop feelings?"

"Maybe at first you don't stop the feelings. Maybe you just stop acting on them."

9

LAUREN

The weekend almost gave me a sense of closure. Sure, Tyler looked sexy as hell and I often found myself daydreaming of the times we had spent together, but overall, it reminded me that I couldn't be with him if he didn't trust me. And from his reaction to Gabe helping me when I was frozen with fear, it was clear that he didn't.

After the night spent in tents, Billie exploded at Hillis and demanded he take us home immediately. His insistence of completing the weekend was no match for Billie's determination and by Sunday afternoon, I found myself unceremoniously dumped at my front door, my duty to attend the Thornton therapy weekend complete and definitely not a success. No doubt Billie would somehow make it my fault.

For the next week, Sadie and I studiously worked on our presentation for Haven's Rest until we were sure it was perfect. Well, as perfect as we could get it. We had completed other jobs and campaigns for small businesses, but to get the contract for Haven's Rest would catapult us into the big leagues. We had fun setting up the room, scattering it with clothes and props to make it look as though a group had just left for a night on the town.

We made the presentation in front of a collection of stony-faced suits who hardly ever smiled. Sadie did most of the talking, but her cheerful disposition did little to warm the hearts of the executives. With little more than a handshake, they dismissed us and we left feeling rather deflated. We were sure we had come up with an interesting concept. It was original and would grab people's attention, but after receiving virtually no feedback, we had picked up takeaway food on the way home and now sat on the couch, watching old episodes of the cooking show I used to be obsessed with. I think that both Sadie and I were hoping that by watching it, some of the contestants' skills might rub off on us. They didn't.

"Do you regret quitting your job with Tyler?" I asked, popping a stale piece of popcorn into my mouth. We had watched a movie the night before and, after devouring our takeout, the leftover popcorn was the only food left in the house. We desperately needed to go to the store, but neither of us could be bothered.

Sadie, eyes glued to her phone, sighed and looked over at me. "Nope," she replied simply. "It's our first presentation, Lauren. We can't expect everything to turn up roses the first time."

"How did you end up working for him, anyway?"

"I thought we weren't talking about Tyler?"

There was an unspoken rule between Sadie and me. I knew she still spoke to Tyler often, but she never mentioned him to me unless I brought him up.

"We're talking about you, not Tyler."

Sadie grinned. "Fine, if that's the way you want to frame it."

I rolled my eyes and picked a stubborn piece of popcorn from my teeth.

"Well, as you know, we met at university. Tyler was this really determined guy, always had a serious scowl on his face, always with his head in a book, or in a laptop. I met him through a friend of a friend, you know how it goes. Well, anyway, he became like this pet project I simply had to corrupt. I mean who went to university to actually study? Apparently no one had informed Tyler that his university years were supposed to be the time he ran amok."

Smudge sauntered into the room and climbed onto Sadie's knee, turning around in a circle five times before curling into a ball on her lap. She waited until he was settled before pushing him off.

"That cat is such an arsehole." Sadie poked out her tongue in the cat's direction as he sat and stared daggers at her, ears firmly planted against his head. "Anyway, back to my story." She adjusted her position on the couch, lying across it rather than sitting on it and crossed her ankles. "You could say I wasn't as well suited for studying as Tyler was and I switched from major to major. In the end, I graduated with a degree in Art history, of which I've done nothing with and can barely remember. Instead, I decided to travel. I kept in contact with Tyler and when I came back home, moneyless and jobless, he was looking for an assistant and asked me to fill in temporarily until he found someone. Six years later, I was still there." She shrugged. "That's how I ended up working for Tyler." Reaching onto the floor, Sadie guided a handful of popcorn from her bowl into her mouth, stuffing it fully until she could barely close it.

"Do you miss it?"

Sadie shook her head, holding her hand over her mouth to stop the popcorn escaping. "Not really. I guess I miss all the functions I used to attend on his behalf. That was fun for a while. Especially when you came along. Before you, Tyler begrudgingly went to almost everything he was invited to as he considered it 'his duty'." Sadie coughed, choking on a stray kernel. "He hated them. I used to have to listen to him moan about all these people I was dying to meet, so when you came along and the requests for me to attend in his place increased, I was pretty happy. Then I realised that it was always the same people talking about the same old shit and the shine wore off rather quickly."

"Did you ever meet his mother?"

"Tyler's?" she asked.

I nodded, keeping my eyes stuck on the television because I didn't want to see the smirk that I knew would be covering her face.

"I thought this wasn't about Tyler?"

"It's just one little question."

The truth was, I was beginning to feel a little Tyler starved. The weekend away had helped give me closure, confirmed that I made the right decision regarding our relationship, but that didn't mean I was completely over Tyler Thornton. He had gone from being my whole world to a distant part of it. There were days when I wanted to pounce on Sadie and demand she tell me every little piece of Tyler related gossip she could muster. My pride never let me though.

"Only the once. At Clark's funeral. She wasn't what I thought she'd be. From the way Tyler spoke about her, I expected this wasted druggy-type, but she wasn't anything like that. She was well presented, well groomed, but I didn't really get the chance to speak to her. Tyler was majorly pissed she was even there." Sadie picked at her teeth. "Did he tell you he's going to visit her?"

"When would he have had the chance?" I shot back, a little more sharply than I intended.

Sadie held up her hands as though I had attacked. "Whoa, calm down. It was just a question. Besides, he told me that he told you on that stupid weekend he was going to go and visit her. He's on his way now. I think he wanted you to offer to go with him."

"I can't go with Tyler to meet his mother. I can barely be around him."

Sadie wiggled her eyebrows. "Because you want to do bad things to him?"

I scowled. "Sadie."

There was a knock at the door and Sadie stuck her thumb to her forehead. "Bags not."

I sighed and lifted myself from the couch, stepping around Smudge who had firmly planted himself in front of Sadie and was engaging in a one-sided staring competition.

"If it's Gabe, don't let him in!" Sadie shouted.

I pulled open the door to find Peta standing on the step, arms laden with bags. "Good," she said without greeting. "You're here."

"And so are you," I replied as she barged past. "Why are you here?"

"It's good to see you too, Ren," she called over her shoulder. "Lounge down this way, I take it?"

I followed as she walked in and dumped her bags on the floor. Sadie shook her head in surprise. "Hello?" she said, looking over at me with a confused expression.

"Sadie, Peta, Peta, Sadie," was my brief introduction. It struck me as strange that the two had never met before. Peta was my oldest and closest friend, and Sadie was fast becoming included in my small circle of friends as one I truly trusted.

The two women eyed each other suspiciously and nodded in greeting. They both knew of the other, but it was the first time they had met. I felt oddly nervous, scared that they wouldn't like each other.

Peta sighed loudly and pulled out a stool from the kitchen counter, sitting down heavily. "I figured I should come and visit you since you haven't come to see me in years."

I laughed and pulled out the stool next to her. "It hasn't been years."

"Years," she repeated, emphasising the word with a pointed glare.

"Any particular reason for this visit? Kids good? Hubby good? Work good?"

Tears welled in Peta's eyes.

"What's wrong?" I said, leaning close and pulling her into my arms. She broke down completely then, and Sadie got up from the couch, declaring she needed to make a trip to the store.

"I'm pregnant," Peta wailed.

"What?" I pulled back and held her firmly by the shoulders. "When? How? Was it planned?"

Peta pulled a tissue out of her pocket and dabbed her eyes, leaving smudges of mascara. "Well, I don't actually know if I'm pregnant yet. I'm late. My boobs are tender, I'm crying at the drop of a hat and I've got this nauseated feeling in my gut. I don't know if it's morning sickness or just worry."

"So not planned then?"

She shook her head. "I haven't even told Shrek. I want to do the test first. I just didn't want to do it with him, this time, you know? All the others were planned. Well, apart from Henry, but the other two were. And now this has happened and I don't want to be alone when I find out, but I also don't want someone there watching and judging my reaction. I really just don't know how I feel. I don't know if I'm going to burst into tears if it's positive or burst into tears if it's not."

I got off the stool and walked over to my bag, grabbing the keys from the pocket. "Come on," I said, dangling them in front of Peta. "There's only one way to find out."

Peta picked up her own bag from the ground and turned it over. Three boxes of tests fell to the floor. "Way ahead of you."

"I'm not coming in while you pee on it."

Peta laughed and hugged me tightly. "Thanks," she said.

"For what?"

"For being you. I've missed you so much, Ren. I don't like you living in the city. I think you should give up this illustrious career in marketing and photography and come back and make coffee with me."

"Believe me, after the reaction we had to our presentation today, it's very tempting." I tugged on her hand, leading her in the direction of the bathroom. I waited, leaning on the other side of the door until she came out again, eyes a little clearer and a white tester held in her hand. "Three minutes. Why didn't I buy the one minute one?"

We flopped back onto the couch. The voices of the cooking contestants filled the space with distracting chatter as we waited.

"I'm sorry to put this on you," Peta said, her hand clutched tightly around the test so she couldn't peek.

"Sorry?" I replied. "I'm pleased you came. I know I've been a sucky friend lately."

"No more than I have," Peta replied. "But I'm sorry because, well, you know."

"This is about you, not me, Peta. So don't you dare apologise for that. You know how I hate it when people try to protect me from anything to do with pregnancy."

"I know, it's just—" her voice cut off in a strangled sob. "I'm not sure if I can do this. I'm not sure if I can go through it all over again. I mean, I love my babies, I really do, but four? I never wanted four."

"How do you think Shrek would take it?"

"I'd say he'd be thrilled. But even though he's the one that looks after the kids the most, he's not the one that has to grow them inside him for nine months."

I glanced at my cell phone, noting the numbers on the clock. "It's time."

Peta's knuckles were as white as the tester they were wrapped around. "I'm not sure I can do this."

"You know the test doesn't make you pregnant, it only confirms if you already are."

"Okay, smart alec. I'm just not sure if I want to—" Before she finished her sentence she ripped her fingers away and left the test exposed in her hand, covering her eyes with the other. "You look. I can't."

I peered down at the little clear window. "What does a blue cross mean?"

Peta's eyes flew open, her hand dropped to her throat, and she let out a sigh of relief. "Oh my goodness, you scared me!"

"No cross." I grinned and patted her knee. "You're not pregnant."

"That was mean." Peta looked at the other two tests she had completed at the same time. None of them showed as positive. Her body slumped as relief overwhelmed her and tears sprung to her eyes again. "Why am I so bloody emotional then?"

I just shrugged.

"I feel so stupid," Peta said, flopping back on the couch. "I got myself all worked up, yelled at Shrek that I needed a break and drove all this way for nothing."

"I'm nothing?"

"Don't make this about you." She grinned, a little of the normal Peta rearing her head. "What now?" she asked, looking around the room as if noticing it for the first time. "Your house is shitty."

"Yes," I agreed. "It is. Drink?"

Peta's eyes lit up. "What are you offering?"

Wandering into the kitchen I pulled open all the cupboards trying to find a bottle of wine. In the end, I admitted defeat and called Sadie, instructing her to come home loaded with wine as soon as possible.

10

LAUREN

"I have arrived!" Sadie announced as she walked through the door, arms filled with bottles of wine, red, white and pink. "I didn't know what you liked so I got everything," she declared.

Peta took one of the bottles from Sadie and held it to the light. "Right now I'd drink anything."

I got the glasses from where they always sat, easily accessible in the closest cupboard, while Sadie unloaded the bottles onto the bench one at a time.

"Are you planning on us having a big night?" I asked, laughing as bottle after bottle was lined up in a row.

Sadie screwed up her face. "Why wouldn't we? Have you got anything on in the morning, because I sure haven't?"

The night started off slowly enough, polite conversation over sips of wine, but the more wine that was consumed, and when the retelling of Peta's pregnancy scare had been told in as many ways as possible, our words began to slur and the topic of my relationships dominated the conversation.

"Wait," Sadie said, holding her hand in the air as she took another sip. We were all piled on the same couch, feet tucked up under our ankles, drops of wine spilt on our clothes. "Who is Derek and why do we hate him?"

Peta high-fived Sadie, though I wasn't sure why. "Derek was her high school sweetheart. The love of her life until she found him humping his assistant on the desk. She literally walked in on them."

Sadie looked at me wide-eyed. "No way!"

I laughed, now able to look back on it with amusement. "His pale, hairy arse was up in the air, clenching and unclenching. It took about two minutes of me just staring before my brain registered what was happening."

"No shit," Sadie said in amazement. "And then what?"

"What do you mean, then what?" I asked, confused.

"And then what happened? Did you drag him off her? Did you yell, scream, kick, punch?"

"I closed the door."

"You fucking what?" she screeched.

Peta's eyes gleamed as she nodded. "She shut the freaking door. I'm not kidding you. There she was, confronted with her fiancé humping some bitch and she just walks back out and shuts the door. She just left them to it!"

I shrugged and took another sip of wine. "Not a lot I could have done to stop it at that stage."

"I would have freaked." Sadie took another mouthful of her wine, only this time it was a gulp. "I would have kicked his arse."

"I didn't see the point."

"The point? The point was to show him you wouldn't put up with that shit."

"I found out later it had been going on for months, right under my nose."

"But you let him finish!" Sadie exclaimed. "You could have at least denied him that. Did he know you walked in? That you saw them?"

I shook my head. "I confronted him at first, asked him if there was anything he wanted to tell me."

Sadie snorted. "Pussy."

"I was in shock."

"You were a pussy," Sadie repeated, punctuating the words.

"But then Gabe came and took all her pain away," Peta sung.

Sadie lifted her eyebrows while talking with her mouth pressed to the wine glass, making her voice echo strangely. "Ah, I always wondered how you two met. You weren't exactly what I would have pictured as a couple."

There were times that I forgot that Sadie didn't know all the details of my life. I only met her when I started dating Tyler. The Lauren that existed in that perfect Tyler bubble was the only Lauren she knew.

"It was all my fault." Peta sighed. "I hired her and Gabe trained her. The rest is history."

"Well," Sadie said, wiggling her eyebrows. "Not exactly history."

"It is," I declared, strong and determined in my new-found drunkenness. "Gone is the old Lauren who flopped from man to man, letting them make her life decisions. Look out world, the new Lauren is here." My voice petered off at the end, contradicting my strong start.

"So, let me get this straight," Sadie said, choosing to ignore my weak declaration. "You went from Derek, who you'd been with since high school, to Gabe and then to Tyler?"

"There were breaks in between," I corrected.

"And another little dalliance with Derek in there too," Peta added.

"Oh," I cried, a little distracted and rather drunk. "Dalliance. I like that word."

"You went back to him?" Sadie gripped the sleeve of my shirt, her red stained lips set in an incredulous line.

"She did," Peta confirmed.

"The guy fucking cheated on you, in front of you, and you went back to him?"

"We were supposed to be together forever. We were engaged. We lost a child."

"Oh, shit." Sadie's voice dropped with remorse. "I didn't know."

"It was years ago." I didn't tell her the full story. I didn't tell her that the reason Derek went into the arms of his assistant so willingly was because I couldn't give him what he wanted.

"Fuck Derek," she shouted.

"Not anymore!" Peta half yelled, half laughed.

"But back to the story, you went back to Derek but you obviously didn't stay with him."

"I should have never gone back to him. It was complicated. It—"

"It was Gabe," Peta finished for me. "He and his body were just too damn sexy. It took her ages to agree to be with him, though. She had this thing with his age and—"

Sadie rolled her eyes. "I don't blame her. He's a decade younger."

"But," Peta held a finger in front of Sadie's mouth, "he loved her. He was good to her. She deserved a little happiness."

"Oh, I'm not denying that," Sadie agreed. "But Lauren never belonged with Gabe. She and Tyler are a far better fit."

Peta lifted her eyes and twisted her mouth in a way which indicated she didn't agree.

"Don't tell me you think Lauren and Gabe are better suited?" Sadie twisted her head to face me. "Please tell me you don't believe that. Tyler adores you. You should see him without her. He's miserable. He does nothing but work now. Nothing. Well, apart from workout but that doesn't count. He's in his office at six-thirty every morning and doesn't leave until at least nine at night. Then he goes home and drinks himself into a stupor."

"He does not," I snorted.

"He does too. He says you've turned him into an alcoholic."

"I thought we weren't supposed to talk about him," I shot back, scared by the overwhelming longing for Tyler that rippled through me.

Sadie held up her hands, her wine glass tipping lopsidedly, the dark liquid threatening to spill once again. "Your rules, not mine. Personally, I don't know why you just don't forgive the guy and get on with it." She saved the wine from spilling by tipping it down her throat.

"Because he can't move past the fact that I was with Gabe before I was with him, and there is nothing I can do to change that. I can't go back and change my past even if I wanted to. I can't make Gabe disappear. I can't avoid him. They're brothers. I was sick of feeling worried when I was around him. I was sick of being made to feel guilty when I've been nothing but loyal to Tyler from the moment we started dating. I was loyal to him while I was still with Gabe, for fuck's sake."

Peta ran her hand down my back as I leaned forward and covered my face with my hands.

"I'm just so sick of feeling guilty. I felt guilty for not being able to give Derek the child he wanted. I felt guilty for wanting Gabe when he was so much younger than me. I felt guilty for breaking his heart and falling for Tyler. I felt guilty when I was with Tyler. And I felt guilty when I saw Gabe while I was with Tyler. I'm just so sick of feeling guilty and I'm sick of missing Tyler so much it hurts."

"Well go back to him!" Sadie declared as though it were the simplest solution in the world. "If you love him that much and he loves you, surely you can work through this."

"But nothing's changed." I lifted my head from my hands. "The weekend away proved that. He gets jealous of Gabe and lashes out at me. He can't control his reactions to his feelings, he told me that."

"Stop," Peta ordered, holding a hand over each of our faces as she sat between us. "There is entirely too much soul searching and not enough drinking going on here. From now on, all conversation regarding men is strictly prohibited." She settled herself, snuggling back into the couch, glass of wine in her hand. "Now, tell me more about Slag."

We talked and drank and danced into the wee hours of the morning. When I woke the following day with a dry mouth and rolling stomach, Peta was already up and in the kitchen. I inhaled deeply, unsure whether the aromas were encouraging or subsiding my nausea.

"You have virtually no groceries in the cupboards," Peta said as a greeting.

"Good morning to you too," I replied. "We mainly eat takeout. Sadie's cooking skills make even my cooking look good."

"That bad, huh?"

"She burned pasta."

"How on earth did she do that?"

I shrugged, and plucked a strip of bacon from the pan. "Beats me."

Sadie waltzed down the hallway, her smile all sunshine and butterflies, wearing a skimpy pair of shorts and a tank top despite the chill in the air. "Morning!" she greeted. "It smells divine in here."

"It's all Peta."

"Duh," Sadie replied. "We've lived together long enough to know it was Tyler who cooked most of the meals at the loft." She looked around the kitchen, bewildered. "What is that smell?" She sniffed, her nose twitching in the air. "It smells like…" She stalked through the kitchen. "Yes! Coffee." Grabbing the pot she lifted a mug down and filled it to the brim. "I didn't even know we had a coffee machine."

"It's a coffee filter and I found it at the back of that cupboard over there." Peta pointed to a cupboard as Sadie took a sip, not caring as the hot liquid slid down her throat.

"Well fancy that," Sadie said. "I've never even seen that cupboard before."

The three of us sat down at the table and ate together. It was the first time the table had been used for its intended purpose since I had moved in. Smudge twisted around our feet, smooching until Sadie relented and gave him a piece of bacon. "I hate you," she muttered, as she stroked his head.

"So what's our plan?"

"Bed," I groaned, rubbing my temples.

"You staying?" Sadie asked Peta.

Peta shook her head. "I've got to get back home. I kind of left in a bit of a state. Shrek will be worried and I told him he wasn't to call. Poor guy."

"You going to tell him?" I asked, tearing a corner of toast with my teeth.

"About the almost baby?" She nodded. "Yes. And then I believe we will be having a conversation that involves sharp objects and his testicles. If yesterday has taught me anything, it's that I'm done having children. Three is the perfect number for me. No need to add any more."

Once breakfast was finished and the dishes done, Peta packed up her belongings that had been scattered around the house at various stages of last night's festivities and waved goodbye. I found tears welling in my eyes again. I had forgotten how much I missed her.

The rest of the day consisted of laying on the couch and watching television. Sadie popped in and out, though I never bothered to ask her where she was going. I tried not to think about Tyler. I tried not to wonder how his visit with his mother was going.

I tried and I failed.

I went to bed early, head still thudding in pain, slight nausea still in my gut. I didn't know how Sadie did it. She managed to drink more than me and still bounce out of bed fresh as a daisy.

I drifted asleep easily and was surprised when I woke to a blackened room, the only light coming from around the curtains. Our streetlight was especially bright. Something had woken me but I wasn't sure what. I rolled over and grabbed my phone off the charger, noticing the little flashing light. There were three missed calls. All from Tyler.

The time read 1:03am and his calls had come through in the minutes previous. I was just about to dial my voicemail to get his message when my phone started to vibrate with another call.

"Hello," I answered when Tyler's image popped up. Gone was the profile picture from his social media account. In its place was a black and white image I had taken of him getting out of the shower. It was a close up of his face. Stubble dusting his chin, hair wet and flopped over his eyes. Dark brows hunched over dark eyes. It made my heart lurch every time I looked at it, which was more often than I cared to admit.

"You answered." His voice was flooded with relief.

"Is something wrong?" I couldn't think of a reason he would be calling in the middle of the night.

"I need you," his voice broke.

"Is everything okay? What's happened?"

Tyler cleared his throat, dislodging the emotion stuck there. "I need to see you. I just can't—I don't know what to do, what to think. I need you, Lauren. Please come over. I would come to you but I shouldn't drive." There was a moment of silence, then he added, "Please." And it was the tone of that word, so desperate, so pleading that had me getting out of bed and pulling on some clothes.

11

LAUREN

I pressed the buzzer at the bottom of the elevator. I had never pushed it before, never needed to. A sound echoed through the exposed lower level of the building and the door clunked as it released in order for me to enter.

My foot tapped impatiently as the elevator rose to the top level, and I slid the door open when the lift jerked to a stop.

Tyler was sitting on the couch, face covered by his hands when I stepped into the open space. His head lifted at the same time as he rose from the couch, striding over to me and wrapping me in his arms. He breathed in deeply as I tried not to melt into his embrace.

"Thanks for coming. I know you didn't have to," he said when he finally released me.

"Is everything okay?" I hadn't seen Tyler this distraught before. He wore jeans and a shirt, but the top buttons had been ripped off as though the shirt had been strangling him. Or maybe someone else had ripped them off. My heart pounded, and I internally told myself to calm down.

Taking my hand, Tyler led me over to the couch and indicated I should sit. He didn't though. He paced the floor, hands running through his hair, eyes wild and glazed.

"Tyler please tell me what's going on. You've got me worried."

"I'm sorry." He sat beside me. "Shit." He ran his hands through his hair again and then reached for the tumbler of whiskey on the coffee table, throwing the contents into his mouth and swallowing painfully.

"I did it," he said finally. "I went and saw my mother."

So that was what it was all about. I sighed in relief. "And it didn't go so well?" I prompted.

"She was better than I thought. Turns out she's got things together. Jake told me she had, but I didn't believe him." He ran his hands through his hair again, tugging at the roots. "Shit," he cursed. "I don't even know where to begin."

"At the start?" I suggested ruefully.

"Drink with me?" Tyler got to his feet and walked over to the whiskey bottle sitting on the bench.

"I don't think I can." My stomach twisted at the mere thought. But Tyler ignored me, or maybe didn't hear me, and poured a shot into the glass, holding it out while he tossed his back.

He sat beside me, although he was restless. "I've missed you," he said quietly. Taking my hand again, he rubbed his thumb in circles over the pad of flesh between my thumb and forefinger. Then turning my hand over so my wrist was exposed, he brought it to his mouth, kissing the tender flesh with feather-like softness.

"Tyler." I pulled away.

"Sorry," he said again. "I just don't—" He stopped and started again. "Do you remember when I told you about that summer I went to stay with Mum?"

"The one where you tried to run back to that girl?" How could I forget? Even though it was years before I met him, my heart still constricted a little at the thought of another woman holding his heart.

Tyler nodded. "Well, that's what really did it for me, the way she dobbed me into my father and he dragged me back home because she didn't want me. I thought she wanted her life free from children, free from family so she could hide herself in whatever substance took her fancy. I found out today that's not exactly what happened. There was a reason she called Dad to take me back. And it wasn't her proclivity for drink or drugs."

Tyler took my hand again, bringing it back to his mouth and pressing his lips against it. Not really kissing, just touching, like he needed to be sure I was there. I was real.

I didn't pull away.

"I arrived at her place unannounced. To say she was surprised to see me was an understatement, but that's the way I wanted it. I didn't want her to have the opportunity to change her life because I was arriving. I didn't want to give her the chance to hide. Anyway, it was just her when I arrived. She cried. She cried and she made me a cup of tea. It was awkward, you know? She sat there with these tears glistening and all I could think about was how I didn't really know her. I knew nothing of the woman in front of me. She looked the same as I remembered. She still wears her hair in the same bob-like cut." He indicated the length with his hands as though it mattered, as though it were an integral part of the story. "But she was nervous. She kept looking at the clock, looking at the door like she was expecting someone. I thought her dealer would turn up or something. I thought catching her unaware had worked out conveniently but only if I left in time before her true nature reared its head again. She was keen to get rid of me, and even suggested I come back later once she'd had time to 'tidy up'." Tyler rolled his eyes. "All these emotions just sort of overwhelmed me. I couldn't understand how a parent didn't want to be part of their kid's life. All this resentment welled up again and I couldn't help think of all the birthdays she'd missed, all the parts of my life she's never shown an interest in. I know that Jake thinks it's my fault we didn't stay in contact, but all I did was refuse to go and see her. I never once stopped her from seeing me." Sighing deeply, Tyler let go of my hand and got to his feet. "I need another drink. You ready for another?"

I looked down at the glass. I hadn't even taken a sip. Tipping the contents onto my tongue, I shuddered as I swallowed the liquid in one gulp and held the now empty glass out for him to refill. Tyler returned with both glasses filled higher than they were before. Even though I'd only had the one, already the warmth crept into my chest and I felt myself breathe a little easier. I tossed the second back, mimicking Tyler.

"No dealer turned up," Tyler continued. "Instead, I found myself face to face with Claudia. The girl I'd fallen for all those years before."

My heart dropped into my stomach. I swallowed nervously, annoyance creeping up my spine over the fact that he had called me here in the middle of the night to tell me he had hooked up with an old girlfriend.

"At first, I was pleased to see her. But she was shocked to see me. She went pale, this sort of grey colour, and kept looking at Diana like they were trying to communicate right in front of me without me knowing what they were saying. It was really strange. Then this kid walked in. He'd just finished school and he dumped his bag down on the floor like he owned the place. It didn't take me long to figure out he was Claudia's kid. He was the right age. It also didn't take me long to figure out that it was like looking in a mirror fourteen years ago."

I looked over at Tyler sharply, unsure if I had heard correctly, but Tyler nodded in response to my unasked question. "He's mine. I have a son."

"But," I stuttered, my head feeling like the sparks of connections were no longer working. "But the baby wasn't yours."

"That's what she told me. Mum found out she was pregnant and told Dad. He then paid her this rather large sum of money so she didn't 'ruin my life.' Claudia said she couldn't refuse. She was twenty-two. She worked at the local shop, with little other job prospects and she had a kid on the way. It was a choice between me knowing and being a part of the kid's life or being financially set up. For both her and Dante."

"Dante?"

Tyler smiled for the first time. "That's his name. Dante." It was a brief smile and he wiped it away with the back of his hand, his eyes dimming again. "So when I went running back to Mum, she already knew what had happened. She knew and she supported Dad's decision to keep it from me. I was only seventeen. I was supposed to take over the company one day, not run away to live with a girl I got pregnant."

Tyler looked at me pleadingly, but I wasn't sure what he was pleading for. The sparking connections of my brain still refused to work, causing thoughts to crash against the walls of my mind rather than fully form. I looked down at my empty glass and rose to fill it again, relishing the clouded fog that folded over me.

"Say something," Tyler urged.

I poured another drink. "I don't know what to say." I drank and poured another. "You're a father."

"I'm a father," he repeated. "Claudia pulled me aside once she realised I'd worked things out and explained everything. Dante doesn't know. He thinks his dad was killed in a mining accident. She asked me not to say anything until she had a chance to explain things to him. If I wanted her to explain things to him."

"What did you say?"

"Nothing. I left."

"You left?"

"After talking to her and learning all this stuff about my life that I didn't know, I just needed to get out of there. I drove straight home, got out the whiskey bottle and then called you. I needed to talk to you. I need you to tell me what to do, how to feel about it all. I'm lost."

Tyler had never looked so small. His dark eyes pleaded with me, his shoulders were hunched and his stance broken. I walked across the space between us and took his face in my hands. "I don't know what to say, Tyler. You are the only one who can decide how you feel. You are the only one who can decide what to do."

"But I need you," he said, bringing his hands up to clasp onto my forearms as I held his face. "I can't think, I can't process this without you." He tilted his head so my hands ran into his hair, and stepped closer, looking up again when he was only inches away, our breath mingling.

Fearing his closeness and my weakness, I took a step back, releasing him. "So what now?"

Dejected, Tyler walked back to the couch. "Claudia said it's up to me. She's content for Dante to continue thinking his father died, but if I want him to know, all I have to do is tell her. She told me to take a while and think about it, this isn't some light decision. But all I could think about was all the stuff I'd already missed out on. His birth. His first smile. His first step. The day he started school. I keep thinking about all the things I don't know about him. Does he play rugby like I did? Does he even like sports? Maybe he's a musician like Jake. If Dad knows and Mum knows, who else knows? Were they just going to keep this from me forever?" With a frustrated groan, Tyler leaned back. "He looks like me. His hair's about the same length as Gabe's and he has this smile that reminds me of Clark, but he's me, through and through. It's like looking into some twisted youthful mirror. And he seemed like a good kid, you know? Shook my hand, looked me in the eye."

"It sounds to me like this isn't really a decision."

"What do you mean?"

"He's yours, Tyler. He's your son. You know your own anger at your mother for not being there for you. How do you think Dante will feel when he grows up to discover his father was alive all this time and didn't want anything to do with him? Because he will find out. Secrets always come out."

Tyler rested his hands behind his head, looking more relaxed and more drunk than he had before. "You're right. As usual, you're right. There is no way I cannot know this kid. There is no way I can just return to life as usual, knowing there is some kid running around out there who is part of me." He sighed and a contented grin spread across his face. "Thank you," he said.

"For what?" I replied. "All I did was listen."

"You turned up. You came." Tyler sat forward, moving closer to me. The effects of the alcohol were plain to see. Glazed eyes, lazy smile. "Stay?" he asked.

I shuffled along the couch, creating distance between us. "I can't do that."

"Stay," he said again, removing the space I created. "Please, just stay with me tonight. I don't want to be alone. I need you by my side, just for tonight." He gripped my face in his hands, the faint scent of whiskey drifting over me. "Please," he said again. Then he kissed me. And the softness and power of his lips dragged me to a place of seduction I had worked so hard to avoid. Pulling me closer, Tyler's mouth danced over mine, our breath becoming heavy as his hands drifted down my cheeks and over my neck and shoulders, settling themselves as tangled knots in my hair. It felt so good, so natural, as though no time had parted since the last time his lips had been on mine, and yet so desperate, as though years had passed. With the whiskey clouding my thoughts and swaying my body, I tentatively lifted my hands, threading my fingers around his neck and getting entwined in his hair. Tyler moaned in a way that sent tendrils of desire shooting through every inch. My body knew that moan. My body missed the way he handled me, the way he demanded everything at the same time as asking for nothing.

Pulling away for a fraction, Tyler's eyes fell to the opening of the dress I had hastily pulled on as his hand moved to the exposed skin of my thigh. "God, I've missed you."

His words broke the spell of enchantment and brought me back to reality. "Tyler, we can't," I said, my words coming out as pants. "This is a bad idea."

"No," he pleaded. The flesh of my thigh burned under his touch. Every cell stood under his attention. Every part of me cried out for his affection. "I need you," he whispered into my ear, his voice alone causing me to clench my legs together as desire twisted. "Just for tonight, let's forget about everything else going on in our fucked up lives and just do what feels right. And this feels so right. I need you. I need this. I've had this tightness in my chest ever since you left, this compression like I can't break free and breathe. Let me breathe. Let me be with you, near you, inside you. Tomorrow we can go back to whatever it is we're supposed to be, but right here, right now, please be with me."

12

LAUREN

Words no longer mattered. Thoughts no longer mattered. All I could see was Tyler. The way he looked at me, the desire and need in his gaze. The strength and desperation of his grip on my flesh. The memory of his mouth on mine, his hands in my hair, his body pressed against me.

Later, I would blame it on the whiskey, on the intensity of his revelation, but the truth was I wanted him as much as he wanted me. My body ached for him. His scent, his mouth, his eyes, his hands, everything about him had me wet with desire and eagerness for him to keep looking at me at the way he was.

His hand rose up the side of my thigh until it dug into the soft flesh of my hip, tugging me closer to his body. Tyler's mouth closed on my lips again and I surrendered fully, almost melting under his assault.

"I've dreamt of this every night since you've been gone," he panted against my ear. "I was afraid I'd forget the way you feel, the way you taste." His mouth moved down to the slope of my neck, leaving the skin he passed wet and prickling with the coolness of the night air. "I was afraid I'd never get to press my mouth to this patch of skin. Never get to feel the way you respond to my touch."

Each sentence was punctuated with the feel of his lips as they dragged over me, never leaving my skin even as he formed the words. It was blissful torture. Desperation grew and I fumbled with the remaining buttons of his shirt, the need to feel his nakedness rising as urgency.

Rising to our feet, we groped at each other's clothing. My hands shook as I undid the remainder of his buttons and slid the shirt over his shoulders, leaving him standing gloriously before me, his eyes undressing me faster than his hands. My dress was pulled over my head and flew across the room as he tossed it aside. His hands immediately undid the latches of my bra as I tugged his trousers to the floor. Tyler was almost reverent in his actions as he leaned down and slid my underwear off. Then he took a step back, his chest rising as his gaze devoured me.

"I just want to look at you a moment," he said breathlessly. With longing and sadness in his eyes, he lifted one hand, a single finger reaching out to stroke the flesh of my breast. My nipple hardened in response and Tyler sighed contentedly.

"I was worried you wouldn't respond in the same way," he said, his eyes fixed on where my nipple protruded. "I was worried your body would forget me."

Judging from the wetness pooling between my legs, it was not possible. "Never," I breathed, and reached out to return his affection, trailing my fingers over his chest. Tyler closed his eyes at the touch, breathing in and out as though it required great focus and concentration.

"Lauren." He stepped forward, looking down into my eyes as I pressed both hands to his chest, fingers splayed, trying to touch as much of him as possible in one movement. I let my hands trail down his sides until the waistband of his boxers tripped under my fingers and I pushed them down his legs. I kept my eyes trained on his as I wrapped my hand around his hardness. Tyler drew in a sharp breath, once again closing his eyes and inhaling deeply. I stroked him, relishing the look of unbridled lust that overcame him. His cock swelled, growing hard like steel. A drop of precum escaped and I rubbed it over his tip, using the lubrication to rub circles over and over until Tyler's body stiffened with tension and his mouth crushed mine.

Desperation guided our movements. Our hands explored each other's flesh as we stood naked in the middle of the room, our bodies interlocking until we resembled pieces of a puzzle joined as one.

Running his hands down my back, Tyler gripped onto the cheeks of my backside, urging me to jump into his embrace. Lifting to my toes, and with the reassurance of his hands on my backside, I rose and wrapped my legs around his waist, my mouth never leaving his. He walked me over to the kitchen bench, lowering my exposed flesh onto the cold countertop.

"I don't know where to start," he said, his fingers gripping onto my chin, directing my gaze straight into his. "I want everything. I want all of you. I want to control you and cherish you. I want to force your head onto my cock at the same time as I want to tease every inch of your flesh until you pant my name."

His words drove sharp pangs of longing into my core and I wrapped my legs around his waist again, tugging him close enough so his hardness pressed against my wetness.

"I just want you, Tyler," I whispered into his ear. "Any way you want to take me."

With a long low moan, Tyler pushed, his head rolling back as he inched inside. I stretched to accommodate him, the exquisite sensation of pain and pleasure mixing as he filled me. Once fully inside, he stopped all movement and looked deeply into my eyes, our breaths in unison as we held each other. It was although we were scared to move. Scared the motion would somehow break this spell between us, the one where memory and pleasure blended into a perfect combination of desire and weakness.

Tyler pushed closer, trying to gain that last inch of depth. His fingers dug into the flesh of my shoulder. "Tell me you want me, Lauren."

"I want you," I said without hesitation.

"Tell me you missed me, that you've lain awake in bed at night remembering how I made your body feel." His mouth trailed over my skin. "Did you think of me?"

I lowered my head and nodded against his shoulder. "Always you," I said quietly. "Only you." I then pressed my lips to the curve of his neck, kissing his flesh, running my tongue up and nipping the lobe of his ear with my teeth.

Tyler hissed a breath of air. "Fuck, Lauren. You feel better than I remembered. And believe me, I've been having some rather vivid memories." He withdrew, not fully, not all the way, just enough for me to feel the emptiness, and then he plunged back inside. "I thought of you in my office, pleasuring yourself in front of me." He pulled out and then plunged inside again with force, eliciting a grunt from me as his body slammed into mine. "I've thought of you pressed to the window in the bedroom, and bent over this bench, and pressed to the bars of the elevator. I cannot forget you. I cannot lose you. You fit me perfectly. You were made for me, Lauren."

I pulled him tight, the desire to somehow get closer to this man filling me so intently it became a need. I gripped onto him with my hands, my arms, my legs and my mouth. Sweat had made our flesh sticky and our skin stuck together as though it belonged there, as though separation was impossible.

"I want to taste you," Tyler growled into my ear. "I need to taste you." He withdrew quickly, leaving me reeling from the loss of him, before he dropped to his knees, pushing my thighs wide apart. "My god, you taste good." His words came out mumbled as he assaulted me with his mouth. His tongue was urgent and lapped at me desperately. His hand gripped my hips, pulling me into him as though he couldn't get enough. I dove my fingers through his dark hair as his head bobbed between my legs.

"Tyler," I panted. The desire to come was welling quickly. "Tyler, Tyler, I'm about to—"

He tore away from me. "No," he ordered. "Not yet."

Grabbing the sides of my face between his hands, he kissed me feverishly before leaving trails of moisture as he made his way down my neck, over my chest and found a home nestled between my breasts. His head twisted from one side to the other as he attended to the soft swell of each breast.

Guiding me from the bench, he pulled me to the ground and I rose over him. As I straddled his hips, the hardness of him rubbed against me. Leaning forward, I kissed his mouth as I ground against him, using his steel-like hardness to pleasure myself. I slid over the length of him, not yet allowing him to slip inside, coating him in my slickness as he groaned into my mouth.

The scent of our sex was heavy in the air. There was a small part of me that told me to stop, that this wasn't what I should be doing. But it was so small, so faint, it was easy to ignore. In that moment, I wasn't thinking of anything else. I wasn't thinking of the way he spoke to me after rock climbing. I wasn't thinking of the awful words he yelled in the casino foyer. The only thing I was thinking was how good he felt. How my body longed and pleaded for him.

Reaching between our sweat drenched bodies, I wrapped my hand around his cock and guided him inside me as I sat upright. Tyler's hands moved to my hips as I rocked back and forth. He did not try to control my movement, he simply rested his hands there, his fingers digging into my skin as I lost myself. The alcohol dulled my whispers of hesitation and I rocked on top of him, my head lolling back and my hands massaging my breasts. I concentrated only on the sensation of riding him, of feeling him inside me. Moving my hips in a circular motion, I ground against him as I bit my lower lip, the need to come overwhelming me suddenly as I cried out, arching my back as wave after wave of pleasure crashed through me. Once done, I collapsed onto his chest, although Tyler remained hard and strong inside me. He wrapped his arms around me, holding me close as he whispered sweet nothings into my ear. Then, he flipped me over, his cock still inside as he rose over the top of me, lifting my legs to his shoulders. I wasn't sure I would be able to take what I knew would come next. My body was drained of everything, leaving me tender and sensitive to his touch. Sensing this, Tyler moved slowly at first, letting his rhythm increase as my tenderness wilted under his need. Rising to his knees, Tyler slanted the curve of my backside off the floor, allowing himself better access as his tempo increased. He plunged into me, my body rippling with each thrust until finally, he too cried out and pushed inside as he throbbed with release.

Maybe it was the alcohol, maybe it was the warmth of the rug under us, or maybe it was the contentedness of our bodies, but we fell asleep there on the floor, wrapped in each other's embrace.

13

LAUREN

I woke in Tyler's bed. I'm not sure when, but sometime during the night Tyler must have carried me there. He was awake beside me when I opened my eyes, sitting on the edge of the bed. Fully dressed.

"Morning."

"Morning." I stretched into the air, scooting across the bed towards him before stopping and remembering we weren't what we used to be. Despite the throbbing in my head and the tenderness between my thighs, he was still Tyler, he was still Gabe's brother and I couldn't be with him as long as he made me feel guilty.

Tyler, having noticed my movement and sudden hesitation, looked at me, his eyes unreadable. "I was just about to head down for a workout. Make yourself at home." Rising from the side of the bed, he strode across the room, the door closing forcefully behind him. I flopped back onto the mattress, tears pricking in my eyes. I knew that it was what I asked, what I required, but his coldness still hurt.

I closed my eyes and breathed in deeply, the scent of Tyler drifting into my mind and bringing back the memory of the night before. Just at the thought of it, my heart beat a little faster and my palms grew sweaty. But it was just as Tyler said it would be. Last night was last night, and this morning everything would return to whatever it was we were now.

There was no point dwelling on it. No point in re-hashing my feelings, or pondering if things could be different this time. With a deep sigh, I tossed the blankets off the bed and got up. I was completely naked, my discarded clothing unaccounted for.

The door opened and Tyler strode back in. "Forgot my drink bot—"

He stopped when he saw me and I froze, unsure what to do. Did I cover myself? Did I act coy and bashful? What I wanted to do was walk over and wrap my arms around his neck, push my body against his until all his resolve melted away and he took me again.

But I didn't. I sort of crossed my legs in an awkward position and clutched my breasts with each hand, which really did little to hide them. Tyler swallowed as his eyes roamed my body, the desire and lust in his expression as plain to see as the bulge in his pants. He didn't apologise for staring and I didn't reprimand him. Tyler opened his mouth like he was going to say something, but then he shut it again and walked into the bathroom to retrieve his water bottle. I hadn't moved when he came back out, just stood there, unsure what to do. Tyler tried to avert his gaze as though it had just dawned on him that I was no longer his. No longer there for his pleasure.

"Are you okay?" I asked.

He looked tired. There were dark patches under his eyes and his hair was tousled and mussed.

He cleared his throat. "Good. Fine." He stopped before walking out, his back to me and his head firmly forward. "Thanks for coming over last night. I needed it. I needed you."

And then he was gone again.

I sunk to the bed, pulling the covers up around my shoulders, suddenly feeling vulnerable, rejected and cold. This is what you want, I had to remind myself. This is what you asked for. Taking another deep breath to harden my resolve, I squared my shoulders and rose from the bed. After taking a shower where I did my best not to think of all the times Tyler had pressed me to the glass walls, I found my clothing and got dressed. I wasn't sure if I was supposed to leave or wait. Did Tyler want me here when he returned? Was his thanks merely a dismissal in disguise? Did he want to talk more? Did he want to—I stopped myself from even entertaining the thought. Last night was a one-off born from too much alcohol and overwhelming news that had left him in need of comfort.

My car was parked on the ground level of the building, waiting for me. All I needed to do was leave and return back to my cramped quarters with Sadie.

Sadie. Had she noticed I wasn't there? Did she know where I was?

I walked towards the elevator door three times, each time stopping myself before sliding the door and walking in. I was torn. Did I stay or did I go?

After almost an hour of deliberation, while I wandered around the apartment stroking Tyler's bookcase, his stack of albums, reacquainting myself with the pictures on the walls, and the scent of his clothing, I finally pulled the elevator door open and pressed the button that I knew would send the lift my way. When it rose to the top and opened, Tyler was in it. He was shirtless and his body drenched in sweat.

He smiled.

When he saw me standing there, uncertainty resting on my face, he smiled. I loved that smile. It was everything sexy, everything wonderful, everything wicked all rolled into one.

"You're still here," he said.

"I didn't know if I was supposed to leave or not."

"I'm pleased you didn't." He sidled past me, careful not to get too close. I wasn't sure if that was for my benefit or his, but either way, just the closeness of him set my heart aflutter.

Walking into the kitchen, he poured himself a mug of coffee. "You want one?" I did, but instead, I found myself shaking my head. I was too afraid to accept anything from this man. If I let him too close again, I knew I would end up in his bed. I knew any resolve I had would melt under his touch.

"Thanks for being here last night." He glanced up at me quickly, before turning away, his voice holding the slightest hint of amusement. "For everything," he continued. "I had, I—" He stopped, pondering his words. "I appreciated it," he finished finally.

"Have you decided what you're going to do?"

"As you said last night, there's really no decision to it. Dante is my son. I want to be there for him. I want to be his father. I'm going to call Claudia and let her know that I want to be part of his life, if he wants me. He doesn't know yet. He might not want to have anything to do with me."

"I doubt that. You will make a wonderful father, Tyler."

I don't know why the emotion crept up on me like it did. I was pleased for Tyler. I knew this wasn't about me, had nothing to do with me, and maybe that was why tears caught in my eyes as I thought of him and his son and the woman who could give him—had given him—the very thing that I never could. I swallowed back the tears and smiled, hoping my true feelings didn't show through.

"I hope I will. Part of me is scared I'll be just like my father. Or like my mother."

"You will be like neither. You are kind and caring and I know you will do right by him."

We stood face to face, keenly aware of the lack of distance between us. I took a deep breath and stood back, plastering what I hoped was a confident smile on my face. "Well, I suppose I should get back home. Sadie will be worried about me."

"I haven't told her yet," Tyler said. "I'd appreciate it if you'd let me be the one to tell her."

"Of course," I replied. "I won't say a word."

"She'll ask," he said.

"Ask what? She has no idea why I left."

"She'll want to know where you were."

"I'll tell her…"

My voice faded as Tyler took a step forward, lowering both his head and tone to whisper in my ear. "You'll tell her you were in bed with me? That last night you rode me?"

I felt a flush of colour race to my cheeks. "I don't think she needs quite that much detail."

Tyler's lips brushed against my ear. "I miss you, Lauren Greer."

I laughed or coughed, it was a noise that sounded like a strangled cry, anyway, and I stepped away before I found myself in his bed again. The man was hard to resist and his voice, his eyes, and his hands did things to me that had me wanting to tear off my clothes and jump into his arms.

"I should go," I said, my voice barely a whisper.

"You should," Tyler agreed, his lips still dangerously close to my skin. "Unless…" he left the word hanging, one eyebrow raised into a question.

"Please don't, Tyler," It was a plea. I knew I was defenceless against him if he pushed the matter. If he touched me. If he chose to dip his head and place his lips on me.

"I won't," he promised. "I won't unless you ask me to. From now on these hands will not touch you unless you instruct them to. These lips will not come near yours until they beg me to. And Lauren, they will beg me." His voice was low and like gravel. My insides literally quivered under the spell of his voice, his words, and my body gravitated towards him.

But resist I did, because nothing had changed.

* * *

"Where the fuck have you been?" Sadie greeted me as she yanked the door open before I even had the chance to insert the key. "I've called you three times already. You had me worried you were face down in a ditch somewhere."

I pushed past her, bumping into her elbow jutting into the hallway as she stood with her hands on her hips. "What if I had been face up?"

"What are you talking about?" Sadie was annoyed.

"You said you were worried I was face down in a ditch. Would you not have been worried if I was face up?"

"Don't try and change the subject. Where were you? I even tried calling Tyler but his phone was off. Why was his phone off? He never has his phone off. Were you with him?" She clapped her hands. "Oh, please say you two are back together. I'm sick of seeing him mope around, talking about you constantly." She rolled her eyes and mimicked a talking mouth with her hand flapping open and closed.

"We're not." I gave her no other information but she still followed me into my bedroom.

"So where were you? Please do not tell me you were with Gabe."

"Of course not!" I replied sharply. "Gabe and I are done. We were pretty much done the moment I laid eyes on Tyler."

"So you were with him!"

"I never said that."

"So why is your dress on inside out?"

I looked down in horror but Sadie merely laughed. My dress was not on inside out.

"You were." Sadie crossed her arms. "You were with Tyler."

"And what if I was?"

"If you were, I'd be thrilled. You know I think you two belong together." She flopped onto my bed. "So how did it happen? Did you grow lonely night after night pining for him and just couldn't stay away any longer? Did you—Hold that thought." Sadie ran into her room to collect her ringing cell phone. "Why hello, Tyler," she said, grinning knowingly at me. "Fancy hearing from you." She pressed the phone to her stomach, covering the speaker. "Don't go anywhere," she warned. "We've got to go check out this office space in a bit, which is why I tried calling you all those times." She lifted the phone to her ear, her wicked grin back in place. "So tell me, Tyler Thornton, what did you get up to last night?"

As Tyler spoke, the grin on Sadie's face faded. "You're shitting me." She walked into her room, closing the door behind her.

When Sadie finished talking she came into my room and sat down heavily on the edge of the bed where I was listening to music. "Well," she said. "That was a bit of a shock."

119

"Tell me about it," I replied, taking the headphones off and placing them on the bed.

"You could have warned me." Sadie laid back, her head flopping over my legs.

I shrugged. "He asked me not to."

"So he's had a kid for all these years. Seems strange to think about it. I mean, it just can't happen for us like that. If you give birth to a kid it's rather hard to not know it happened." She sat up again. "Fuck Hamish Thornton. He had no right to take that decision away from Tyler."

"I'd really prefer not to."

Sadie looked over at me, confused. "What are you talking about?"

"Fucking Hamish. I'd rather not."

"You're in a weird mood today."

I didn't tell her it was because while receiving the shocking news of Tyler's son, I had also succumbed and spent the night with him. A night that I was struggling to get out of my mind.

"By the way, your sister called. She wanted to make sure you've remembered that you've got to pick Madi up tomorrow evening."

"Shit. I'd forgotten."

"She said you would. Why is she coming again?"

"She's got a hockey tournament on Friday and Morgan didn't like the look of the people that volunteered to have the girls stay. She didn't trust them, she said, so she asked if Madi could stay here instead."

"She's met you, right? I mean she knows you're probably less trustworthy than those strangers."

I threw a pillow at her. "Let's just go see this office space."

14

LAUREN

Sadie and I had been looking at office spaces for weeks and this was the closest we had come to getting what we wanted. And, at a price we could afford. It was just outside the city centre with plenty of space for parking and good street frontage. It was a new building with clean lines and modern spaces, leaving most of the interior up to Sadie and me to plan. Since it was the best we had seen, and our need to move out of meetings at coffee shops and have our own office was increasing with each new client, we signed on the dotted line and would be in our new premises one week after we found out whether we got the job at Haven's Rest. The wait had been torture for us both. We were unable to take on new jobs, unable to plan until we knew how much of our time, if any, would be taken up by Haven's Rest. They were letting us know at the end of the week.

Part of me thought Tyler might call, might pop over to check in on me, or, at least let me know any updates regarding his son. But he didn't.

* * *

Madi was all smiles when we greeted her off the plane. She was immediately taken with Sadie, gushing over everything from her hair to shoes. Sadie revelled in the praise, in return commenting on how in-tune Madi's powers of perception were.

On the way home, we grabbed some takeaways and spent the night tucked up on the couch, watching some television show that Madi declared the best thing on TV. I wasn't so convinced.

The next day, I dropped her at the hockey turf at seven o'clock in the morning for a warmup before the day's competition. It was good to see my niece on the field. I hadn't seen her play since she was a little girl. Her skills were ruthless. I watched my phone for most of the day, checking and hoping that Sadie would call with the news of whether we got the Haven's Rest contract, but no call came.

It wasn't until I walked into the house, an exhausted Madi trailing behind me, and saw the selection of wine on the kitchen bench that I knew the news was good.

"So we did it? They went for our campaign?"

Sadie took a swig out of an open bottle before handing it to me. Congratulations Slag!" she crowed. "We did it. They loved your idea. They said it was the best by far and we're supposed to start in a couple of weeks."

I hungrily slurped on the wine, wiping my mouth when a little ran down my chin. Madi tried taking the bottle off me, but I jerked it away. "No way. Your mother would kill me."

"But I'm eighteen. I'm allowed," she whined.

"Just," I amended. "And there is no way your mother would let me live if you got drunk under my watch."

"Drunk? Who said anything about getting drunk? I just wanted a little sip." Madi pouted delightfully and I had to laugh.

"Oh, go on," Sadie crowed. "Let her just have a little."

"No," I said firmly. "Do you know what sort of trouble I'd get in? Do you know what sort of trouble Madi would get in? And then every family gathering I'd have to hear about it over and over again. Nope," I said at Madi's pleading look. "It is not going to happen."

"And I thought you were the fun one," Madi huffed. "Well, if you're not going to let me join in the fun, I'm going to my room."

"My room, you mean," I called after her.

"Would it have killed you just to let her have a little sip? Surely you were drinking at that age."

"Me? Of course I was. But she's Morgan's kid, not mine. And yes, I do think it might have killed me."

"Always with the sarcasm lately. Is there something going on in your life I'm not aware of? Something you're missing maybe?"

"Just shut up."

Sadie held her hands in surrender. "Fine. I won't say any more. Well, not for a while at least. Goodness knows what will come out of this mouth of mine once we've had a few drinks."

"I can't drink much."

"What do you mean?" Sadie asked, horrified. "We're celebrating. There is either sober or wasted. No in between tonight."

"I'm supposed to be babysitting, remember?" I said, jerking my thumb in Madi's direction.

"You heard the girl, she's eighteen. There is zero effort required in babysitting an eighteen-year-old, in fact, you can hardly call it babysitting. It's more just having your niece to stay, so grab a glass, sit down and celebrate with me, bitch!"

Three wines later, I crept into the bedroom to check on Madi. She was lying on the stretcher, headphones over her ears and a sullen look on her face. I smiled and waved but she merely scowled back at me.

Once nearly at the end of our second bottle of wine, Sadie's face was beginning to sway in my vision and the show on the television was a lot funnier than I remembered. In the back of my mind, something was warning me that the recent increase in my drinking was probably not a good idea, but I didn't want to listen to that voice. Right there in that moment, I was happy and content. Sadie and I had won a huge contract, things were looking up. I didn't need Derek or Gabe or Tyler in my life. I had things sorted.

My phone rang and Gabe's image flashed across the screen.

Sadie dove on top of it. "Don't answer!" she screamed. Then, realising how loud her voice was, she whispered, "Don't answer it."

Pushing her off the couch, I slid to accept. "Hey, Gabe!" I greeted cheerfully.

Music blasted in the background as Gabe shouted down the phone. "Lauren? Can you hear me?"

"Loud and clear," I shouted back.

Sadie tore the phone away and pressed it to her ear. "I really think you need to give up, Gable Thornton. Did you know she spent the night—"

I grabbed the phone back, frowning exaggeratedly at Sadie. "What's up?" I asked.

"Ah," Gabe mumbled down the line. "Is Madison supposed to be up here at the moment?"

"How did you know?" I asked. "She's here for some hockey competition or something. I watched her today. She's good." Then it occurred to me that there was no way Gabe should know this. "Why?"

"Because she's currently on the dance floor right in front of me."

Leaping from the couch I ran to the bedroom and threw the door open. "Shit," I cursed when I found it empty. Madison had managed to sneak out while Sadie and I were drinking. Some responsible babysitter I was. Sadie was right. Madi would have been better off with strangers. At least they didn't let her crawl out of windows and go downtown in the middle of the night.

"Has she seen you?"

"No, I've kept my distance. But you better get down here quick. She's off her face."

"Right. Okay." Panic was beginning to slice through my drunkenness. "I'll be there soon."

I hung up after getting the location of the club and ran back out to Sadie. "We've got to go," I said, grabbing my jacket from the back of the chair.

"Go where?" Sadie asked.

"Madison's currently getting her groove on down at some club. Gabe's there and he saw her."

"Go her!" Sadie shouted.

"No, not go her. We're supposed to be looking after her and instead, she's out drinking with goodness knows who."

"Correction." Sadie's finger hovered in the air. "You were supposed to be babysitting her."

I rolled my eyes. "Come on."

"Come on where? Both of us have had way too much to drive to drink." She furrowed her brows but couldn't quite make out what she'd said wrong, then an idea replaced the confusion. "I'm calling Tyler. He can drive us."

"No!" I lunged towards her. "I'll call a taxi." But Sadie hovered out of my reach, dashing away each time I came close, and she appeared to be less affected by alcohol than I was.

"Hey Ty," she cooed down the phone. "We got the contract!" she shouted, grinning stupidly at me. "And we've also had a lot to drink and need a ride." There was silence for a moment as Tyler responded and then she shouted, "To the club," in some strange deep voice. "Apparently Madi isn't allowed to have a life, so Lauren is insisting we go and collect her." She rolled her eyes in my direction. "Yes, she knows I called you. She's right here. You want to talk to her?" She shook her head at me. "Okay, we'll see you soon. Yup. Bye."

"He's coming?"

"He sure is. You don't want to go put on something a little nicer? Something that shows a little more skin perhaps?"

I threw her another scathing look but still glanced down at the jeans and light sweater I was wearing and shook my head. "We're just friends."

"I bet that's not what you said the other night."

"Shut up."

Sadie rolled her hands in the air in some elaborate fashion and bowed deeply. "As you wish, my lady."

Tyler tooted when he arrived and I begrudgingly followed Sadie out to the car. I headed for the backseat, glaring at her to get into the front. She did. Tyler met my gaze in the rear vision mirror.

"Hey," he said.

"Hey," I replied.

"Madi, huh?"

"Madi," I replied. "Thanks for driving us. I would've just called a taxi."

"I don't mind. I wasn't up to much anyway, just working out."

I wished he hadn't told me that as unwanted images of him shirtless, muscles straining and flexing as he lifted weights, came unbidden into my mind. I crossed my legs and looked out the window as the streetlights blurred past.

Tyler didn't say anymore and neither did I. Sadie did enough talking for the both of us. I suggested they wait in the car while I went into the club, but they ignored me, following me through the single red door. The beat of the music vibrated the floor. Lights flashed in neon colours. Gabe spotted me immediately and strode across the floor, a wide grin on his face. It faltered a little when he saw Tyler, his gaze flickering to him momentarily before regaining his composure. Jake followed him, lifting a bottle of beer and tipping the contents down his throat. One eye was swollen and black.

"What happened to you?" I asked, momentarily distracted by Jake's appearance.

He shrugged and took another gulp of beer. "Some people have hard knuckles."

"She's over there." Gabe stood close and pointed in the direction where Madi danced, surrounded by a group of men egging her on as she toyed with discarding the first layer of clothing.

"Madi!" I called out. "Madi!" I started walking across the floor, but a strong arm held me back.

"It's probably best if someone else goes to get her," Tyler's deep voice sounded. "Let Gabe go. If she sees you coming she might slip out of here and it could be hours before we find her again."

I wanted to protest, but with a sigh I agreed. Gabe sauntered over to Madi, tapping on her shoulder. She twirled around, and after seeing who it was, threw her hands around his neck, plastering her mouth to his. Gabe reeled back, shocked, looking over at me and holding his hands up, declaring his innocence.

Sadie, having walked over to the bar, came back with drinks. I took mine eagerly, there was no point in pretending to be sober now, and chugged it back.

"Whoa," Tyler warned from behind me. "Slow down."

"That's not what you said the other night," I shot back, surprised at the heat to my voice.

I didn't look at Tyler when he responded, but I could tell from his tone that a slow smile spread across his face. "You have me there."

Burning with confidence from the supplied drink, I took a step back, pressing closer to Tyler's body, pretending I was unaware of my actions. My backside brushed against him, and I heard a hiss of air escape between his teeth.

Gabe, having managed to wrestle Madi away from her new-found friends, returned with her in his arms, batting away her hands from where they travelled over his biceps. "She's had a lot," he said, although the words were unneeded. It was plain for anyone to see what sort of a state Madi was in. Morgan would kill me if she found out. Conservatism was valued in our family.

Spinning around at such a speed I was surprised she didn't fall, Madi inspected the people before her.

"Where do you find these men?" she asked me. Her whole body swayed as she attempted to keep upright. Leaning forward, she peered into Jake's face. A lazy smile drifted across her mouth. "Well, hello my sun and stars," she said.

She attempted to kiss him also, but Jake caught her by the shoulders, firmly directing her attention away. Madi sulked. Until she saw Tyler.

"And who are you? I know Gabe and I've now met the hunkish specimen who's beside him, but I have no idea who you are. And I think I'd like to."

"Tyler," he replied. "I'm the other brother."

"You're Gabe's brother?" She looked over at me with a shocked expression and I couldn't help laughing.

"They're all brothers," I confirmed, nodding.

"Wait." Confusion crossed over Madi's face. "You are brothers. All of you?"

Tyler nodded.

"And Aunty L used to date Gabe?"

Tyler nodded again and I swallowed the uncomfortable lump that rose in my throat.

"Tyler." Madi mused on the name. "It sounds so familiar. Tyler. Tyler. You're the one she dumped Gabe for! I overheard Mum telling someone on the phone about it. Oh, Aunty L, you're a nasty girl!" Madi laughed and walked over to Gabe, slinging her arm around his shoulder. "Poor, poor Gabe," she cooed. "Do you want me to comfort you?"

"I think it's time we got you home." I took her arm and tugged her towards the door, but she didn't budge.

She screwed up her face and repeated my words mockingly before snorting. "You sound just like Mum, Aunty L. And I thought you were supposed to be the fun one."

Sadie pressed another bottle of some premixed drink into my hand. "Yeah," she said. "We thought you were the fun one. Go on, let her stay for a bit. Just one more dance? We're here now anyway."

The room was already swaying, my thoughts already blurred and my nerves heightened from the pleading looks Gabe gave me, while Tyler's were filled with venom. I couldn't please them. I couldn't keep any of them happy, so what was the point in trying.

"Fine. One more dance," I relented. It felt good to just give up. Let Madi do what she wanted to do. Let Tyler glare at me. Let

Gabe look at me with those pleading eyes and Jake look at me with amusement. I took a sip of the drink, letting the music sway me on my feet. "Shall we?" I said, looking over to Sadie.

"Hell, yes," she shouted, taking Madi's hand and leading her to the dance floor. "Here's to being the fun Aunty!"

15

LAUREN

Tyler's eyes never left me as Sadie, Madi and I succumbed to the hypnotic beat of the music. Madi moved freely in the middle of the dance floor as Sadie and I kept her from latching onto random strangers that happened to encroach on her personal space. One dance turned into two. Another drink got pressed into my hand and soon I found myself face to face with Gabe as he danced closer to me, a wicked grin on his face.

I was aware of Tyler's gaze, but I still danced with Gabe. I didn't get close, I didn't touch him and he didn't touch me, but he stayed near. I was filled with drunken bravado and out to have a good night. I no longer cared what either of them thought. Or so I kept telling myself.

After taking a swig of his beer, Gabe leaned forward, trying to communicate over the deafening volume of the music. "I quit," he shouted.

"Quit what?" I yelled, leaning forward just enough to speak the words into his ear.

"Thornton Industries." Gabe lifted one brow and grinned. "I realised I wasn't exactly there for the right reasons. I was trying to be someone I'm not, so I quit."

"But what are you going to do now? Are you staying in the city?"

He nodded his head over to where Jake and Tyler leaned against the bar. Jake's posture was relaxed, his elbow propped against the counter, drink held casually in his hand. Tyler stood straight, eyes creating a piercing line in my direction. The muscles of his jaw clenched as he watched. There was something appealing about seeing him like that. Something that told me in spite of his cold shoulder since I spent the night, his mind had not been free of me.

"I've got a job at a coffee shop just down the road for the meanwhile," Gabe was saying, "But Jake and I are going to open a gym together. We've got a place in mind and everything. We've just got to come up with the start-up cash. Hence, Jake's black eye."

"Sounds great!" I shouted enthusiastically. "But what's money got to do with Jake's black eye?"

Gabe attempted to answer, but his words were lost to the music.

"What did you say?" I shouted, leaning closer to Gabe than before.

Grabbing my shoulders, Gabe pulled me close so he could speak into my ear. "I miss you," he said. "I miss us."

"Gabe don't." It was strange to shout the words. I usually spoke them so quietly, so softly as not to hurt him. Gabe had been good for me. He helped me see myself in a way I had forgotten. But he wasn't who I wanted. We weren't meant to be. "You know it's over between us."

"Yeah," he shouted back. "But I wish it wasn't."

A hand snaked around my waist and pulled me back against a hard body. "Are you purposely trying to drive me insane?" Tyler's low growl brushed against my ear. His hand was splayed across my stomach possessively, my back pressed against his chest, my head pulled into the crook of his neck.

For a moment I was trapped between the two. Tyler's body warmed me from behind, his hands firm and covetous. Gabe's eyes bore into mine, pleading, begging for me to pull away from Tyler. It would only be a fraction of a movement. Forward or back. Gabe or Tyler.

I leaned into Tyler's body, relishing the comfort and excitement it brought even as the hurt registered over Gabe's eyes. As Tyler moved me through the throng of people, his legs guiding, pushing against mine, his hand snaking its way up my torso and crushing my breast, Gabe gave me one final glance before retreating. Madi found him and wrapped her arms around his neck. Without looking back, Gabe encircled her waist and threw back his head in laughter.

"You shouldn't do that," Tyler growled once we were in a more secluded part of the bar. "You know what it does to me."

"Oh, so you're talking to me now?" I shot back, inwardly cringing at the bitchy tone to my voice, but outwardly unable to stop it.

Tyler spun me around to face him, a frown creased between his brows. "What are you talking about?"

"A couple of nights ago ring any bells? You seemed quite content to fuck then forget."

"Are you fucking kidding me?" He pulled me tight against him, his mouth moving over my neck as he spoke, his breath hot. "You were the one who broke up with me, remember? I was simply following your lead. I was desperate for you that night, just like I am desperate for you right now." He moved from where his lips brushed over my neck and pressed his forehead on mine, his eyes blurring to darkness from the closeness. "You are the one who chose this, not me. I would have been content for you to drive me insane with jealousy for the rest of my life."

His hands gripped the flesh of my upper arms. His eyes bore into mine. My heart raced erratically, and in that moment, I couldn't remember a single reason why I had broken up with him. The words he had said to me that morning after, raced through my mind. "Kiss me," I dared.

Tyler didn't need any further invitation. His hands clasped my cheeks, his mouth crashed onto mine and I lost myself in the sensations of lust that rippled through me. His hands found their way into my hair, bending and melding me to his mouth. His tongue wrapped around mine and desire burned between my legs. I needed this man. I wanted this man.

I tore away, breathless. "Take me home," I panted. "Fuck me."

Smiling slowly and taking my face in his hands again, Tyler said, "No."

The word struck me like a whip. "No?" I repeated. "Why not?"

"Because you're drunk."

"I was drunk the other night and it didn't stop you."

"True," Tyler mused. "But you weren't this drunk and you weren't babysitting your niece."

Even though he was smiling, even though he was being sensible and responsible and I knew it, his refusal still pissed me off. Probably more from the alcohol flowing through my system.

"Well, fuck off then," I said, pushing against his chest.

"No," he said again, though this time his infuriating grin was gone.

"Leave me alone," I ordered. "There is no need for you to be here."

"How are you getting home?"

"I will call a taxi."

"Don't be stupid," he snorted.

"I'm not being stupid. I don't want you here, Tyler. I was doing just fine before you waltzed over here and put your hands all over me."

"I'm not leaving," Tyler said firmly. "I'm taking you and Madison home."

"No!" I took a step back, crossing my arms over my chest in defiance.

"Lauren," he warned, advancing on me.

I took another step backwards and banged into someone, sending me sprawling to the ground. Tyler reached for me but I jerked away from his touch. "Just leave, Tyler Thornton," I shouted.

Tyler glanced around the crowd, nervous of the attention I was drawing, and waited as I found my feet. "I'm only trying to look after you, Lauren."

I wanted to stop the words coming out of my mouth but I couldn't. The alcohol had some strange power over my actions and words that I couldn't control, despite inwardly cringing at my behaviour.

"I'm going to find Gabe," I yelled. "At least he knows how to let loose and have a little fun once in a while."

"Like fuck you are. This is why I can't stand for you to be around him. I don't know what you're going to do." He reached for my hand but I jerked away violently.

"You don't know what I'm going to do?" I almost shrieked, then I glanced around the room, becoming aware of all the eyes watching. It was the casino opening night all over again, only this time I was the one doing the yelling.

Tyler pulled me close, pressing his body against mine. I could feel the slight surge of his hardness and I closed my eyes and breathed in deeply, but I didn't pull away.

"What are you afraid I'm going to do, Tyler?" I asked. "Is it based on past behaviour? Because I don't recall ever once fucking Gabe after we broke up. Not once. I didn't hold his hand. I didn't kiss him. I didn't do anything but love you, Tyler Thornton, and you made me feel like shit for it. You knew I had a relationship with Gabe when you pursued me and yet you never forgave me for it."

I glared at him, anger colouring my expression. Enough was enough. Sure, I had made a mistake by not telling him about that one time I danced with Gabe, but other than that, everything had been initiated by Gabe. I had not instigated, or been a willing participant in any of it.

Tyler's chest heaved. His eyes flashed with a mixture of anger and lust. We stood facing each other, not touching, but standing dangerously close. So close that I could feel the heat of him, inhale the scent of him.

"Fuck," Tyler cursed. "I'm powerless against you, you know that?" And then his lips were on me again, his hands wrapping around my waist and falling to cup the cheeks of my backside. He held me against his body before tearing himself away once again.

"We're leaving," he instructed. And before I had the chance to respond he took my hand and pulled me after him through the crowd. Tapping Madi on the shoulder, he jerked his head towards the door, letting her know we were going. She hugged Gabe then clutched onto Tyler's arm, looping her own through the crook of his elbow and followed him outside with me reluctantly dragged behind.

"Where the fuck is Sadie?" Tyler said. He stood in the entrance, eyes scanning the heads of the crowd with Madi and I either side of him. The surge of adrenalin the alcohol had given me before was beginning to fade. Swaying with the power of the music, I breathed deeply again, hoping the increase of air to my lungs would dull the sudden wave of nausea.

Disengaging himself from Madi's grasp, Tyler pulled out his phone and called Sadie. After getting hold of her, he dragged us both outside. "Sadie's staying with Jake," was his only explanation.

Madi, still perky and bouncy, jumped into the front passenger's seat while Tyler helped me into the back. I lay on the cold leather, counting my breaths. In and out. Slow and steady.

The rolls and sways of the ride home did little to quell my sickness and I was grateful when I looked up at the familiar streetlight outside my house. It had a piece of its cover missing and the exposed patch of light shone brighter than the rest.

Cold air blew over me as the door was opened and Tyler's hand tugged on my legs. "Come on," he said, more gentle than he had been at the club. "Let's get you into bed."

I was hoisted into the air and found myself in his arms. Pathetically kicking my feet, I told him to put me down, but he insisted I wouldn't make it to the door, and when I saw the steps, I had to agree.

The next place I found myself was flopped onto my bed. I closed my eyes as the sound of the stretcher getting dragged across the floor faded. The bed dipped and Tyler sat on the edge, tugging his boots. The movement made my stomach lurch.

"You don't have to stay," I said sullenly.

"I'm not leaving you like this."

"Where's Madi?" I asked, aware she should be in the room with me.

"She moved her stretcher into the lounge when she realised I was staying."

"You're staying?" I repeated.

Tyler chuckled. "We've just been over this. I'm not leaving you like this."

"You're staying in my bed?" My voice was croaky.

"Would you prefer it if I slept on the couch?" By this stage, he had removed his shoes, socks, and shirt, and was tugging the waistband of his jeans. I twisted from the position I had been flopped down in to get a better look, and watched as his jeans slid to the floor and he was left mainly naked. The light shone in through the window and danced shadows across his smooth flesh. I moaned and Tyler chuckled again.

"Do you see something you like, Miss Greer?" he asked as he slid into the sheets. Leaning forward, he tugged the blankets out from under my body, wrestled my shoes off my feet and tossed the now freed blankets over the two of us.

I scooted across the mattress and nuzzled into his side, letting my hand roam across his chest. Tyler picked it up and removed it, placing it back next to my side. Finding a sudden burst of energy, I sat up and threw my top off then my bra, wiggled out of my jeans and left only my underwear on.

"What are you doing?" Tyler asked, his eyes glued to my chest. My nipples tightened under his gaze. I slid my hand over his chest again, caressing the smooth flesh as I trailed it over the swells of his pecs, the shadowy undulations of his stomach and followed the v-line down to the waistband of his boxers. But again, he caught my hand and held it away. "Lauren," he breathed. But I was unsure if it was a warning or an invitation.

Moving to straddle him, I took his wrists and pulled his hands to my chest, squeezing the flesh of my breasts so it bulged through his fingers.

"My god, this is torture for me, Lauren."

I bent down, hovering my mouth above his. "Please fuck me," I begged.

Tyler moaned. One of the gloriously wicked moans that quickened my pulse. "You're so beautiful," he said in a reverent tone.

Beneath me, I felt the hardness of his erection press against my wetness. Tyler sucked in a breath, before shaking his head and holding my hand away from him again. "No," he said. "I'm not fucking you tonight only to have you curse me tomorrow."

"But I want you." Something in the back of my mind told me to stop begging, attempting to remind me how I'd feel in the morning. "I won't curse you in the morning."

"As much as I want to take you right here, right now, I'm not going to, Lauren. No matter how much you beg."

The words shot out of my mouth before I could stop them. "Gabe would've."

Ice sliced through me.

"Fuck!" Tyler twisted his hips, tossing me from him. "Why would you say that, Lauren? What on earth would possess you?"

"Maybe it's because I'm sick of feeling guilty for a part of who I am. I can't change my past, Tyler Thornton, no matter how much I would want to. I slept with Gabe. There's nothing I can do about that."

Tyler was quiet for a long time. I expected him to get up and leave, but he just lay there, flat on his back, eyes glued to the ceiling, his chest rising and falling. "You're drunk," he said finally. "Get some sleep."

* * *

When I woke the next morning with a wicked hangover and a throbbing headache, Tyler's side of the bed was cold. I let my hand travel over the space, feeling more nauseated from the memory of my behaviour than from the drink. Pressing my face into the pillow, I let out a frustrated sigh. I was more confused than ever. It seemed that even though the sensible part of me, the practical part, told me to stay away from Tyler Thornton, the rest of me couldn't. Nor did it want to.

A hot shower brought some life back into my body, but my stomach still cramped and my head still throbbed. Madi and Sadie sat at the kitchen table when I entered, a full array of food before them.

"Tyler went grocery shopping," Madi said happily. Too loudly, and too perky, but happily.

"He's still here?" I was surprised at the violence of the sudden lurch in my heart.

"Nah," she said, stuffing her mouth with fresh melon that had been sliced and arranged on a plate. "But he did say he thought it would be best if Mum didn't arrive to a house with no food in it and three hungover women." She chewed loudly, the green flesh of the fruit visible in her open mouth. "I told him I was fine, though. No hangover for me!"

"I, on the other hand," Sadie added, "am not quite so fortunate."

"You and me both. What time did you get to bed?" I reached for a piece of dry toast, not yet trusting myself with anything else.

"I haven't yet," was Sadie's reply.

The lounge had been tidied. Madi's bags were neatly stacked in the corner, her stretcher had been put away and the array of food on display was impressive.

Because of Tyler, my sister would never know of the indiscretion of Madi sneaking out. I must thank him sometime. If I saw him again.

My voice begging him to fuck me replayed in my mind. I wasn't sure if I could ever look him in the eye again. I had begged and been rejected.

16

GABE

The way she looked at me. The way she leaned back into him. Her actions said it all. I had lost her. And I was foolish to think I could have ever won her back.

I was heartbroken when Lauren broke it off with me. At first, I delved into my usual response, drink. Drew sat to the side and watched as I drank and fucked my way through the heartbreak, but it was what I did next that surprised him the most. We had been friends for years, he had helped me through a lot of tough times, but when I announced I was going to the city to work for my father, he laughed. It only hardened my resolve. I would work for Dad and make my way up the rungs of the company ladder. I would prove to him, to her, to myself, I was capable. I would win her back.

Only she didn't want to be won back, and I hated who I was trying to become. Tyler didn't make it any easier. He despised me and I despised him. He stole my girl and now I was trying to steal her back.

Lauren had always let me down gently when I'd tried to sidle my way back into her good graces. She'd always been sweet, gentle.

But last night in the club, she'd spoken to me harshly. She was sick of my advances. Sick of me constantly trying to get my hands on her, make her remember what we used to have. And it cut deeply.

I was back working at a coffee shop now. Dad had been surprisingly calm when I told him. In fact, he'd been surprisingly calm ever since the night he crashed the car and got arrested. I think it shocked him, made him realise what he'd become. A money-hungry, grumpy old bastard who cared more for Thornton Industries than his wife or children. He told me he was going to do right by Oliver. I hated him and loved him for saying it. Hated him because he never tried with me. Loved him because he was going to try for the wee dude that had never known him like I did. Hopefully, he never would.

The coffee shop wasn't nearly as fun to work in as Peta's, but that may have had something to do with my lack of interest in the co-workers. None of them were Lauren. It was only temporary though. After giving up my job at Thornton Industries and realising I could no longer afford the rent on my apartment, Jake let me crash on the floor at his place. There was only one condition. I couldn't tell Tyler, even though he lived on the level above.

Then Jake had an idea. We should start up a gym together. We both excelled at sport. We both liked to workout. We could both box, and we knew plenty of personal trainers we could beg to come work for us if need be. There was only one thing stopping us. Money.

That was why I was back working at a coffee shop. Sure, it didn't bring in the big bucks, but with Tyler footing the bill for the building and most of the utilities, we had very little expenses and the money Jake and I earned could be ferreted away for that dream.

We could have asked Dad, but neither of us wanted to do that. This was for us. We didn't need Dad getting involved on any level.

There was one problem. The way Jake earned money.

Ever since his return, he had been restless, uncertain of his place in the world. I think a part of him longed to go back to wherever it was he went. But then on the night he woke, yelling out in his sleep, begging with some unknown person to stop whatever it was they were doing to him, I knew as well as missing it, there was a part of him that feared it. Pushing himself physically became his way of escape. And fighting was his sport of choice.

He'd been fighting in the underground ring for a while now. He didn't tell me much about it, but then again, Jake didn't say much about anything. He came home with split lips and bleeding noses, but would always fling a wad of cash onto the table, so I never really asked too many questions. I did earlier on though. After he'd disappeared from the club, leaving me with Sadie—who wasn't nearly as much of a bitch as I originally thought—he returned home and folded over on himself, hand clutched to his side. I whistled low and long. Sections of his face were swollen, the skin broken in places, and one eye was almost fully lost to the engorged wounds on his face. When he told me he had another fight that night, I knew I had to do something. It was one thing to fight for money. It was another to get the shit kicked out of you and keep going back for more. We weren't that desperate no matter what demons he thought he was keeping at bay.

But Jake wouldn't listen to me. He kept repeating that he needed to do it to feel alive, but I knew that was all bullshit. I was no stranger to fighting when I was pissed, both emotionally and because of drinking, but Jake didn't have either of those excuses. He drank, but he rarely got drunk, well, not that I saw. He was doing it to punish himself or make himself forget. Neither were working.

There was only one person he would listen to and that person had no idea what was going on. Jake wanted to keep it that way but I knew he needed help. I knew if he set foot in that ring tonight, he might not ever be able to set foot in it again. It was plain to see from the way he clutched his side that his ribs were bruised, if not broken. There was also a suspicious tilt to the set of his nose, and a nasty gash over his eye.

It was like he didn't care. Like he almost welcomed it.

Steeling myself, I picked up my cell phone and dialled Tyler. It rang and rang but he didn't answer. Can't say I was surprised. It was no secret that there was a loss of love between us. I guess loving the same girl did that to brothers. It drove them insane. But it was time to put it aside because this wasn't about Tyler, or about me for that matter. This was about Jake.

I left a message. It was hard asking for help, but not as hard as sitting back and watching Jake destroy himself. After finishing the voicemail and asking him to call me back, I grabbed my jacket from where it lay on the floor and draped it around my shoulders. I wasn't exactly sure where the fights were held, but I had a rough enough idea.

Pulling open the door, I stopped short when I found Tyler, ready to knock. He looked up, no surprise on his face when he found me standing there.

"We need to talk," he said gruffly.

"How did you know I was here?"

Tyler grunted or snorted. "How could I not?"

"So you got my message?"

"What message?"

"The one I left on your phone. The one about Jake."

Tyler pulled his phone out of his pocket and cursed when he saw the missed call. "I had it on silent."

"So you're not here for Jake?"

"What's happened to Jake?" he asked.

"I'll tell you on the way." I closed the door, locking it behind me. "If you didn't want to talk about Jake, what did you want to talk about?"

Tyler cleared his throat uncomfortably as we thundered down the stairs, two at a time. The metal steps and concrete walls echoed our footsteps loudly.

"Tell me about Jake first."

I figured I may as well get straight to the point. Tyler and I had never been ones to exchange small talk and now didn't seem like a good time to start. "He's been fighting for money."

Tyler, also not keen on small talk, barked out, "Where?"

"In some shed out on Styx Road. He's in bad shape. He needs to stop."

"Why didn't I know about this?"

"Probably because no one told you."

Tyler grunted behind me but didn't say any more. He walked over to his vehicle, a late range Mercedes that was almost the exact opposite of my jeep, and we drove in silence.

Once we pulled onto Styx Road, I decided I needed to update him on the situation, let him know what we were walking into and warn him of Jake's determination to fight, regardless of what shape he was in. Tyler's mouth was drawn into a tight line, his eyes glued to the road. The knuckles of his hands were white from being wrapped around the steering wheel.

"Here," I said, pointing to a group of buildings on the side of the road. "It's in here somewhere."

We pulled to a stop on the gravel and got out. There were no cars, no sign of people, but a low hum of noise came from the far building. Tyler dug his hands into his pockets and stalked in the direction of the noise. Stopping under the light over the door, he looked back at me, one eyebrow raised. "So what's the plan?"

I shrugged. I didn't do plans. "Go in and stop him from fighting."

A lecture flickered across Tyler's expression, but he must have dismissed it as he merely opened the door and walked in.

The noise was deafening and I was greeted by a sight I wasn't expecting. Sure, there was a ring in the middle of the room, people gathered around the sides, shouting and yelling and waving dollar notes in the air above their heads as some sort of strange incitement for the fighters. As though they were hookers that could be lured with cash. But the thing that surprised me was the people. Men in business suits and women in glamour gowns all screaming at the fighters with blood-crazed lust in their eyes.

Tyler appeared unimpressed by it all, but I did notice him nodding to the odd person as we made our way through the crowd, trying to search out Jake. He knew some of them. These were his people. The sort we did business with at Thornton Industries.

"Can you see him?" I yelled across the space between us.

Rising to his toes, Tyler scanned the crowd. "The fighters are at the back."

We pushed through the throng of people, earning scowls of disapproval when we walked between a person and their view of the ring. The fighters were kick-boxing and the power of their blows had me wincing. Half the crowd were cheering for the man in red. The other half for the man in blue. It gave me flashbacks to my fight with Lauren's ex-fiancé, Derek, and the pounding I had given him. It was nothing like these fights though. That fight was controlled with strict rules. These fighters were savage. I didn't know if there were any rules.

The fight stopped before we made our way over to where a rope segregated the fighters from the spectators. The crowd cheered. Money was exchanged and the losing fighter was being helped from the ring by his friends.

"We can't let him fight," I said, my eyes on the man's body as he was dragged away, a hand held to his nose in an attempt to stop the bleeding.

When we reached the fighters, we found Jake in the corner, jumping up and down restlessly on his feet, punching into the air in front of him and trying to hide the pain.

"Jake," Tyler said.

Jake whirled around, his face a measure of both shock and annoyance. "What are you doing here?" he growled.

"Stopping you before you get completely fucked up," I replied.

"And you had to tell him?" Jake jerked his head in Tyler's direction.

"I knew you wouldn't listen to me."

"Well, I'm not going to listen to him either so you can both fuck off back home."

"Jake look at you," Tyler said. "You've had the shit kicked out of you. You can't possibly step back into that ring again."

Jake rolled his shoulders, rocking his head from side to side. "I can and I will. I need this."

"You need it why?" Tyler asked.

I leaned over, lowering my voice. "We're starting a gym. This is the start-up money."

"It isn't about the money." Jake's voice was low and deadly as he glared at us.

A man with a pock-covered face and dressed in a smart pinstripe suit, walked over to Jake, a roll of tape extended. "You ready?" he asked and Jake nodded.

"He's not fighting," Tyler stated.

"And you are?" the man asked.

"His brother. Look at him. He's in no state to be fighting. Another fight will land him in hospital."

The man shook his head, pushing tape around and around Jake's hands. "Not my problem. Jake signed a waiver. He agreed to this fight. It will fuck my whole line-up if he sits out. It's just not possible. I'd lose too much money."

"Come on," Tyler urged. "Just look at him. One knock and that split above the eye will break open and blood will go everywhere. He won't be able to see, let alone fight. And look at his ribs."

The dark coloured swelling was more prominent now. Jake was glaring at Tyler, mentally telling him to shut the fuck up. I'd had bloodlust before. I knew of the need to feel flesh under my knuckles but this was something else. This was stupidity.

"I'll lend you the money you need for the gym. I'll be a silent partner and won't interfere at all. But there is no way you're stepping into that ring."

"It's not about the money," Jake repeated, shoulder barging past Tyler.

Twisting to step in front of Jake, Tyler placed a hand on his shoulder. "This is not happening."

At the signal of the man who placed the tape on Jake's hands, two large men stepped over to Tyler and glared down at him, almost begging him to lay another hand on Jake and give them the excuse of taking him out.

"How much money?" Tyler asked, reaching for his wallet.

The man in the pinstriped suit laughed. "You don't have as much as I'll make off this fight so take your pitiful wads and leave before I have you escorted off the premises."

Tyler looked at me desperately, but I shook my head. There was nothing I could do. That was the whole reason I needed Tyler in the first place. Jake wouldn't listen when I talked to him. Tyler was my last option.

"What can I do?" Tyler asked the pock-faced man. "What can I do to stop this?"

"Just leave," Jake said, his words mumbled by a mouth guard.

But the man put his hand across Tyler's chest. "If Jake doesn't fight, his opponent doesn't fight. I know this might look like some backwater fighting arena to you, but each fight is carefully planned. Each fighter is matched. Each style of fighting is carefully considered. I make a lot of money off these fights and the fighters make a lot of money off me. In order for Jake to sit this one out, I would need a fighter to take his place. Do you two care to volunteer?" He raised one mocking eyebrow.

"Who?" I asked. "Me and Tyler?"

"I don't see anyone else involved in this conversation, do you?"

"I'll be fine," Jake insisted. "Just get out of my way and let me do this."

"It might be worth considering, Jake," the man said. "The way you're looking at the moment, you're not going to last. Fuck, the way you're looking you might not be back in the ring for a long time and I don't want to lose you as a fighter. Do you really want this to be your last fight?"

"Fuck," Jake cursed and started unwinding the tape from his wrists. "Well, you heard the man. If you don't want me to fight that means you two have to."

I looked over at Tyler. He was taller than me, bulkier too, but I was sure we could put on a good enough show to entertain the crowd, and the thought of having the chance to exchange blows with him was therapeutic in a sense. "Shall we?" I asked.

"I don't want to fight you, Gable," Tyler growled.

"Yes, you do." I could see it in his eyes. I could remember the feel of his fist against my face from not all that long ago, and I knew there was a part of him that would relish doing it again. All he needed was a little prod. I leaned in close and whispered in his ear. "Just think of me fucking Lauren and I'm sure you'll find it in yourself."

Tyler's jaw clenched. His teeth worked over each other as he glared at me. He turned to the pock-faced man. "Give us five minutes and then you're on." Jerking his head in my direction, Tyler guided me over to the corner of the room. "That's what I came to talk to you about," he said.

"What?" I taunted. "Fucking Lauren? Did you want to compare notes?" I knew I was playing a dangerous game, but since the thought had been put into my mind, there was nothing more I wanted other than to take Tyler down a notch or two. Excitement had started to buzz in my blood.

"Would you fucking shut up for a minute?" Tyler was angry and it was just the reaction I was looking for. I grinned and it angered him more. "I love Lauren," he continued. "I want her back. But she said something last night that made me realise it could never happen unless I sorted out shit with you first. She said that I made her feel guilty about a part of who she was. You. You were a part of her life. You were a part of her. Are a part of her. You shared something and I need to deal with that in order to move on, so basically, what I came to ask for was a truce. I will stop being such an arsehole if you stop trying to win her back. I care for her, Gable.

I want to make her happy. I want to spend the rest of my life with her and I can't do that if there's constantly this thing between us. I want a truce, but first I need to ask your forgiveness for stealing her from you in the first place. Because of you, I now know what the threat of that feels like." He held out his hand. "I'm sorry."

I looked down at the hand extended towards me. There were two parts of me wrestling with the situation. There was the little boy who screamed at Tyler while begging for his attention, and there was also the part that still wanted Lauren and would have wanted nothing less than to knock his block off and claim her for myself. There was one problem with that, though. Lauren didn't want me. She wanted Tyler.

Fighting the urge to spit in his face, I cautiously held my hand and placed it in his, shaking firmly. "Apology accepted. I'll keep my hands to myself in the future."

"And your eyes and your fucking mouth."

I grinned. "And my eyes and my fucking mouth."

Tyler nodded once. "Right, well let's celebrate this new-found truce by getting into the ring and punching the shit out of each other."

17

LAUREN

Tyler stood at the door, blood trickling from a gash above his eye, his nose swollen with a dark bruise appearing over the ridge, and his bottom left lip drooping dejectedly.

"My god! What happened to you?" I reached for him, pulling him inside. My stomach twisted at the state of his face but he was smiling. Well, smiling as much as he could with his misshapen lip.

"I did it," he said. "I sorted things out with Gabe."

"By fighting him?" I couldn't escape the horror in my voice. This was not what I wanted. This was not what I asked for.

Tyler realised his error and waved my concern aside. "No, no. I didn't mean like that. I mean, we did fight, but not like you think. We did it for Jake."

I shook my head in confusion. "Are you sure you're okay. You're not making a lot of sense." I closed the door. "Come down to the lounge, I'll get some ice for your face. And a cloth." I shuddered as another trickle of blood dripped over his cheekbone.

Tyler took my hand. "No, listen to me, Lauren. I don't need ice, I don't need to be cleaned up—"

"Yes you do," I insisted, turning away from him.

"Please," he said, stopping me by tugging on my hands. "Just listen to me first. I heard what you said last night."

Colour flamed up my cheeks.

"I heard you when you said you were sick of feeling guilty about part of who you are. I get that now. I understand. All this time I've been petrified of losing you instead of just being grateful you chose to be with me. You didn't have to. You were happy before I met you and probably would have gone on being happy with Gabe if it wasn't for me."

I started to shake my head. "I don't think—"

But Tyler silenced me. "Let me finish. I was wrong to hold you accountable for Gabe's actions. I want you, Lauren. All of you. Every part of your life, your past and your future, and I'll be fucked if I let my jealousy of Gabe's relationship with you ruin that. I was wrong. I was stupid. I let my jealousy and fears control my behaviour and I promise I won't do it again. I'm yours, Lauren Greer. Yours fully and completely. If you'll have me."

I stood in the hallway, my hands in Tyler's, staring up into those steel-grey eyes as he pleaded. I could barely compute the words coming out of his mouth. They were the words I wanted to hear, but they didn't make sense. Why had they fought? Why was Tyler standing here, bruised and injured?

"Say something." Tyler's expression was desperate.

I shook my head, pulling my hands away from him. "I don't get it."

"Don't get what?" He took a step forward. "I'm apologising. I realised what an arsehole I was and I wanted you to know that. I want you back. I want us back. I don't want to face the next stage of my life without you."

"But why are you all beaten up?"

Tyler rolled his eyes and grinned. "This isn't going quite how I expected. It's a long story and I promise I'll tell you, but would you please just kiss me? I've been thinking about this a lot, and if I'm being perfectly honest, your lack of affection is rather ruining the moment."

"So you and Gabe are good now?"

Tyler lifted one brow, wincing. "I wouldn't say good, but definitely better with the chance of improving."

He stepped closer again, cupping my face with his hands. "Kiss me, Lauren Greer."

I lifted my face away from his hands and folded my arms. "Not until you tell me everything." I still didn't get it. I got that Tyler thought he had everything sorted in his mind, but I didn't understand what had changed, how it had changed.

"Seriously?" Tyler let out a breath of air and ran his hands through his dark hair. "You are ruining all my fantasies here."

Taking his hand, I led him to the bathroom. "Sit," I ordered, making him perch on the side of the sink. "I'll sort your face while you tell the story."

He started the story from when he left my house to when he returned again, explaining the bizarre events that led up to the fight.

I gently wiped away the trickles of blood dried to his face. "So Jake's been fighting for money?"

Tyler nodded.

"And you and Gabe sorted things out and then fought so Jake didn't have to?"

"He was in a bad way."

"So are you," I scolded. "So who won?"

Tyler smiled. "Gabe."

I was surprised by his response. It was hard to imagine a world where Tyler would have let his younger brother beat him, but judging from their past scuffles, there was no way Gabe would have won.

"You let him beat you?" I asked.

"Don't you think that was best? I stole his girl, the least I can let him do is get in a few decent punches."

"It's just so different from the stance you've taken in the past. I'm struggling to believe it."

"It's the truth. I swear. Ask Gabe." Tyler pulled his phone out of the pocket. "Talk as long as you want."

I narrowed my eyes, not sure about the sudden change in attitude.

"Look." Tyler rose from his perch on the edge of the sink. "Sometimes it takes a while for things to sink in. All I was thinking about was how it made me feel when you were around Gabe. It took a while for me to figure out that how you felt and how Gabe felt was different. I finally saw my behaviour the way you did, the way Gabe did. I'm begging here, Lauren. All I want is you."

I crossed my arms again, not letting him know how much I loved hearing those words and leaned back against the wall. "Take your shirt off."

Without hesitation, Tyler wrestled his t-shirt over his head and tossed it to the ground. "As you wish," he said, a wicked glint to his eye.

"Are you injured anywhere else?" Slowly, I ran a single finger over the rise of his shoulder. Tyler shuddered and pressed his lips together, drawing in a deep slow breath.

Could it be true? Could it be this simple? One fight between the two brothers, some words exchanged and a change happens in them both? There was still hesitation and doubt in my mind but as

I walked a circle around him and he stared at me with those steel-grey eyes, every part of my being wanted to believe him. Needed to believe him. Tyler was everything I wanted.

I let my fingers trail over his skin, studying his body for signs of injury at the same time as drinking in his beauty. My heart began to hammer with lustful familiarity.

When I skimmed over his left side he winced. "Gabe got in a good one there," he said, though his tone had changed. It no longer held the teasing lilt that it had moments earlier.

Standing behind him, I pressed my lips to his skin, twisting my head to rest my cheek against his shoulder blade as I snaked my hand around his waist and splayed my fingers over his body. His chest rose and fell with each laboured breath, and his hand covered mine.

Lowering his head and turning to the side, he whispered, "I missed you, Lauren. I missed the feel of your hands on me. I missed waking up to your body pressed against mine. I hated going to bed at nights and finding it cold and empty."

The sound of his voice vibrated through his chest as I leaned against his back. There was no way I could resist him. Not when he was standing before me broken and bruised. Not when the words on his lips were the very ones I had been dying to hear.

Snaking my other hand around his waist, I let it fall lower, dipping to the waistband of his jeans and fumbling with the button until it released and I was able to push his jeans over his hips. His boxers followed suit, falling to the ground, and I released my hold on him, once again trailing my fingers over his flesh until I stood facing him, looking him up and down as he had done to me so many times before.

His cock stood tall and hard, straining to get closer to me. But I stood still and let my eyes slide over him. He reached out to me and my body wanted to lurch towards him, throwing myself into his arms and crushing my mouth against his, but I backed away.

"Lauren, please don't torture me like this. Let me touch you."

Mimicking the wicked grin he had given me so many times before, I shook my head. "No touching." And then I began to undress. Slowly. One item at a time sliding across my skin and falling to the ground. Tyler took himself in his hand, gently stroking back and forth as I undressed. His eyes danced over my body, watching my movements as my clothes fell away and I was left naked before him.

"Can I touch you now?" he asked almost reverently.

I stepped so close I could feel the heat radiating from his body. "No," I breathed, running my lips over his with the faintest of touches.

Groaning, Tyler's hands moved to the curve of my waist.

"No touching," I scolded, batting them away.

A devilish desire had overtaken me. I wanted to torment him. I wanted to make him suffer. As I sunk to my knees, I let my breath fondle his skin, skimming over his chest, his abdomen, and down the valley that led to his erection. Letting my hot breath wash over him, his cock twitched under my attention, straining hard, almost throbbing in anticipation. I kissed the insides of his thighs and pressed my mouth to the tender flesh of his groin. Moaning once again, Tyler's hands pushed into my hair, but I plucked them away, warning him with a daring look. Instead, he ran them through his own hair, pushing out his chest as he took in a deep breath, his cock surging towards me. Teasing and taunting him with my hands and my mouth, I carefully made sure I touched him everywhere but the place he wanted it most. I let my tongue swirl over his salty skin as he breathed and moaned, wanting to take control. But this wasn't about his control. It was about mine.

Getting to my feet once again, I walked behind him and pressed the length of my body against his, my breasts crushing against his back, my hands again curving around his waist and dipping low until they found his hardness. A sharp hiss of air escaped him when I finally took him in my hands. His head rolled back as I worked him and a rush of desire soared within me. Wetness pooled between my legs. He was so hard, so virile. And he was all mine.

"Lauren, please," he begged.

Lifting to my tiptoes, I held my mouth against his ear as I spoke. "I have missed you too, Tyler Thornton. I have missed the way you made me feel. The insane amount of desire that I felt every time I looked at you. I missed your mouth, your hands, your—"

"Now," Tyler said sharply, all the begging and pleading of his tone long gone. "I need you now. I want you now." He twisted in my embrace, my hands leaving his cock as he took my face in his hands and crushed his mouth against mine. His movements were urgent and demanding, despite his injuries. His hands feverishly explored every part of my body as though it were the very first time. They were knotted in my hair, clutching the soft flesh of my breasts, fondling the cheeks of my backside, slipping into my folds. His mouth joined the assault. He was everywhere.

My body turned to fire.

My breaths turned to pants.

My skin glistened with desire and sweat and longing.

"You feel so good," Tyler growled. Spinning me around, his hard cock pressed against my backside, his hands gripped to my breasts. "You have no idea how I've dreamt of this. How many nights I've lain there and imagined being inside you again."

Sliding himself over my entrance, I opened my legs, allowing him better access, urging him to take me. The time for teasing had gone and I was desperate to feel him. Not needing any further encouragement, Tyler thrust inside me, plunging in without preamble and sinking himself with a contented sigh. He withdrew slowly, allowing me to feel every inch of hardness until there was only the tip remaining pressed against my entrance, and then he plunged back inside again, causing moans of pleasure to fall from my lips. He felt so right. My body welcomed him, tingling with the sensation of longing that had built for so long.

As Tyler dove into me, somewhere at the back of my mind, I became aware of the sound of keys jiggling in a lock. Then the familiar creak of the front door sounded and Sadie's cheerful voice floated down the hall and into the bathroom. I had forgotten that she was due home.

Tyler froze, his cock still hard but his movements stilled. "Fuck," he cursed, withdrawing. "What's she doing here?"

With the sweat and lust of our encounter still covering my body, I laughed as he fumbled around the floor, looking for his clothes.

"She lives here."

Holding his shirt to his chest, Tyler quickly pulled me to him. "Let's go to my place."

I bit the lobe of his ear, sending shivers through his body, all the while being aware that the bathroom door was still open. Sadie could appear at any second. "No. Let's get dressed," I replied, pushing him away.

"Are you fucking kidding me? Look at this? There is no way this is going down." He peered at his erection still standing strong as I gathered clothing off the floor and hurriedly tried to pull it on. "Let's sneak into your room before she sees us," he suggested.

"There you are," Sadie's voice greeted us at the doorway. "Oh my!" Her voice rose an octave. "Oh my," she said again, covering her eyes. "I did not want to see that. Tyler is that your naked arse in my bathroom?"

"You wouldn't have to see it if you walked away."

Sadie moved her fingers, peeking through the gaps. "But where would the fun be in that?" She winked at me, barely able to control her laughter. "Oh, please tell me you two were not just about to have sex in my bathroom." Then she added, "And what happened to your face?"

Tyler, having covered the indecent parts of himself, grinned wickedly. "Not just about to. Already—"

"Stop!" Sadie shrieked. "Okay, you win. I'm officially more embarrassed than you now. I'm going to the lounge. I don't care what happened to your stupid face. Join me when you're finished." Her eyes flew wide. "Not finished, finished. Finished as in decent." She let out an exasperated sigh. "Just get dressed, okay?"

As soon as she left the doorway, Tyler's clothes dropped to the floor again and his lips were on my neck. "I think we should finish before I explode."

Laughing, I pushed him away. "I am not having sex while Sadie is out there waiting for us. She'll know exactly what's going on."

"And?" Tyler asked, still attempting to convince me.

"And nothing."

Dropping his head into his hands, Tyler groaned. "I can't walk out like this."

"I can still hear you guys," Sadie yelled out. "Remember the walls are paper thin in this house."

"This is not the reunion I was expecting," he sighed grumpily. "How long until—"

I folded my arms and glared at him teasingly.

"Okay," he said. "I get it. It's not happening right now. Curse you Sadie Anderson!" he yelled. Sadie's laughter drifted down the hall. "But as for you." Tyler wrestled with his jeans. "I will be dealing with you later if my balls haven't fallen off by then."

Tyler sunk glumly to the couch when we finally made our way into the lounge. His displeasure was not lost on Sadie and I think she enjoyed the torment she was putting him through. Picking up a cushion from the couch he placed it over his crotch.

"So I take it you two are back together?" she asked sweetly, batting her eyelashes innocently but not waiting for an answer. "Well there needs to be some house rules if you are to be spending time here, Tyler. First of all, no having sex in places that I could possibly walk in on. I do not need to see that pale, naked arse again. Got it?"

That brought a grin to Tyler's face. "Sure thing."

"And no making sex noises, you know? Keep things quiet. I don't want to wake up in the middle of the night to hear Tyler grunting and groaning as he—"

"Okay, okay." I laughed. "No more details. I think we get it."

18

LAUREN

Sadie insisted on hanging around the house with the sole purpose of pissing off Tyler. He could barely concentrate, his hands slipping to my body every chance they got, but then Sadie would notice and clear her throat loudly until he pulled himself away and then she would laugh until she was breathless.

By the time evening faded into night, Sadie had had enough of her teasing and left to go out for dinner with some friends, but not before listing off rules of where we could and could not have sex in the house, grinning wickedly the entire time.

When she yelled her goodbyes and the door shut behind her, Tyler stood from the couch, grabbed my hand and pulled me into the bedroom, firmly shutting the door behind him. Spinning me around, he pushed me against the back of the door, his hand either side of my face, caging me with his body. He didn't speak. He didn't do anything other than stare at me for a very long time. The intensity of his gaze sent sparks of desire fizzling under my chest and down to the depths of my being. I didn't move though. There was something challenging and demanding in the way he looked at me. Something so scorched with lust, I was frozen, trapped by the demand of his eyes, waiting for the command of his mouth.

Tyler's chest rose and fell as he reached out and trailed a single finger over my cheek, down my neck, between the swells of my breasts under the fabric and then toyed with the hem of my shirt, lifting it just high enough for a strip of flesh to be exposed. He lowered himself, eyes locked on mine until his mouth found the exposed skin and left moist trails of desire in its wake.

I drew in a breath of air as his mouth worked across my belly. His lips danced along the waistband of my jeans, before moving upwards, no flesh left unattended until finally, he found my breast. Taking as much of the soft flesh in his mouth as he could, his tongue swirled around my nipple, and I caught my lip between my teeth, breathing deeply as the sensation overwhelmed me.

"My god, Tyler," I moaned under his attention.

At the sound of my words, his mouth moved away and he tore at my clothing, suddenly desperate. He fumbled, my t-shirt getting tossed over my head and floating to the ground and my jeans following suit. He moved quickly and fluidly until I was naked before him, and he was naked before me. I didn't even see him remove his clothing, but there he stood, still encasing me with his body as I leaned against the door.

"Kneel," he commanded.

My body trembled as I obeyed, all the times he had used that tone, that voice of command with me before, racing through my head. But there was something different about this time. It was a command and a question. A wish, not an expectation. I knelt before him, heart beating rapidly, excitement pooling as I waited to be told what to do next. I loved how he could do this to me. I loved how one movement, one word, could demand so much and have me quivering to please him. I missed pleasing him. I wanted to please him. I ached to please him. It was a physical need, an emotional longing.

Tilting my chin so I looked into his eyes, Tyler bent down to kiss me gently and softly. "You are the most beautiful thing in the world."

A million emotions ran through me. Excitement and terror. Pleasure and torture. Lust and longing.

"Tell me you want me, Lauren. I need to hear those words come out of your mouth."

His finger was still under my chin as I spoke. "I want you, Tyler Thornton. Only you. Always you."

Submitting to the pressure of his finger, I rose from kneeling on the backs of my legs and lifted as his mouth found mine. His hand dipped between my legs and he groaned against my mouth when he discovered how wet I was.

"What will you do for me?" he asked.

"Anything," I replied. I was under his spell, ready and willing to do whatever he wanted. Anything. Everything.

He cupped his hand to my cheek, then dragged his fingers over my jawline until he gripped my chin between his fingers. "Open."

I did as asked, and Tyler guided himself into me, his hands knotting in my hair as I took him in my mouth. I squirmed as I bobbed up and down, the desire welling inside me so strongly, I felt the need to quell it before I came without him even touching me. Tyler's hands moved to the back of my head, pulling me to him, suffocating me on his hardness. He held me there for the briefest of moments before releasing, letting himself fall from my mouth as I gasped for air. But it only made me eager for more. I moved to take him in my mouth again, but he pulled me to my feet, his mouth claiming mine as he turned me and walked me backwards until the bed hit the back of my knees and I fell onto the soft covers. Gripping my thighs, Tyler pulled until my backside was perched on the edge of the bed. Then, with the pressure of his hands on the inside of my thighs, he opened me, his eyes darkening with lust when I was fully exposed. Hot breath teased my flesh. The stroke of his tongue was as light as a feather at first, teasing and toying before applying pressure and diving into me. It was almost too much. My body had been on alert since our encounter in the bathroom, longing for him as we sat on the couch, trying to keep our hands to ourselves, and now, finally, after all the build-up, I was afraid I was about to explode and shatter all over him after a few masterful strokes of his tongue.

"You taste so good." His mumbled words vibrated over my sensitive flesh.

His finger joined the assault, slipping inside me, back and forth, slick with my arousal.

"Tyler, careful," I moaned, not wanting the sensation to push me over the edge just yet.

"No," he said, inserting another finger and increasing the pressure. He put his mouth over the apex of my sex, sucking as his fingers worked inside. Looking down at his dark and mussed hair between my legs, his mouth latched to me, and his eyes flicking up to meet mine was too much and I cried out loudly as an orgasm ripped through me.

"Tyler!" I panted as the waves of pleasure crashed over me.

Rising from his position on the floor, Tyler climbed over me. "I love hearing my name on your lips like that."

Grabbing himself, he rubbed his cock back and forth over my clit, the softness and the hardness contrasting in a way that made my body jerk and twitch, overly sensitive. And then he guided himself in, moaning delightfully as he sunk in deeply. My walls clamped around his hardness, the feeling almost too much after my recent explosion, and I gripped his hips with my thighs, preventing him from pushing in any further.

"Relax," he said, increasing the urgency of his penetration.

"I can't," I panted. Every cell was on edge. Every nerve tingled.

Tyler's hands wove into my hair, knotting themselves and jerking my head backwards so he could kiss my neck. When he reached the tender curve, the dip of my neck he loved so much, the feeling of his mouth melted my body and Tyler sunk in deeper, sighing as he pushed in all the way. Moving back and forth slowly, he allowed time for me to recover as our bodies pressed against each other with each rock and thrust. When all resistance had left me, when my body was warm and subdued to his touch again, Tyler sat back on his knees so he could watch where our bodies joined.

"Play with yourself," he said.

Needing little encouragement, I moved to the wetness, toying with myself as he rocked within me, his eyes trained to where I pleasured myself. His movements became harder, faster, sharper as he thrust into me, giving little heed to the way my bed rocked and banged against the wall.

"You're getting tighter," he said as the pressure inside me built. "Come for me, Lauren. Let me feel you."

And I did, panting out his name once again as he held his hand over my mouth, releasing his essence into me until he was finally spent and lay over me, our bodies slick with sweat.

Having excused myself to the bathroom, I slipped back under the covers, relishing the warmth of Tyler's body. I snuggled into his side, one leg splayed across his, arm draped across his stomach and head resting on his chest. Placing a kiss on the top of my head, Tyler squeezed, his arm crushing me closer to his side.

"Thank you," he whispered.

The light from the lamp on the street shone through my window, casting strange shadows across the bed.

"For what?" Sleep was pulling me into a lazy haze of comfort.

"For taking me back. For understanding. For forgiving me."

"I would have waited forever," I said. And in that moment I knew it to be true. There would be no other man for me. Tyler was my everything. All I ever wanted. Even though I had broken up with him, I knew I would never be able to stay away from him forever, but I was still glad we had that time apart. Time for me to reflect on what I wanted, what I needed, and time for Tyler to do the same. Gabe was merely a brief part of my past, one that we needed to accept, but one that no longer mattered. Both Tyler and I knew what we wanted.

And what we wanted was each other.

"She's telling him tomorrow." Tyler didn't need to say who. The revelation of his news was never far from my thoughts.

"When are you going to meet him?" I whispered.

Tyler shifted under me as he reached for the floor, pulling his cell phone out of his jeans lying discarded on the ground. "Claudia wants to give him a bit of time to wrap his head around this new development in his life. I'm going there next weekend. That will give him a week to adjust to the idea. Part of me wonders if he would want to wait that long. I know if I found out that the father I previously thought was dead was suddenly announced as alive, I wouldn't want to wait that long to meet him. But it's Claudia's decision. She's been there for this kid his whole life. I'm just an unexpected interruption to it."

I moved to lie on my back, my head supported by the crook of his armpit. "That wasn't your choice though. You were never given the choice of knowing him."

"I just hope he understands that."

"I'm sure once he meets you everything will be fine. How could he not love you?"

Entering his passcode, Tyler brought up the social media account for his son. Unwanted tears rushed to my eyes when I saw the picture of the smiling boy. I wasn't sure why.

"This is him," Tyler said, tilting the phone so I could see the image better. "This is my son."

There was no mistaking that he was Tyler's. He had the same dark hair, the same smirk for a smile, the same straight teeth and ever so slightly crooked nose. With his hair styled at the same length as Gabe's, it was hard not to see him in the boy too. He reminded me a little of all the brothers.

"Does Hamish know you know yet? Have you told any of the rest of your family?

Tyler shook his head, the movement jiggling his arm. "Not yet. I want to meet him first. Give myself time to wrap my head around it all before I confront Hamish, or tell anyone else. At the moment I've only told you and Sadie. I do wonder whether Diana's been on the phone to Hamish though. I didn't think they had any communication since they divorced, but clearly, I was wrong about that."

Flicking through the photos that were available, Dante's profile showed a kid heavily into sport. He appeared to play both rugby and hockey during the winter, as well as cricket and water polo over the summer. With a smile constantly on his face, Dante had his arms slung around the shoulders of his friends in most of the pictures, a happy and carefree teenager.

"Will you come with me to meet him?"

"You want me there?"

"I wouldn't have asked if I didn't. It would just be for the weekend. We'd leave on Friday night and then come back home on Sunday."

"Then I'd love to."

"I want him to meet us together so he knows right from the start that you are a part of my life, a part of his, too. I'm in this for the long-haul, Lauren."

19

LAUREN

It was still dark, the light from the lamp pouring in the little squares of window, casting the patchwork of the frame on the bed. I had been asleep, lying on my side, Tyler cocooning my body with the warmth of his own. One arm was draped over my side protectively, even in sleep his grip not loosening as though he were afraid that I would leave. I turned in his embrace when he relaxed his hold for a moment, rolling to my other side so I could study him.

Today was my birthday and I couldn't ask for a better present. Tyler was mine again and I was his. I had planned on spending the day ignoring the fact it was my birthday, ignoring the phone calls and the text messages, and watching an entire season of my favourite cooking show with the curtains pulled and the door locked. Somehow I suspected my family wouldn't turn up unannounced this year. But now, I would get to spend it with Tyler.

It was strange seeing him in my small bedroom. He looked out of place, like he belonged only in his oversized bed with the dark sheets rather than squished into my smaller one, the hideous pink and silver duvet Sadie had bought, tucked beneath his chin. The shadow of stubble grazing his jawline had deepened. His hair, a haphazard mess, pressed into the pillow. Knowing he was naked beneath the covers elicited a tingle of excitement as my hand searched the darkness in the space between us before resting on the dip of his waist. His skin felt smooth as I ran my hand over his hip, letting it fall until I found him. I didn't know if he was half-awake or merely having a dream which excited him, but he was semi-hard and sprung to life as soon as I wrapped my fingers around his length. He stretched a little, moving to his back, my hand on his cock creating a tent with the covers. His eyes weren't open, his breathing was still deep, rhythmic and controlled. I toyed with him, stroking up and down, encouraging his full length and hardness to come to the fore. He moaned. His moans controlled a direct line to between my legs and I shuffled closer to him, pressing my naked body against his.

It wasn't until I straddled him, resting my exposed body on his hips that he opened his eyes. He smiled at me lazily, sleep still holding onto him, eyes glazed by a curious lust. Slowly the sleep fell away and Tyler focussed on me, the glazed curiosity of before replaced with a burning need. Without a word, he reached between us, guiding his hardness inside me. I gasped with the fullness of him, closing my eyes as I rocked slowly, relishing the hardness of him, feeling every steel-like inch. Resting his hands on my hips, Tyler let me control the speed of our movements. I chose slow and gentle, circling my hips, savouring the feel of him inside me.

Tyler watched as I rode him, eyes lowering to my breasts as I pulled his hands to them, content to forget everything but the sensations rippling through me. Moving slowly across my skin, letting his fingers drag and create friction as he pulled them downwards, his thumb found my clit, and I stopped all movement. I sat impaled on his cock as it surged within, responding to his thumb dipping into my wetness. He worked in circles, mimicking the movements I had been making with my hips. My head fell back and my hair tickled the flesh of my back as I arched my chest high into the air, pressing towards him, encouraging his attention. Every few seconds I lifted my hips, withdrawing from the length of him before sliding back down again, a small moan escaping every time I allowed him full access.

The slow, constant repetition of his thumb soon had the delicious tingle of completion looming. Feeling the rise in my arousal, Tyler increased the speed of his attention and I began to pant as sparks fizzled in my depths, building and spreading to every part before erupting into a glorious orgasm that overwhelmed me.

Tyler stayed still, letting me squirm and grind against him until I came down from my high, my limbs turning to jelly. Tugging me forward against his chest, he held me tight as he rose his hips, thrusting into me time and time again until he too cried out, his mouth pressed to the top of my head as he came. I flopped against him, spent and undone, letting myself relax as the last spurts of him throbbed inside.

I think we fell asleep like that, me lying on top, breasts pressed to his chest, head tucked beneath his chin, him still inside me. But when I woke in the morning, I was alone with his side of the bed cold, but I could hear rustling coming from the kitchen, music playing faintly in the background. I smiled to myself, snuggling down into the blankets, relishing the warmth for a few more moments before tossing the covers aside, wrapping a dressing gown over my shoulders and pressing my feet into fluffy slippers.

Tyler stood in the kitchen, jeans on, top bare and Sadie's pristine and unused apron tied around his waist. The blush of a bruise could be seen spreading across his side, the darkness under his left eye had deepened and the split on his lip had not sealed over, due to the activities of the night before.

"Morning, sunshine." He walked over, planting a generous kiss on my lips before returning to the stove top and winking. "It's a good thing I went to the store the other day because there is nothing in your cupboards other than canned spaghetti. There is no way I'm eating that. And I thought you should have something nice for your birthday breakfast."

"You know it's my birthday?"

Tyler snorted. "Of course I know it's your birthday."

As he stirred the pot, I perched myself on one of the kitchen stools, watching him from across the bench. I wanted to sigh with contentment. I wanted to smile. I wanted to press my nose to his skin and inhale his scent. Mint and musk.

"Who started round two last night?" he asked, chuckling under his breath. "I woke with you on top of me and no idea of how it happened. I don't know if I reached out for you in my sleep, or if it was you reaching out for me."

"That might have been me," I said somewhat sheepishly, the memory of my actions appearing a little brazen in the bright light of day. "Just call it an early birthday present."

"For you or me?" Tyler stopped stirring the yellowish sauce and walked over, leaning across the counter to place a kiss on my nose. "For the record, you can wake me like that anytime you please. I'm not sure if I have ever been woken quite so..." He stopped, pausing to find the right word as he walked back to the pot on the stovetop. "So enticingly," he finished.

Leaning over the kitchen bench, I peered at the food on offer. There appeared to be some sort of fish sliced thinly, salmon I thought. I despised salmon.

"Before you complain," Tyler said, noticing I was inspecting what was on offer. "It's smoked trout, not salmon. It tastes cleaner. I think you'll like it. I've got bread in the oven and a hollandaise sauce on the go. I'll start the eggs once the bread's done."

"I knew there was a reason I wanted you back," I joked.

Tyler held out a spoonful of the sauce. "Open," he said and I couldn't help the thrill that rushed through me, my body automatically responding to the memory of the night before when he had used that command for an entirely different reason.

It tasted delicious. Just the right amount of lemon and mustard which I only knew it contained thanks to Peta. "Yum," I responded, licking my lips. Tyler's eyes became stuck on the movement, and he visibly adjusted the bulge that emerged in the front of his jeans.

"You shouldn't lick your lips like that near me," he growled tenderly, stalking around the kitchen counter until he stood in front of me. His kiss was soft, the flavour of the sauce still dancing on my tongue as he toyed with my bottom lip, biting it ever so gently.

"Who's licking what?" Sadie appeared in the doorway, her body covered by petite shorts and a crop top, seemingly oblivious to the temperature of the crisp morning. She leaned against the doorframe, one ankle crossed over the other, her arms folded over her chest. "Actually," she said, peeling herself away from her leaning post. "Don't answer that. I don't want to know. I was all for you guys getting back together, honestly, I was. But now that it's all going on right in front of me," she waved her hand in a circle in front of my face, "I'm not so sure."

Tyler laughed. It was a hearty and carefree laugh that I hadn't heard in a long time. "Well, get used to it," he replied and my heart soared.

"So you sorted your shit with Gabe then?" Sadie dipped her finger into the sauce and licked it, her eyes blinking in surprised approval.

Tyler nodded, pulling the bread out of the oven and placing it on the bench. The scent that drifted over caused my mouth to salivate. "You could say that."

"Is he the one that did that—" this time she waved her hand in front of Tyler's face, "—to your pretty little profile?"

"I object to being called pretty," Tyler replied.

"But it's what you are," she cooed. "You're so pretty." She drew out the words, laughing at Tyler's disgusted expression. "He's pretty, isn't he?" Sadie said, turning to me.

"You are very pretty," I replied.

Tyler batted his eyelashes and smirked wickedly. "One egg or two?" he asked, changing the subject.

"Two," Sadie and I replied at the same time. "So?" Sadie continued. "You never answered. Was Gabe the one who did that to your face?" She ripped the end of the bread off and stuffed it into her mouth, poking her tongue out when Tyler scolded her.

"Only because I let him." He broke an egg into the simmering water.

Sadie laughed. "Right. You 'let' him." She placed air quotes around the word let.

"I did," Tyler started to protest, but then realising Sadie was trying to get a rise, he shrugged it off. "Think whatever you want, Sadie Anderson, you are not going to ruin this for me. Gabe and I reached an understanding. I agreed not to act like an arsehole and he agreed to stop harassing Lauren. It was after that the fists flew, and I know you probably won't believe me, but we did that for Jake."

Sadie just lifted her eyebrows, claiming scepticism without speaking.

"Believe what you want, but it's true."

"Whatever you say." Sadie shrugged and winked at me again. "But for god's sake would you please put a top on." She rubbed her fists into her eyes. "I think you've scarred my eyeballs."

The smoked trout with fresh bread, eggs and hollandaise sauce was divine. We ate with plates balanced on our knees, Tyler still defiantly topless, much to Sadie's outspoken disgust.

After announcing she was going out for a run and reiterating the rules she had stated the night before, Sadie jogged out the door, buds pressing into her ears, her head bouncing in time to the unheard beat.

"The sooner you move back in with me the better," Tyler said, bending to load the dishwasher I didn't know we had.

"One step at a time."

He looked up, surprised. "What do you mean? You're not going to stay here, are you?"

"I was intending on it, yes."

"But it's so small. And cold. And messy."

I wrapped my arms around his waist from behind, squeezing tightly, before remembering the bruise blushing over his side and releasing my grip a little. "But it's mine. Well, really it's Sadie's, but I pay rent so it's mine too," I replied. "Besides, I kind of like seeing you here, all uncomfortable."

"So, what you're saying," he replied, pulling apart the hold of my arms and spinning to face me. "Is that you like seeing me suffer."

"Suffer is taking it a little far, don't you think?" I let a look of faux horror pass over my face. "You mean the shower is over the bath," I mocked. "Heaven forbid!"

One corner of Tyler's mouth turned upwards. "I never said that."

"But you thought it, didn't you?" I teased, knowing I was right.

"I guess I'd have to try it out first. Care to join?" He stepped away, jostling the waistband of his jeans down as I watched from behind, each step letting them fall further, his boxers following suit until the pale skin of his backside was exposed. Turning around, he leaned with one hand pressed to the bathroom door, the other on his hip, grinning seductively as he stood completely naked in the hallway, his erection strong.

Screwing up my face, I pretended to weigh my options before laughing and running down the hall, jumping into his arms as his hand braced my backside, my legs wrapping around his waist. He winced a little when I hit the tender patch on his side. "Sorry!" I squealed.

"I didn't feel a thing," he lied, lips moving towards mine. We kissed as he walked into the bathroom.

Lowering me back down, he undid the tie of my gown and let it fall to the floor. "My god, I love looking at you. One day I want you to spend the entire day naked. Nothing, and I mean nothing, covering you."

Reaching behind the tacky shower curtain, I turned the facet, allowing the water to cascade into the bath. "Ready to lower yourself to the insufferable torture of a bath-shower?" I stepped in, the base feeling gritty under my feet.

"I guess you've got to try everything once." Tyler stepped in behind me, circling his arms around my waist as I stepped under the stream of water, letting it flow over my head, flattening my hair to my scalp.

The bathroom was in stark contrast to the sleek lines of Tyler's Scandinavian inspired ensuite. Little patches of mould that simply wouldn't budge despite any amount of scrubbing grazed the ceiling. The wallpaper was ripped in places, jagged edges hanging from the walls. The mirror was old and mottled, green around the edges. But Tyler ignored all that as his mouth found my neck, my head falling to the side as the sensation of the warm water travelling over my body and Tyler's attention melted my insides.

The birthday I had planned on ignoring was turning out to be my best one yet.

20

LAUREN

Tyler finally tore himself away from me to go to work around lunchtime, promising to return later. At two o'clock a knock sounded at the door, and Sadie bounded to answer it, returning with a bouquet of bright orange lilies in her hand and a scowl on her face.

"I take back everything I said about wanting you to get back together with Tyler," she announced, unceremoniously dumping the flowers on the bench. "If this is what you've reduced him to I want no part."

I moved to pluck the note accompanying the flowers out of her hand, but she sidestepped me and cleared her throat. "I hope these flowers brighten your birthday even just a fraction of the way you've brightened my life. I love you. Tyler." Sadie started to gag, holding the note away from me. "It's sickening." Then she froze. "It's your birthday?" she questioned. "Why didn't you tell me?"

"Because I planned on ignoring it," I replied, finally ripping the note from her hand. Yes, it was cheesy. But that's what made it special. Tyler was being all cheesy and romantic just for me. I ran my fingers over the ink, then turned it over when I noticed something scrawled on the back. "Please join me for dinner?"

My phone buzzed in my pocket and a text message from Tyler displayed across the screen.

Tyler: Please say yes.
Me: Yes.
Tyler: I will pick you up at seven. Love you.

I must have had one of those dopey, happy and contented smiles on my face because Sadie made another gagging sound. "I guess I'll cancel the party I had planned."

I narrowed my eyes. "You didn't even know it was my birthday."

"But," she said, holding a finger up. "If I had, I might have planned a party."

"Liar."

Sadie moved to the couch and flopped down, blinking at me expectantly. "So," she said, drawing the word out and resting her chin in her hands. "Where's he taking you? What are you going to wear?"

"Maria's, I imagine," I replied, before realising she was mocking me.

"Well don't mind me, here, alone, while you two go out and celebrate. I'm sure I'll find something to amuse myself."

I rolled my eyes and she laughed, leaning back into the couch and resting her hands behind her head. "I'm actually going out for dinner myself."

"A date?" I asked, surprised. Sadie had not been on one single date that I knew of since I'd moved in. I'd heard the odd man sneak out of her room at horrendous times of the night, but she insists they were all nothing but a way to relieve an itch.

"Sort of." She shrugged then grinned. "My little sister, Roan, is in town. She fancies herself a writer and she's heading away to do some sort of travel article thing on this old bed and breakfast we used to stay in. She wanted to catch up before she left."

A frown creased. "I didn't know you had a younger sister."

"And I didn't know it was your birthday." She wiggled her eyebrows. "Guess we both learned something new today." Sighing, she got to her feet. "Don't forget we're meeting that new client tomorrow," she called as she walked down the hall. "I wouldn't want you to get all distracted tonight and forget about it."

"I love how much you trust my professionalism!" I called after her.

After receiving a sung version of Happy Birthday from Peta and her boys, complete with a tambourine, and enduring an awkward conversation with Mother where I told her I was back with Tyler, I started to get ready for my date. It was a strange sensation. Something I had never done before. Things had developed so quickly between us, and we fell into the sexual part of our relationship so easily, it had never occurred to me that we had pretty much missed the dating aspect. But things would be different this time. There was no urgency. No sense of guilt about Gabe. There was just us.

* * *

Tyler knocked on the door. Dressed in a dark suit, hair slicked back from his face and a black box between his fingers, he took my breath away.

"Hi," I said, suddenly feeling self-conscious.

"Hi," he breathed back. Stepping forward he held out the box and placed a chaste kiss on my cheek. "Happy Birthday," he whispered in my ear. My heart fluttered as his scent invaded me, flooding me with memories of every time we had been together. Mentally scolding myself, I took a step back, allowing him into the house. I played with the box, between my hands, running my fingers over the ribbon that held it together, all the while my eyes flicking up and down to meet Tyler's.

"Are you going to open it? His smile was teasing. Even though this nervousness had descended on me, it hadn't on Tyler.

I laughed and it sounded odd and strained. Plucking at the end of the ribbon, I pulled it away from the box.

"Wait," Tyler said, his hand moving to cover mine. I looked up at him again, a question in my eyes as he brought his hands to my face, cupping it gently as he lowered his mouth to mine. When our lips touched, all of the nervousness and tension released from me and I melted into him.

"There," he said when he finally released me. "That's better." And it was.

Inside the box was a fine platinum chain, with a single tear-drop shaped diamond hanging from it. I gasped at its elegance, my hand coming to cover my mouth. "It's beautiful," I said, almost in a hushed whisper.

"Happy birthday," he said again, taking the necklace and moving behind to loop it around my neck. "I've had this for a while. I was going to give it to you for your birthday whether you were with me or not. But I am mightily pleased you agreed to have me back."

"Mightily pleased?" I teased.

"Mightily pleased," he repeated, stepping closer. Without warning, the playfulness left his eyes and his stance became taut.

His eyes darkened with lust and he gave me a look that had me wanting to melt into a quivering mess of desire. Instead, I cleared my throat and placed my hand on his chest with a warning glare. "Enough of that, Tyler Thornton. You promised to take me to dinner."

A smirk slowly overtook his expression. "And take you to dinner I will," he said, stepping back and holding out the crook of his elbow. "Shall we?"

Looping my arm through him, he led me to the car waiting complete with driver to whisk us away. Tyler slid into the back seat beside me, reaching out to take my hand and running his thumb over the soft flesh of my palm. "You look divine, by the way."

"Divine?" I repeated.

"Like an angel." Lifting my hand, he brushed a kiss across my knuckles.

The dress I had chosen was admittedly one of Sadie's, but one she had never worn. It was white, with little embellishment and had a low scooping back that I knew Tyler would love. "If I'm an angel, what does that make you?"

My mind flew back to the first time I had met Tyler. I had been hidden behind Gabe, peering at him from over Gabe's shoulder and it had struck me how different the brothers were. Gabe had been so sweet and light, I considered him my angel at the time, making me believe that the dark intensity of Tyler had to be more of the devil. I knew better now. Devil or angel, I didn't care. The only thing that mattered was that he was mine.

"Who made the angels fall?" Tyler asked, lifting that one brow.

"I believe they made that decision themselves, though I'm sure Lucifer helped," I replied, casting my mind back to the bible stories my mother had drilled into me as a child.

"Well, call me Lucifer," he replied and winked wickedly. "Though there is only one direction I want you falling and that is straight into my arms."

I couldn't keep a straight face at that and threw my head back in laughter.

"Too much?" Tyler questioned.

"Definitely too much," I replied. "I think you would have had Sadie running to the bathroom for that one."

Tyler screwed up his face in confusion but I kissed it away.

The car didn't take us where I had expected. Instead, we pulled up at a restaurant renowned for its exclusivity and long wait lists. "How did you get us in here?" I asked, stepping out of the car, careful to lift the hem of my skirt.

"I would like to say, I have my connections, but I booked-in months ago and could never quite stand to cancel. I guess, deep down, I was always hoping that you would find your way back to me."

"Or," I suggested. "That you would come to your senses and get over your jealousy of Gabe."

"Or that," he agreed.

Dinner was a more accurate use of the word divine than my appearance. Or, at least in my opinion. Every dish was exquisite. Every morsel mouth-watering.

We discussed Hamish and Billie and little baby Oliver, and Gabe and Jake's desire to start a gym. Tyler told me how he didn't really hear from his father anymore, he was too busy being super-dad and a health-nut, even taking the baby to music and movement classes. We laughed over the pictures Billie had posted on social media.

But there was something distracting Tyler. He wasn't as in command or as relaxed as he normally was. Every now and again, I could feel the vibrations as his leg jiggled under the table and he would chew on his bottom lip. As much as I loved watching his mouth work like that, I knew something was bothering him and it could only be one thing. One thing he hadn't mentioned and I suspected it was because he didn't want to taint my birthday with his drama. But what he didn't understand was that I wanted to be a part of his life. Every part of his life.

"Are you nervous about the weekend?" I asked once the last mouthful of some delicious dessert with a strange name had slipped down my throat.

His shoulders slumped ever so slightly. "I'm sorry." He reached across to take my hand. "I didn't want to talk about this on your birthday."

"I want to hear." And then I added an, "honestly" when he looked at me sceptically. "She told him today, didn't she? Have you heard how it went?"

Tyler cleared his throat. "She called earlier." He paused for a moment. "It was a shock, obviously but she said he's keen to meet me and looking forward to it."

"Of course he is," I said, giving his hand a reassuring squeeze. "You're his father." I think I said it more to remind myself than Tyler. "Did you tell her that I was coming with you?"

Tyler's eyes jerked to mine, a frown crossing his expression. "No. Should I have?"

I sighed deeply. "Yes," I replied. "It probably would have been a good idea. She's agreed for you to meet him. You. His father. Not his father's girlfriend."

Tyler scoffed. "Girlfriend. It's such an inconsequential word for what you are to me."

"Nevertheless," I replied. "It's exactly what I am."

"I'll call Claude again tomorrow then and let her know."

My heart winced a little at the familiarity of her shortened name. It hadn't really struck me before, but I was about to meet his ex-girlfriend. The only one who Tyler had told me ever meant anything to him. His first. But I pushed away that uncomfortable feeling. She was the mother of his child. There would be no avoiding her if I wanted to be with Tyler. And after all the lectures I had given him on his jealousy of Gabe, envy was not going to sit well on me.

"Is there a Mr Claudia?" I asked cautiously.

"Mr Claudia?" Tyler paused for a minute. "I never thought to ask. I guess there could be. Dante could already have a father figure in his life. I hadn't thought of that. Oh, god." He ran his hands through his hair. "I really hadn't thought of that. What if he thinks I'm trying to take his place? What if Dante's happy with his step-father and doesn't want anything to do with me?"

"You don't even know if the man exists. I wouldn't start worrying just yet."

Tyler took a deep breath, his chest rising and falling. "You're right. Let's just put it out of our minds and enjoy ourselves for tonight. Are you ready to go?"

"Go where?"

"It's a surprise." Tyler winked and gathered his jacket from the back of the chair, tossing it over his shoulders.

We walked out into the coolness of the night and Tyler took my hand, pulling me towards the centre of the city. "It's not far," he assured me.

We strolled through the city, under the twinkling lights that decorated the cafés and bars along the edge of the river until we stopped in front of the old movie theatre.

"The movies?" I asked, peering up at the old-fashioned cinema, with the movie titles proudly lit over the entrance.

"We never really did date," Tyler said, looking down at me. "I thought of lots of different places to take you, but in the end, I thought a classic first date, dinner and a movie was the best place to start."

I laughed, thinking how similar his thoughts were to mine.

"Do you hate it?" he asked, his face wincing in anticipation of my displeasure.

I took his cheeks between my hands and planted a loud kiss on his lips. "It's perfect."

"We can go somewhere else if you prefer. I could take you dancing. I could take you to the museum, I know someone who would let us in and we could stroll around without anyone else there, or I could—"

I cut him off with another kiss. "It is perfect," I said again, looking him straight in the eye. "What are we going to see?"

"Whatever you want," he replied. "I booked an entire theatre."

"You what? That's hardly first date material."

"And here I thought I was being romantic," he said with a sly grin.

In the end, we slid into the back seats of the empty theatre, but I barely saw any of the movie as I couldn't concentrate. Tyler was too close. His hand was too warm resting on my thigh, and the only thing I wanted to do was take him home and devour him. And as soon as the movie finished, that's exactly what I did.

21

LAUREN

Tyler was a mess. His knuckles were white as they gripped onto the steering wheel. The muscles of his jaw were clenched and tight, though every now and again he would unclench them long enough to chew on his bottom lip so hard I was afraid it would start to bleed.

There was very little I could do to help, other than sit by his side, ready to talk, ready to do anything to help ease the anxiety twisting within him. I couldn't imagine what it would be like meeting the son you never knew you had.

I was nervous as well. Not only was I going to meet Tyler's son, I was also meeting his ex-girlfriend and his mother. No pressure. I had almost laughed out loud when it occurred to me. But no matter what I was feeling, this meeting wasn't about me. I was here for Tyler. I was here to lend him strength, to give him someone to lean on.

We were to meet at his mother's house. Tyler and I would arrive around six o'clock in the evening, and Claudia and Dante would arrive later. Tyler had assured me that he had called ahead and let Claudia know that I would be with him, but he never told me her reaction to the news.

We pulled into the driveway of a modest house. It was nothing like the mansions that Hamish chose to live in. It was a simple block-styled house, weather-beaten but loved. The door swung open with a creak as soon as we stepped out of the car, and a lady with salt and pepper hair styled into a short bob smiled at us from the front porch. Tyler approached and held out his hand, but she pulled him in for an embrace, despite his obvious resistance.

"And you must be Lauren." She walked over, arms open and ready to hug me. I glanced Tyler's way, but he was too busy pacing the small porch, his jaw once again bulging in and out.

"It's wonderful to meet you Mrs—" I stopped, unsure what to call her.

"Please, just call me Diana. Tyler does." She shot a look Tyler's way, but he didn't notice. "Come in," she urged. "Make yourselves at home. Claude and Dante won't be arriving for a little while so I've got the kettle on and we can all have a cup of tea."

I'm not sure what I was expecting of the mother of Tyler Thornton, but this woman who moved around the small kitchen with ease, ragged jeans adorning her legs and an over-sized woollen jersey hanging off her shoulders was not it. There was nothing about her that reminded me of Tyler. I couldn't imagine her in the Thornton world at all. She chatted easily about nothing, the weather, the flooding that had recently passed through the town and she asked about Sadie and the company we had started. For someone who hadn't had much contact with her son, she sure knew a lot about his life. I guess that was because of Jake. She informed me that he called every week to keep her up to date, although he was yet to come and visit her since he had been home. She said he had demons he needed to chase away first.

Tyler sat silently through it all, only speaking when his mother directly asked him questions. And even then his answers were as short as possible to the point of being rude. She didn't seem to notice or at least acted as though she didn't, but there was an eagerness in her eyes that was hard to miss. She was desperate for contact with Tyler. She would take anything she could get.

There was nothing about her to indicate her past apart from a lone plaque on the wall. The mantra that many addicts lived by. A prayer of sorts. There was no twitch to her movements. I don't know why I expected one, but from the way Tyler had described her, I imagined a woman desperate for release. A woman who was only holding on by a thread to her sobriety. Instead, she was a woman like any other, and I felt shamed by my assumptions.

When tyres crunched on the gravel, Tyler's shoulders tensed. He looked over at me, his eyes darting between mine, searching for something, maybe strength, maybe reassurance. Whatever it was, I hope he found it. Taking his hand, I squeezed tightly.

"You okay?" I whispered as Diana opened the door and called out a cheerful greeting.

With a deep breath, Tyler nodded. "I have never been so desperate for someone to like me before I've even met them," he said, his words getting caught in his throat.

In the doorway, Diana wrapped her arms around someone and dark hair appeared over her shoulder. Tyler closed his eyes for a moment, as though sending up a silent prayer and stepped forward as Diana released Dante from her embrace. Turning with a wide smile on her face, she spoke. "Dante, I would like you to meet your father. Tyler, this is your son, Dante."

It was like the entire house held its breath as the two of them looked at each other with the same expression on their faces. Tyler was the first to step forward, offering his hand to the boy and clearing his throat. "Dante, I can't tell you how good it is to meet you."

Dante shook his hand before breaking into an ear-splitting grin. "I guess now I know why I don't look like my mother."

Tyler laughed nervously and turned to me. "Claudia, Dante, I'd like you to meet my partner, Lauren."

"Gidday," Dante said easily as I held out my hand.

His mother greeted me from the doorway with a cool, "Hello," and a nod of her head. Her eyes narrowed as she looked me up and down, and I got the impression that Tyler's announcement of my accompanying him didn't go all that well.

"Where are your bags?" Diana asked, breaking the start of what was about to be an awkward silence. "I've made up the spare bedroom for you two."

"I've booked the hotel in town," Tyler replied, his eyes never leaving his son.

"Nonsense," Diana dismissed. "Why would you stay there when you can stay here?"

"I thought it would be more comfortable for everyone."

Diana gave Claudia a knowing look then plastered a smile back on her face. "Well, why doesn't everyone take a seat and get to know each other. Lauren, would you like to join me in getting some refreshments while this little family reacquaint themselves."

Family. The word struck my heart. That's what they were. A family. I cleared the knot in my throat, reminding myself internally that this was about Tyler and Dante and not about me, and smiled politely.

"Of course." I started to follow but Tyler gripped my hand.

"Please," he whispered under his breath. "Stay with me."

I looked between him and his mother, torn. Diana folded her arms and looked at me expectantly until finally, Claudia placed her hand on Tyler's arm, forcing him to release his grip of me.

"This way," she urged. "We've got a lot to catch up on."

By the time the kettle had boiled again and I had helped arrange cucumber sandwiches (which Diana assured me were Dante's favourite) on a plate, Dante and Tyler were chatting easily in the lounge. Tyler's eyes were bright. He leaned forward, elbows resting on his knees as he and Dante discussed their playing positions on the cricket pitch. Of course, they played the same position.

They laughed when Tyler asked which sports he played. Dante replied, "Rugby in winter," and then they both added with the same tone of voice, the same mannerisms, "Cricket in summer."

Claudia sat beside Tyler, leaving no room for me, so I moved to the only chair left spare, content to sit in the background. As much as I kept telling myself this was about Tyler, the way Claudia leaned into him and the way she threw looks my way had me worried that she didn't feel the same. There was no way a 'Mr Claudia' was in the picture. I was afraid I was going to have to eat my words in regards to my scolding of Tyler's jealousy. Just the way she was looking at him was driving me insane. And it didn't help that she was gorgeous. She was tall, a lot taller than me. And skinny. And blonde. And beautiful. And she had given Tyler something I never could. A son.

But each time I looked at Tyler, all that worry faded. His eyes were fixed on his son. Everything about him gravitated towards the boy and it made my heart swell.

Dante was the same. It was like staring at the same person, years apart, facing their former and future selves. But Dante lacked Tyler's seriousness. He was laid back and laughter fell out of his mouth easily. He was also a performer, many times rising to his feet to re-enact a story he was telling. He invited Tyler to his cricket game the next day and Tyler promised to be there. He wanted Tyler to meet his friends. He wanted to show Tyler his world.

It was late into the night when Dante asked how Tyler and his mother met, and it was Claudia who answered.

"Tyler and Jake came to stay for the holidays with Diana," Claudia started.

"Jake?" Dante repeated. "Who is Jake?"

"Your uncle," Tyler replied.

"I have an uncle?"

"You have two uncles, actually. Gabe and Jake."

Dante grinned and nodded. "Sweet. When do I get to meet them?"

"Slow down," his mother warned. "You've only just met your father. Let's not go rushing into things."

Dante shot Claudia a sharp look. "Rushing? You lied to me for years about his existence. I don't think it's possible to rush meeting your own family."

Claudia swallowed her guilt and darted a look Tyler's way.

"Hey," Tyler said, reaching out to pat Dante's knee. "I know what that's like. My mother lied to me too and I wish I'd known about you earlier, but your mother is right. There is no need to rush anything. You've got me forever now."

That made Dante grin and he sat back with his hands behind his head, crossing his legs at the ankles, reminding me so much of Tyler it hurt.

"Well," he said, wiggling his eyebrows at Claudia, his annoyance discarded quickly. "He came for the holidays and?"

Claudia let a smile spread across her face and turned to Tyler. "You should have seen him back then. He was quiet and serious and ever so innocent. He was such a good boy. I couldn't help but want to ruin him a little."

"Did you leave before you found out?" Dante asked, turning to Tyler. "Before you knew she was pregnant."

Tyler glanced Claudia's way before answering and she nodded her permission. "I knew she was pregnant but I thought you were someone else's. Your mother faced a difficult decision and I was just a boy back then. I wasn't ready to be a father, even if I was never given the choice."

Claudia reached out and took Tyler's hand in her own. "Your father and I did what we thought was best."

Surprise lit Tyler's eyes and he pulled his hand away, but he didn't correct her.

"So you knew this whole time?" Confusion passed over Dante's face.

"No," Tyler said firmly. "I never knew about you. I would have wanted to be part of your life if I had."

Shaking his head, Dante looked between Claudia and Tyler. "I don't understand. If you didn't know about me, how could you know what was best for me?"

Claudia sighed. "It's a long and complicated story, Dante, and one day I will tell it to you. But not today. Today all you need to know is that you have a father and a mother and we both want what is best for you."

"But—"

"No buts!" Claudia said sharply. "It's time for bed."

"It's only—"

"Bed now!" she ordered and then turned to Diana. "Is it alright if we stay the night here, Diana? I'm not sure I can handle going back to an empty house tonight and if Tyler isn't going to stay…"

She let her words fade and glanced my way as though it were my fault that Tyler insisted on staying at the hotel.

"Of course, my dear. You know you and Dante are welcome in this house whenever you want."

Dante got to his feet, letting out a resigned sigh. "Fine. But you will still be here tomorrow, won't you? You'll come to my game in the morning?" he asked, turning to Tyler.

"I wouldn't miss it for the world," Tyler replied, getting to his feet. Dante's eyes skipped around the room. "I've actually got a match on this Monday if you wanted to stay and—"

"Dante," his mother warned.

"I know, I know. Bedtime. But I can't believe you won't even let me stay up when—"

"Goodnight," she said firmly.

Dante grinned and pushed his hair back from his face. "Goodnight," he said to everyone. "Guess I'll see you tomorrow."

"It was wonderful to meet you, Dante," I replied, returning the boy's smile. "I look forward to seeing you in action."

"Good. I'm worth seeing."

I chuckled at his confidence as he walked over and threw his arms around Tyler, startling him for a moment before he returned the bear hug.

"Tomorrow," he repeated as he clapped Tyler on the back. He tried to act casual but emotion caught in his throat as he uttered the words, "Night, Dad."

Tyler looked over Dante's shoulder as he hugged him, eyes shining brightly as they met mine. "Night, son."

"Well," Diana said as soon as the door closed behind Dante. "That went well. Don't you think it went well, Claudia?"

"It would have been nice for you to back me up a little more, Tyler," was Claudia's reply.

"What?" Tyler replied. "I'm not lying to him. I'm not pretending that I knew he existed when clearly I didn't. I won't have the boy thinking that I deserted him."

"Like you deserted your mother?" Claudia threw him a challenging look.

"My mother chose you over me." Tyler's voice was cold. "It wasn't the same thing."

"I did no such thing, Tyler," Diana said quietly. "You are the one who avoided me for all these years. I've always been here."

The tension in the room grew so thick I could taste it.

Tyler's voice was quiet but controlled. "You lied to me for years, Diana."

"I didn't have to lie. I never saw you. Besides, it was what your father wanted."

"And you've always done what my father wanted?"

"We agreed together that it would be what was best for you."

"It wasn't your choice to make," Tyler growled.

"Don't be too harsh on your mother, Tyler," Claudia spoke up. "I know this has been difficult for you, and I understand that you feel hurt by it all, but your mother has been there for me and Dante in ways I can never repay. She pulled her life together for us. She's been here for us. She's been more of a mother to me than my own mother has."

"Well, I'm pleased she was a mother to you," Tyler said bluntly. "I wouldn't know what that felt like."

Getting to my feet, I attempted to relieve the situation by suggesting we leave for the night.

"Yes," Claudia agreed. "That might be best. I would also suggest you don't attend Dante's game in the morning," she added, turning to me. "It would be good for Dante to spend some time alone with his family. It's quite enough for him to wrap his head around having a father, let alone having to compete for his affection with the girlfriend."

I waited for Tyler to object but he didn't.

"Whatever you think is best," I replied, swallowing the rising anger that I wanted to direct Claudia's way. For Tyler's sake, I wouldn't bite.

"Till the morning then." Claudia got to her feet and pressed a kiss to Tyler's cheek. "I will see you at the game. I'll text the address."

It was only then that I truly grasped what it must have felt like for Tyler to see me with Gabe, knowing the history we had shared. Seeing him with Claudia was hard enough even knowing that their history was years in the past. If it had been more recent, I don't know how I would have reacted.

22

LAUREN

"Do you think I've been too harsh on her?"

Tyler and I were lying in bed in the small hotel, Tyler with his back pressed to the headboard, hands behind his head. He had talked non-stop about Dante. I couldn't recall so many words coming out of his mouth in such a short amount of time.

"Who?" I asked, struggling to keep up with his train of thought. So far I had heard a summary of every word that had come out of Dante's mouth and every thought Tyler had on those words.

"Diana," he said. Adjusting his position, he scooted down in the bed so he was closer to me and huddled into my side, his arm wrapping around my waist. "I always took Hamish's word about who she was, the problems she faced. But now, when I think about it, I can only recall one specific story about her habit. And it came from Hamish. Maybe she was never as bad as I thought. Maybe I've blocked her out of my life for all these years because I blindly believed Hamish was telling the truth. What if all this time he was purposely trying to keep me from her so I wouldn't find out the truth?"

He glanced up at me but I could tell he didn't expect me to answer. His entire life had been turned upside down. It was natural for him to question everything. He was unable to lie still, his foot twitching against the restriction of the sheets, his fingers skimming my side. He only stayed like that a moment before throwing the bed covers off and getting to his feet. He started pacing the room, lip pulled between his teeth, eyes flicking restlessly.

"Why do you think she named him Dante? Why Dante? Did she have a thing for The Divine Comedy? Did she just like the sound of it?" He let out a frustrated sigh. "It fucks me off that I've had no say in his life. Not even an opportunity to have a say." He stopped pacing and ran his hands through his hair, leaving it sticking up in strange places. "It was one thing learning I had a son, but it was quite another meeting him, seeing myself in him. It's changed everything. I'd never thought about it before, you know? Never considered that I had a child out there in the world. It wasn't even a possibility. The news of it hit me hard, but today, seeing him, meeting him, talking to him and realising there really is a part of me that exists that I didn't know about, well I feel like I'm on top of the world. But there's also this part of me that's terrified. Where to from here? What does having a son mean for my life? What does having a father mean for him? How often will I be able to visit? How often would Dante even want to see me? Will he come to visit me in the city? Is there the possibility he'd ever want to live with me?" Tyler rubbed a hand over his face, leaving it covering his mouth as he let out a long breath of air. "Basically, I'm completely freaking out." He kneeled on the bed, looking to me as though I had the answer. "I've never felt like this before. I don't know what to do. I'm all excited and tight in my chest at the same time as feeling like I might be sick." He looked over at me, his jaw working back and forth, thoughts running through his mind. "I think I might go for a run."

Tossing the covers off and rising to my knees, I took his face between my hands, staring into the grey. His gaze flicked between my eyes, dancing from left to right. I moved closer, pressing my forehead against his and slowed my breathing. He stopped jostling. The rise and fall of his chest slowed until it matched mine and his gaze dropped to my lips.

"If you're looking to expend a little energy, there is one way I can think of," I said, biting my lip and releasing it slowly in an effort to show him my intention.

He rushed towards me, desperate to devour me with his lips, but I held him back, held him firm, our heads pressed together, our noses touching just the slightest bit. His eyes blurred in my vision with the closeness and I dipped my head to the side and pressed my mouth to his with the lightest of touches. The moan that escaped his mouth and bled into mine reverberated throughout my entire body. We kissed softly and gently, his mouth exploring mine as my fingers dug into his scalp, the controlled desire pulsating through us as a steady heartbeat.

The longer we kissed, the more desperate Tyler became. His hand wound into my hair, pulling me closer, forcing our mouths to collide in reckless passion. He tugged, jerking my head back as his mouth moved along my jawline and down to my neck. He sucked, moulding my flesh to his whim as my breathing quickened to panting. Teasing the lobe of my ear, he released my hair as his hands fumbled with my clothing, lifting the hem of my nightshirt up and over my head. And then his mouth was on my breasts, his attention changing from one to the other, not wanting to leave any part of me untouched. Pushing him back, I climbed onto his lap, wrapping my legs around his waist as his head dove between my breasts, his arms pulling me closer, tighter. His erection pressed against me, hard like steel, and I pushed against it, eliciting another moan to fall from his mouth.

"I needed this," he said, his words mumbled by my flesh. "I needed you."

Standing with me still wrapped around him, he turned and lowered me to the bed. Space invaded between us and I almost cried out at the lack of him, but he pushed down his pants, freeing himself, and climbed over me and everything felt right again. Running his hands down my sides, I lifted my hips, allowing him to push down my shorts, my underwear. Then he lay over me, every inch of me covered by his body, his cock hard and heavy between us. He rocked slowly and his hardness slid over my wetness. Reaching between our bodies, he guided himself inside. I gasped, arching as he filled me. Pushing himself in fully, he held himself in place as I squirmed, adjusting to his length and clenching around him. Gripping onto my chin, he lowered the tilt of my head so I looked him in the eye. And then he went back to rocking, slow and gentle, in and out, his gaze never leaving mine. Pushing himself further up my body, he pressed our foreheads together again, our mouths meeting in a messy fumble of passion.

He stayed like that. Slow and gentle. Rocking back and forth until my need grew. Feeling the intensity rising within me, Tyler drew back to look me in the eye again. I arched towards him, my head rolling back but he gripped my chin again.

"Look at me." He pushed in fully and held himself there until I obeyed. "Don't look away," he whispered, pressing a kiss to my lips. "I want to see you."

It was almost too much looking into his eyes. The closeness of him. The feel of his skin pressed against mine. Our connection. Sparks of desire began to burst like fireworks at the innermost part of my being. They built, rising within me until they exploded and I shattered beneath him. Forcing my eyes to remain open, the sparks reflected in his gaze, my body tight and taut as finally the fireworks subsided and I softened beneath him, feeling as though I was melting into the mattress. It was only then that he moved again. Just a single thrust of the hips and he came undone, his lip caught between his teeth, his eyes resisting the urge to roll back in his head and remaining fixed on mine instead.

When he finally breathed again, when his body softened, he pressed his lips against mine again before collapsing against me, our hearts beating in unison.

"I needed that," he repeated as he rolled off and lay back on the bed, spent and content. He only lay still for a few moments before twisting over and laying one arm across my waist. "What about you?"

"What about me?" I repeated.

"How are you feeling about all of this?"

Reaching down, I ran my fingers over his shoulder, then up into his hair, pushing it back from where it hung over his forehead. "I think it's amazing. I think Dante is amazing and you're amazing and I'm so happy for you."

A flicker of doubt passed over Tyler. "Are you sure?"

"What's not to be sure about?"

"Well, for one thing, it's not just about you and me anymore. I want Dante to be part of my life, part of our lives."

"And that's what I want too. There is no way I would ever keep you from your son."

He sat, his back pressed against the headboard once again, his chest bare and his hard stomach on display. I resisted the urge to reach out and touch him. "Are you sure? This changes things. You never asked for this."

I let annoyance press my brows together. "Of course I'm sure. What sort of a question is that?"

"But what about—" Tyler cleared his throat and adjusted his position so he could better look at me. "What about kids of your own, our own?"

My gaze flicked away from his. "You know I can't have children."

"But do you want to? There are other options we could consider."

I laughed and got up from the bed, feeling uncomfortable with the conversation. We had only just got back together. We were yet to have any serious talks about our future and I didn't feel like now was the time. Tyler had enough to deal with. I had enough to deal with. Dante. Diana. Claudia. Work. And goodness knows what would happen when he told Hamish.

"How about we concentrate on the son you've just discovered, rather than worrying about any children you may want in the future." I started to walk towards the bathroom, finding the room claustrophobic, but Tyler leaned over the bed and gripped my arm. That familiar feeling crept up my skin. That one of being unable to move, trapped by his touch, lost in his attention.

"Talk to me," he encouraged.

I shrugged, resisting the urge to pull against his grip which was now burning into my skin. "I don't know what you want me to say."

"I want you to talk to me. I want you to tell me what you want, what you envision for your future, Lauren."

I dropped my eyes to the ground, suddenly finding the patterned carpet mesmerising. "I don't know."

Pulling himself over to the edge of the bed, Tyler never let go of my hand as he sat, turning me so he could grasp my other hand and hold me in front of him. "Look at me," he urged.

Taking a deep breath I looked into his steel-grey eyes. "Talk to me," he said again. "I want to know what you want. Where you see us in five years' time, ten years' time."

Chewing on my bottom lip, I dropped my eyes to the ground once again. Why was I finding this so difficult? Why did I suddenly feel pressured, trapped?

"I can't have children," I said again quietly. "And I'm not sure if I'd want to explore other options or not. Right now, all I want to do is build the company with Sadie. Make something of myself without worrying about children or anything like that. I want to travel. I want to see the world. I want…" I let my voice trail off. "I'm not sure what I want, to be honest." Tugging my hands out from his, I sat down on the bed beside him. The softness of the mattress caused his body to dip towards mine. "Is that okay? That I don't know?"

Picking up the hand that was now discarded on my lap, Tyler pressed his lips to my knuckles. "Yes. But just so we are clear, Lauren Greer, what I want in life is you. That's it. I've got other goals, other things I want to do, want to accomplish, but mostly, all I want is you. I don't care whether we have children or not. I just want you."

Tears came unbidden.

"Hey," he said, reaching out to brush a tear away from my cheek. "Hey, I didn't mean to upset you. I just wanted it to be clear. I just wanted to let you know that I don't care about any of that other stuff. After discovering that Hamish and Diana have lied to me for all these years, I don't ever want to put someone else through that. I am in this one hundred percent, Lauren, whatever that means. Whatever our lives bring."

The tears came in force then. I don't know what overcame me. Maybe it was the way he was looking at me so intently. Maybe it was because I feared that his declaration was merely a reaction to the recent revelations in his life. Maybe it was because his questions were making me confront choices and decisions I had purposely put from my mind.

"Lauren?" he questioned, pulling me to him. "Did I say something wrong? I didn't mean to upset you."

I was sobbing. Giant breaths of air got stuck in my throat. Fat tears rolled down my cheeks. I needed to get a hold of myself but I couldn't shake this feeling of dread.

"Lauren, tell me what's wrong."

Tearing myself from his embrace, I walked towards the door, not meeting his eye as I pulled a sweater over my head, threaded my arms through the sleeves and put on some shorts. "I need a minute," I said over my shoulder, my throat tight. "I just need some fresh air."

23

LAUREN

Shutting the door behind me, I walked out into the night. There was a single lamp post on the road outside the hotel. The rest of the street was deserted. Hugging myself and willing some warmth back into my body, I walked along the edge of the road, staring down at the pebbles of gravel beneath my feet.

This wasn't fair on Tyler. I was here to be his rock and yet I crumbled at the mere mention of children. I had blocked the memories out for so long, shoved them to the back of my mind and now they had come flooding back. The reason I had felt such guilt. The reason I had crumbled when that little life was lost was because I used to think I didn't want children. I remember the first time I voiced it. I was fourteen and my mother had scolded me. She had yelled and told me that children were a gift from God and I should not shun His gifts. She told me I would change my mind. But I didn't. Even when I fell pregnant, there was that little voice in the back of my mind reminding me of those words that I had uttered all those years before. And then, when that little life was taken, I knew it was my fault. My punishment.

Another sob caught in my throat and I fell to my knees. I didn't know what I wanted. I didn't know if I wanted to try for a child in the future. I didn't know if I wanted to try other options, if I wanted to face the heartbreak of being refused at an adoption agency or the stress of finding a surrogate. I wanted to be his. I wanted to be a step-motherly figure to Dante. I wanted to run my company. I wanted to be an aunt, a sister, a daughter and one day a wife. But I didn't know if I wanted to be a mother. Even saying it within my head had swells of nausea crashing through me.

Would Tyler still want me? Would I be enough?

As if he knew the thoughts racing through my head, I heard footsteps crunching over the gravel. He didn't say a word as he lowered himself to the ground and sat beside me.

"Lauren?"

His fingers brushed my hair away and I lifted my tear-stained face. He was so handsome it hurt. The cold wind of the night danced over his skin causing goose bumps to erupt. His dark hair fluttered in the breeze. His eyes locked on mine and he took a deep breath.

"Lauren," he said again so quietly it almost got lost in the night. "Everything about my life has changed. This news, it's made me look at things differently. It's made me realise that I don't want to waste a minute with the people I love. You are everything to me, Lauren. I love you. I want to spend my life with you and there is only one thing I can think of that will show you how serious I am." He took another deep breath, a wide smile transforming his face. "Lauren, will you marry me?"

Shock sliced through me. "No." The word out of my mouth before I could stop it, like a gush of air.

"No?" Tyler repeated, his eyes still locked on mine.

I blinked. Once. Twice. Now was not the time to be discussing this. Not when we had only just got back together. Not when Tyler was on this strange high. Not when I wasn't.

"You don't want to marry me?" There was hurt in his tone.

"No," I said again as my heart started to thump. The word just kept coming out with no explanation. I swallowed. "Yes. No. Maybe." I stumbled to my feet. "It's not supposed to happen like this. You're not thinking clearly, Tyler. We've only—"

"I am thinking clearly." Tyler got to his feet, his hands reaching out to grasp my shoulders. "Everything makes perfect sense. I want you. I need you. There is no doubt in my mind I want to marry you."

My head shook of its own volition. "Tyler, please no, not now. Not with everything that's going on. We've only just got back together. You've just discovered you've got a son."

A frown passed over his expression and his hands dropped back to his sides. "You don't want to be with me?"

"Of course I do," I rushed to assure him. Nothing was going right. My words weren't coming out right. Why did he have to do this? Here? Now?

"We can be a family. You, me and Dante." Tyler was pleading.

"And I'm sure Claudia would be really happy about that."

"Is that what this is about? Claudia? You've got to know I have no feelings for her. Not in that way. In fact, the only feelings I have for her right now are resentment for keeping this from me for so long. You are the person I want to spend the rest of my life with. You are the person I love."

Waves of panic began to wash over me. Trying to sort out my thoughts was like wading through thick syrup, they slid around my mind, never solidifying. "I can't think." I started to walk away but Tyler turned me to face him.

"What is there to think about? Do you not love me?"

"Love you?" I laughed and it sounded a little hysterical in the darkness of the night. "Love you?" I said again. "Tyler, I love you more than I have ever loved anyone. But you don't mean this right now. You're in an emotional place. You—"

"You're the one who walked outside after starting to cry. Tell me what's wrong. Tell me what you're thinking, what you're feeling, Lauren. I wanted to let you know that none of this, Dante, Claudia, none of this changes how I feel about you."

"We've only just got back together," I started to say.

"And yet I know I want to be with you forever." He was firm.

I continued, ignoring him. "It was only weeks ago that you were so jealous of Gabe that we couldn't be together."

"I've changed." He took a step forward.

"So quickly?" I scoffed.

Tyler's jaw tightened. "You don't believe me?"

"I—I—" I reached a rock on the side of the road and slumped down to sit on it. "I'm scared, Tyler. When Derek left me, I had to rebuild my life from scratch. There was nothing of me without him." I took a deep breath and looked up to where he glared down at me, the light of the moon illuminating him like a halo. Silently I begged him to understand. "I can't go through something like that again. I promised I would never put myself in that position again. And then, when you—"

"So that's it? You're just never going to trust anyone?" Lowering himself to the ground, he crouched on one knee in front of me. "I'm not Derek, Lauren. I'm not Gabe and I'm not anyone else you might fear I am. I won't ever desert you. I won't ever leave you like he did."

Closing my eyes, I swallowed the knot of panic in my throat. "You already did once." I looked up at him and saw the pain flood his features. I rushed to continue before my strength left me and I found myself submitting to everything this man wanted. "I don't know if I want children, Tyler. I might someday, but I might not. I know that might make me selfish, but I can't put myself through something like that again. The guilt…"

"I want you, Lauren. Just you. Only you."

Every part of me wanted to surrender. Every part wanted to whisper that one little word. Yes. But I didn't. I couldn't. Not yet.

Taking my face in his hands he pressed a kiss to my lips. "All you need to do is say yes."

I placed my hands over his. "I can't," I said, pulling his hands away. I couldn't say yes simply because he wanted me to. It had to be because I wanted to. I wasn't ready yet. And even though he didn't agree, neither was he. He was too hopped up on life. Too drunk on the knowledge of his son. "Not yet," I whispered.

And then I walked into the night and left him on one knee, crouched at the side of the road. I stumbled down the strip of gravel on the roadside, aware of the solitary figure I was leaving behind.

I loved him.

He loved me.

Shouldn't that be enough? Shouldn't the choice be simple?

But it wasn't. Not for me. Not for him. He wasn't thinking clearly. He wasn't remembering the way he used to feel, the way he might still feel when confronted with Gabe. He wasn't thinking of the rumours that would be whispered at our wedding.

I didn't know where I was going. I didn't even know where I was, but I needed to get away. I needed my thoughts to stop tossing around my head, nauseating me.

I'm not sure how long I wandered. There was no fear of being lost, there was only one road. A couple of cars drove past, their headlights cutting across the tarseal. Someone stopped and asked if I was okay and that was when I turned back. Tyler would be worried.

Having forgotten to take a key with me, I knocked on the hotel door. It swung open immediately and relief flooded Tyler's expression as he pulled me close.

"I was worried."

"I know," I said against his chest. "I'm sorry. I just needed time to clear my head."

He pulled me back at arm's length and studied me as though I'd been away a long time and he'd forgotten how I looked. His eyes scoured my body as though looking for injuries and it occurred to me how I must have looked to the man on the road who stopped to ask if I was okay. I was dressed in shorts and a baggy sweater. My hair was wind-tossed and knotty. My feet were bare.

"Here's the thing," Tyler started, but I stopped him by pressing my lips to his.

When I broke away he smiled. "What was that for?"

"To let you know I love you. You know that, right? You know that—" This time it was Tyler who cut off my words with a kiss.

"Yes," he said after slowing down our tangled lips. "I know." He smiled against my mouth. "So does that mean you'll say yes?"

I pulled away. "Tyler." He looked so hopeful. "I can't."

His smile fell. "I don't understand," he said. "You say you love me, you say you want to be with me but you're still saying no."

"I'm not saying no," I replied, looking into his eyes and pleading for him to understand. "I'm saying not yet."

He nodded. "Okay then." He forced a smile. "Not now. I can live with that." Reaching for the door, he pulled it open again. "I think I'll just head out for that run now. I need to clear my head."

* * *

He woke me with a coffee. The scent of it hung heavily in the air and I stretched.

"Morning beautiful," Tyler said and I heard the cup getting placed on the table beside the bed. "You ready to get up?"

Finally opening my eyes, I looked over at the clock. "It's early."

Tyler smiled but it was tight, forced. It didn't reach his eyes. I didn't know what time he had returned from his run. I had fallen asleep after an hour of waiting for him to come back.

"Dante's game starts in an hour. I don't want to be late." His voice was flat.

Frowning, I rubbed the sleep from my eyes and sat up, grabbing the coffee from the table and bringing it to my lips. It was hot, a little bitter, but just what I needed. I inhaled its aroma and looked back up at Tyler.

"I thought I wasn't coming."

"Why not?"

"Because Claudia said so."

"She did?"

I nodded and took another sip of coffee.

"Huh." Tyler looked confused, as though he couldn't recall the conversation and got to his feet. "Well, I want you there." Then he looked back at me. "That is if you want to come. The weather is not all that nice out there. Raining."

"I'll come," I replied, stifling a yawn. "I'll just jump through the shower first."

I showered quickly and threw on some clothes. Jeans, a sweater and the boots Tyler had given me for the worksite all those months ago. Tyler was quiet on the ride there. If he caught my eye he would smile but it was another of those forced ones. I knew our conversation from the night before was weighing on his mind. It was weighing on mine too. But I didn't know what else to say. How do you act once you've turned down a proposal?

We arrived at the field and Dante waved us over, introducing us to his teammates, a smile plastered on his face as he called Tyler his dad. He had inherited Tyler's height. At fourteen, he stood almost as tall as his father.

The rain was only a light drizzle but I shivered with the cold as the little droplets stuck to my hair.

"Here." Tyler shrugged out of his jacket and draped it over my shoulders. I hadn't thought to bring one.

"Morning!" Diana called cheerfully as the boys left to warm up by running around the field.

"Mum." Tyler nodded in her direction quickly before training his eyes back on Dante.

Diana froze, her eyes searching out mine. I could almost see the thoughts racing through her mind. She walked over and stood close. "Did he just call me mum?" she asked beneath her breath.

"I believe he did," I replied, warmth spreading within me at the brightness of her smile.

Diana tugged her jacket and hugged her arms around herself. "And how are you today, my dear? Sleep okay in that horrible wee motel?"

I wanted to reply that my sleep was wrought with worry. That I woke feeling stiff and sore and sick. But instead, I smiled and replied, "I slept fine, thanks."

"You're here." Claudia's voice sounded behind us. I knew it was directed at me, but it was Tyler who answered.

"I said I would be."

Claudia narrowed her eyes, flashing a look my way but then went to stand beside Tyler. "I had thought that you would spend some time with your son today. Alone," she emphasised.

Tyler didn't even look at her. "He looks good out there, doesn't he?" He nodded to where Dante ran around the field with his teammates, each of them running to an unheard beat, their footsteps thumping in time.

Claudia pulled her jacket tighter. The wind had come up and blew her hair around her face. Droplets of rain splattered onto the ground. "He's a good player," she said. "Like his father."

Tyler laughed coldly. "You never even saw me play. You barely knew me at all."

She lowered her voice, but not enough that I couldn't hear. "I would have liked to."

He turned to look at her then. "You never gave me the chance," he said coldly. "To know you, or our son."

"Tyler, you know that—"

"Yes, I know," he cut her off. "You were young and single and didn't have a penny to your name. My father's offer was too much to say no to."

"He made me promise not to contact you. He said if I ever did, he would take everything away. My house, the allowance, Dante's trust fund."

Tyler left her side and came to stand by me, wrapping his arm around my shoulder. "Warm enough?" he asked.

I smiled and nodded, huddling into his side. Tyler was acting as though nothing was wrong, that our conversation wasn't on replay in his mind but he couldn't quite pull it off. His arm was too tense around my shoulders. His actions too stilted.

"Have you told him?" Tyler asked, looking over my head at his mother.

"Who?" she asked, feigning ignorance. But you could tell by the tightness in the set of her chin, she knew exactly who.

"Hamish."

"No," Diana shifted a step away. "I thought I would leave that to you. I know I've interfered enough in your life for someone who hasn't been present for most of it. I'd like to change that."

Tyler's jaw rocked. "Thanks."

The bell sounded, the boys walked onto the pitch and the batsman knocked his bat against the ground, ready for the first ball to be bowled. Tyler released me, stepping closer to the sideline, his eyes locked on Dante.

24

LAUREN

The only place we could go for dinner in the small town was the local pub. As soon as we walked in, curious eyes slid in our direction from over handles of beer. It was a place for the locals. Strangers didn't usually walk in and ask for a table. The waitress frowned a little and flicked her hand in the direction of a few empty tables in the corner of the room. She smiled at Dante, nodding in acknowledgement and simply asked, "Who are these two?" without acknowledging Tyler or me at all. The rest of the pub twisted towards us. The chatter fell silent.

Dante straightened his stance. "This is my father, Tyler Thornton and his partner Lauren," he said proudly. It was as though when Tyler or Dante uttered the words father or son, they stood a little taller, smiled a little harder.

"You're the father, huh?" the waitress said, grabbing a plastic covered menu from the stack on the bar. "Fancy that."

Little more was said and it amazed me that the town was so willing to accept Dante's announcement with such few details, but heads nodded, a few whispered words were exchanged and then mouths dipped back to their drinks and the chatter started again.

We followed the waitress over to one of the empty tables and pulled out the chairs as she tossed the menus onto the stained tablecloth. "I'll be back to take your orders later," she said, then turning to Dante, she added, "Good game," and cuffed him over the head.

"So," Dante sat down and Tyler and I followed suit, "when do I get to see where you live? When do I get to meet my uncles?"

Tyler laughed, outwardly pleased with Dante's eagerness to be part of his life. "I guess we will need to discuss that with your mother."

Dante's shoulders slumped a little. "Great," he muttered.

"This will all be a bit of a shock for her." Tyler bumped his elbow into Dante's. "She'll need a while to adjust to things. She's had you all to herself for so long, having me around is going to be hard."

The waitress came back without giving us time to even look over the menu, so we echoed Dante's order for the hamburger.

"Do you two live together? Will I get to come and stay? I finish school in a couple of weeks for the Christmas holidays, maybe I could come and stay then. Maybe I could come and spend Christmas with you guys?"

"We'd like that," I replied, and Tyler looked over at me, a question playing in his eyes. I didn't tell Dante that we didn't live together. I didn't tell him that we'd only just got started dating again, that we were working through things, that Tyler had asked me to marry him and I said no.

Hamburgers and fries were dumped on the table before us. This waitress wasn't capable of simply placing something down. Plates were dumped. Menus were tossed. Drinks were splashed.

"So, are you two, like, serious?" Dante asked, taking a large bite of his burger.

"Yes," Tyler and I replied at the same time. Dante lifted a single eyebrow, a trait I now associated solely with Thornton men, and flicked his eyes between us.

"Okay," he said slowly around his mouthful of food. "So when are you guys heading back to the city?" He swallowed almost painfully. "Not that I want you to go," he added. "It's just that I've got this cricket game on Monday, it's a school thing, we play the team from the next town over every year and it's sort of a big deal, the last game of the year and all that."

"I'd love to watch. I'm pretty sure I should be able to juggle a few things around at work in order to stay," Tyler replied. "Lauren?"

"Sadie and I have a meeting with a client on Monday." I poked at my burger. "I don't think I can."

"S'all good," Dante said, although his shoulders slumped and his hair flopped over his eyes a little. He took another bite of his burger just as the waitress brought a bottle of tomato sauce to the table.

"I forgot," was all she said.

I glanced out the window and sure enough, rain splattered onto the glass. It hadn't stopped all day. "Maybe I could call Sadie…"

Tyler shook his head. "No, you need to get back for that meeting. I will stay on and you can take the car back. Maybe Diana can give me a ride home, or I could hire a rental."

Dante grinned again, pieces of burger showing in his teeth. "You would do that?"

"Of course. I'd love to watch your game and as long as I can shift a few meetings around at work, it will be fine." Pushing back from the table, Tyler's chair scraped loudly on the floor. "I'll go make some phone calls now. Lauren, you'd be okay with driving home on your own?" But he didn't wait for my reply. He lifted his phone to his ear and walked away.

I rolled my eyes and gave Dante a teasing grin. "I'm pretty sure I can manage to drive a car."

Dante tore another mouthful off his burger. Once he was done chewing, he nodded to where I hadn't even started mine. "Don't you like it?"

Hesitantly I picked up the burger and took a mouthful. It tasted a lot better than it looked. "Not bad," I mumbled, my hand coming to my mouth when some of the burger threatened to spill out.

Dante let out a loud laugh. "Don't lie. The food here is terrible. People only really come here to drink. They only offer food to get the alcohol license."

I placed the burger back down on the plate and swallowed the remainder of the bite I took. "Yeah," I replied. "It's not that good."

"It's shit," Dante said.

I narrowed my eyes a little at his language and then shrugged. "Okay, it's shit."

"So tell me what he's like. You know. For real like."

"For real?" I repeated.

"No bullshit, you know?"

I sat back in my chair. "Your father is wonderful, Dante, no bullshit. He works really hard and takes pride in it. He's kind, always helping people out when he can, even if he tries to hide it, but he's also strong and determined, always standing up for what he believes in, which, despite the crap he's had thrown at him, is his family. He loves his family, even his crappy father."

"Hamish, right?" Dante had memorised all the names of the members of the Thornton family like he was studying for a test. "And he's married to Billie?"

"That's the one."

"Not sure if I want to meet him. I overheard Diana and Mum talking. I know he's the one who paid Mum to keep quiet about me."

"I guess he thought he was doing what was right. He didn't know how much it would mean to Tyler to know he had a son."

"You like him?" The last of Dante's hamburger was shoved into his mouth.

I looked at him and screwed up my nose. "Honestly," I said, leaning forward. "Not really. He's a pompous arse, but he is Tyler's father, so I like him simply because he made Tyler. He's just had another child and I think it's softened him a bit, so who knows? Maybe he's changed."

Dante laughed and slapped the table. "Another kid?"

"A wee boy called Oliver."

"So I have an uncle that's a baby."

I let a grin spread across my face. "It's a rather messed up family."

"I'm good with that. Mum's family aren't around anymore. Diana is all we've got. I like the fact that I've got more people now, you know? Even if they are a little messed up."

I thought of my own mother, her strictness, her bluntness. "I think most families are."

* * *

We dropped Dante home to a slightly annoyed Claudia who complained about the lateness, but she gave me the smallest of smiles, and I hoped it was a sign that maybe one day we could be friends. Probably not soon, but hopefully, once she realised I was here to stay, that I would be a part of Dante's life, it might give us the chance to develop some sort of rapport. If I was here to stay. Tyler still hadn't brought up our conversation. Neither had I.

The following day was spent at Diana's house. She cooked us a simple lunch, taking pride in the vegetables from her garden, and again, I struggled with the thought that this woman was ever married to Hamish Thornton.

It wasn't until late in the afternoon that I loaded my bag into the boot of Tyler's car and kissed him goodbye. He kissed me back but it was as though his lips were cold, even though they weren't.

Diana had agreed to drive him home late Monday. I think that secretly she was thrilled, although she did her best to remain casual when Tyler asked her.

The sun was low in the sky as I started the trip home. I turned the volume up and sang until my throat began to ache. I tried not to worry. I tried to push it out of my mind, but the pain and confusion in Tyler's eyes when I uttered the word 'no' kept repeating. I just hoped he would understand. The thought of losing him again made me almost sick to my stomach, but I couldn't race into something merely because he wanted me to.

I slowed down as I reached the stretch of road that ran around the side of the lake. It twisted and turned so I pushed down the volume, needing the quiet as I concentrated on manoeuvring Tyler's car around the tight bends. By now the sun had set and my headlights cut across the road. Ahead of me, a car was twisting its way towards me, the beams of its lights on high, blinding me each time it caught in my vision.

I slowed down further, muttering under my breath at the idiot on the road. I was grateful I was on the inside curve, knowing that there was no way the approaching car could push me into the lake.

The speed of the car was erratic, fast in the straights and then slowing down with each corner. When it rounded the bend in front of me I cursed as the headlights blinded me. Everything was bathed in light. Tyres squealed on the road. My body was thrown to the side, my head hitting the glass of the window. Pain enveloped my body.

25

TYLER

I had a son. I was a father. The words still sounded strange to me even if they were only rattling around in my head, rather than being spoken. Dante was everything I wanted in a son I never knew I had. My heart swelled with pride from just looking at him. He was a good kid. One to be proud of even if I hadn't had anything to do with his upbringing. That was going to change. Now that I knew about him, I would never let him go.

I guess that's what made me utter those words to Lauren. It was foolish. I know that now. I knew it then. I was overwhelmed with delirium, dizzy with the emotions racing through me and I needed somewhere for them to spill.

Still, I never expected her to say no.

I wanted Lauren. I wanted more than anything to make her my wife, declare to the world that she was mine. But the moment that flash of panic darted across her eyes, the moment she uttered that word 'no', my heart broke. For an instant, I thought I'd lost her again. My high plummeted to a low within an instant, and I cursed myself.

It was only once she walked away, once I'd had time to think of what I'd asked, of how I'd asked it, of when I'd asked it, that I realised Lauren wasn't saying no to me. She was saying no to marriage. She'd already refused to move in with me again so quickly, what the fuck was I doing asking her to marry me?

Even though I knew all this, I still felt like shit.

I wanted to suck the words back into my mouth, as though it were possible to undo them. But I couldn't. And now I had to live with the fact that I had asked and she had refused. It annoyed me that my usually rational thought process was completely and confusingly irrational in regards to Lauren.

My jealousy of her past was gone. I knew that I just needed time to prove it to her. I would never treat her the way I had again. I would never speak to her like that. I almost lost her because of it. And now, more than ever, I knew I needed her in my life.

She was my life.

Lauren and Dante.

We would be a family one day.

In my mind, we already were. I just needed to convince her.

Walking back into the motel room that seemed so much smaller now that Lauren wasn't in it, I pulled the bottle of whiskey that I had bought from the pub out of its paper bag and poured some into the only thing I could find. A coffee cup. It would do the job.

Flicking the television on, I jumped onto the bed, pushing at the heel of one shoe with the toe of the other, letting them fall onto the floor. My eyes fell to where they had dropped. I sighed and leaned over the edge of the bed to arrange them tidily.

I must have drifted off at some stage as I woke to my phone ringing. The room was dark, lit only by the TV screen and Lauren's face as it illuminated the screen of my phone. "Hey you," I greeted her, doing my best to keep my voice light, happy, as though her refusal hadn't cut my heart into a million little pieces.

"Hello, is this Tyler?" a strange voice replied. It was noisy in the background. The lady, whoever she was, was shouting over the roar of something but I couldn't make out what.

I sat up in the bed. "Tyler Thornton." I cleared my throat. "Who is this? Why are you on Lauren's phone?"

"Tyler, your number was in Lauren's phone as her emergency contact. This is Katie and I'm a paramedic. Lauren has had an accident and we are currently on our way to the city hospital."

Panic dropped like rocks in my stomach. I found myself on my feet. "What?" I shouted down the phone, matching her volume. "Is she okay? Is she hurt?"

"She's unconscious at the moment and has sustained some injuries to her left side. I would suggest you make your way to the hospital as soon as possible. We should be arriving there in about half an hour."

The roar in the background suddenly became clear. It was the roar of an engine and the whack of helicopter blades.

"Is she okay?" I shouted again.

"At this stage, we believe the only injuries she has are to her side. We will know more once we reach the hospital. Have you got some way of getting there? Where are you currently situated?" A beep sounded in the background and the woman's voice became muffled.

I let the phone slip through my fingers as I dove into action. Tearing through the room, another wave of panic washed over me when I couldn't find my shoes. It was such a small thing. Inconsequential. But at the time it seemed important. It was like my brain refused to single in on the most important information.

Lauren was hurt, and instead, I chose to focus on the fact that I couldn't find my shoes.

"Fuck!" I yelled into the empty room, folding over on myself as the pain of dread gripped my stomach. "Fuck!"

The whiskey bottle beside the bed caught my eye. I had only had a couple of drinks earlier and I was tempted to throw the rest down my throat in an effort to remove this feeling within. This panic. This dread. This terror.

I shook it off and reached down to collect my phone. "Hello?" I said into it, but the woman, whoever she was, was gone. My hands shook as I scrolled through my contacts, pressing on the number once it came into view.

It rung once, twice, three times. I started praying. "Please pick up. Please pick up," I muttered until finally, I heard a tired "Hello?" on the other end of the line.

"Mum," I said, my throat growing tight. "Lauren's had an accident. She's been hurt. I need to get to her. I need—"

"I'm on my way," Diana replied. "Gather your things, Tyler. Do you hear me? Collect your stuff and I will be there soon."

"Thank you," I breathed.

It felt like forever before I saw the flash of her headlights approaching. Images kept flashing through my mind. Lauren lying on the ground, a wound on her head, blood creeping out onto the dirt. Her face twisted in terror as she plummeted off the road. Some maniac crashing into her and her body flying through the windscreen. I had packed my bags, throwing clothes and toiletries in without even comprehending what was going into my bag. For all I knew, I had half the hotel's belongings in there.

Opening the door before the car had even rolled to a stop, I jumped into the passenger's seat and tossed my bag over the back.

"How is she?" Diana asked.

"I don't know." I let out a breath of air, pushing away the hair that fell in my eyes. "I tried calling her phone again but no one answered."

Diana reached over and patted my knee. Her hand felt strange, unfamiliar, but it did lend some comfort. "She'll be okay, Tyler."

I prayed that she was right. I no longer cared that she had said no. I no longer cared about anything other than if she was okay.

Diana kept talking to me for most of the journey but I didn't remember what she said. I must have registered her conversation on some level though, as I found myself replying to questions, though I don't know what my answers were. I only heard my voice as some sort of muffled drone in the background.

When we started around the road that hugged the edge of the lake, my heart twisted in my chest. Up ahead were lights. Flashing lights. My car, the one that Lauren had been driving, was ploughed into the side of the road. Rocks above had crashed into the side of the car, pushing over to where Lauren would have been sitting.

My stomach lurched. "I think I'm going to be sick."

"Roll your window down," Diana ordered. "Take in a deep breath of air."

I did as she instructed, grateful to have someone to tell me what to do. My brain was scrambled. All I could think about was Lauren lying in a hospital bed, face white, and covered with blood. It would be another three hours before I saw her.

I stared out the window at the men sweeping glass from the road. Another car was getting loaded onto a tow truck. It was obvious that the other driver had been the one to cause the accident. It had travelled across the line, directly into Lauren, shunting her into the side of the cliff, causing the rocks to slide down and... I stopped myself from thinking any more. I couldn't think about her lying there alone.

Alone.

The word rattled through my mind. I could do something about that. Grabbing my phone, I pushed the contact for Sadie. She didn't answer. So I called the next person I could think of who would be close, who would look out for Lauren no matter what, who cared about her almost as much as I did.

"Gabe?" I said after his bleary hello.

"Tyler?" There was a muffled sound and then his voice became clearer. "Why are you calling me? Is everything okay? Is it Jake?"

"No, Jake's fine. But I need you to do something."

"Sure," he replied hesitantly.

I swallowed the swell of panic that rose to the back of my throat again. "Lauren's been in an accident. She's at the hospital. I'm on my way but I'm not going to get there for another couple of hours. Would you go to her? Make sure she's okay."

There was nothing but silence on the end of the line.

"Gabe?"

"I'm here," he replied. "I'm on my way."

Relief flooded me and for a moment the panic and dread and terror subsided. I could breathe.

"Ty?" Gabe questioned. "Is she okay?"

Tears pushed. "I don't know." My voice was hoarse.

"Keep your phone close. I'll call you as soon as I know anything." Then he hung up and I stared at the blank screen. My mind immediately went back to Lauren. I pictured medics doing CPR. I pictured the slackness in her features as they tried to force life back into her.

I needed to stop thinking.

So I concentrated on the other driver and hoped that they had died. It was a horrible thing to wish death upon another human being but it calmed me. Gave me a sense of control as my world was spinning. More than anything, I just wanted to hear her voice, know that she was okay.

It wasn't until we reached the city boundaries that I thought of calling her family. And Peta. They would need to know. But know what exactly? I had no news to give them. Nothing other than the fact that she had been in an accident and was injured. I decided to wait until I had more information. They were hours away and there wasn't a single thing they would be able to do to help. It was better to spare them this pain of the unknown. My phone rang, startling me, even though I was staring at it.

"How is she?" I asked Gabe as soon as I pressed the phone to my ear.

"I haven't seen her yet. She's still in surgery."

"Surgery?" Nausea rained down on me once again.

"Apparently something hit her side and cracked her pelvis. They are unsure if there's any damage to her internal organs." Gabe's voice was tight. Strange. Almost as though he was finding it difficult to speak. "Are you almost here, Ty? She'll want you when she wakes."

I looked out at the lights flashing by. "About forty minutes away," I estimated, gauging from the familiar landmarks passing by in a blur.

"Second floor," Gabe said. "I'm in the waiting room. She's been in there for a couple of hours."

I let the phone fall to my lap once he was done talking. I just wanted to be there with her. I needed to be there.

Diana's hand rested on my knee and I jumped a little. "She's going to be okay," she said for the millionth time. But this time it didn't reassure me. It did nothing but panic me more. She didn't know if Lauren would be okay or not. None of us did.

As soon as we arrived, Diana dropped me at the entrance of the hospital and I ran inside, up the stairs, taking them two at a time and ran breathlessly into the waiting room. It was empty. I scanned the area and spied a nurse walking down another hallway so I sprinted to her.

"Lauren," I called out, panting. "Lauren Greer. She was just in surgery. She had a car accident and—"

"Oh, yes," the nurse replied, smiling brightly. I wanted to push her against the wall. Yell at her. Scream. Demand she tell me where Lauren was this instant. She pushed buttons on a device. "Yes," she said, flashing me another smile. "She's back on the ward. One level up. Room 318."

I didn't thank her, I simply tore away and headed back for the staircase, hauling myself up the steps as fast as my body would allow. The numbers on the rooms were hard to read in the dim light, but eventually, I found her room. Gabe was standing beside her bed, her hand in his, a nurse adjusting the drip hung above her.

I froze.

Gabe smiled. "She's okay," he assured me. "The doctor said she's going to be okay."

Life drained out of me at his words. My body slumped. My throat grew tight and a giant sob escaped. Attempting to blink away the tears, I stepped towards her and Gabe transferred her hand from his to mine.

"Lauren?" I whispered, bringing her fingers to my lips. Her skin was cold and pale. A drip was inserted into the vein in her elbow. A clip was clamped over her finger with a dull red light illuminating the tip. A reassuring beep sounded periodically in the background.

"They said she woke up in recovery, but fell back asleep before they transported her here," Gabe said, taking a step back and allowing me closer.

"And she's okay? You sure she's okay."

Gabe nodded, walking over to take a seat near the window. "The doctor said he'd come back in a few minutes to discuss everything, but he wanted to wait until you arrived as you're listed as her emergency contact." Slumping back into the chair, Gabe let out a long breath and rubbed his hands over his face. "Did you call her parents?"

I shook my head, my eyes stuck on Lauren. She was so pale. Even her lips were white. Scratches marked the left side of her face. Bruising was visible on her shoulder. A pale blue blanket covered the rest of her.

"I didn't know what to tell them."

"You want me to do it?" Gabe asked.

I shook my head again. "I'll call them soon. I just need a minute." I concentrated on the rise and fall of Lauren's chest, reminding myself that she was alive. She would be okay.

She moaned and her face twisted in pain. Her eyes fluttered open, blinking a few times before focussing on me. "Tyler?" she said, a smile stretching across her face. "Is that you?"

Relief escaped as tears. "It's me, baby. Are you okay? How do you feel?"

"Baby?" She moved in the bed and tensed a little when she discovered she couldn't move the lower portion of her body properly. "You've never called me baby before. It's weird." Her eyes had trouble focussing but then she smiled up at me brilliantly. "I feel fantastic."

I laughed, wiping tears away from my eyes and lifting her hand to press kisses to her knuckles.

She looked around the room, giving Gabe a large smile, her wide and dark eyes looking at everything in wonderment. "Where am I? What happened?"

"Ah, you're awake." A doctor walked into the room, dressed in blue. "Are you Tyler Thornton?" He held his hand out.

After I shook his hand, he moved to Lauren's bed, his hand resting gently on her right leg. "How are you feeling?"

She grinned again. "Great."

"That will be the morphine." The doctor looked at me and wriggled his eyebrows.

I wanted to grab him by the neck and thrust him against the wall. "Is she going to be okay?" I asked instead.

The doctor patted her leg again. "She's going to be fine."

Walking over to the wall, he flicked on a light that illuminated a panel and took x-rays out of her file. Pressing them against the lightbox, the stark black and white images shone back at me.

"Lauren has sustained injuries to her pelvis. As you can see, it has been cracked in two places." He ran his finger along the faint line that I wouldn't have noticed unless he pointed it out. "Unfortunately, the places they occurred meant that the fractures were unstable, and we have had to place pins to repair the damage and hold everything in place. She should make a full recovery. Other than the injuries to her hip, she only sustained cuts and bruising to her left side. She's a very lucky woman."

I no longer wanted to throw him against a wall. I wanted to hug him. He kept on talking, but I barely heard a word he said. Tracing across Lauren's forehead with my fingers, I pushed her hair away from her face. "Did you hear that?" I whispered. "You're going to be fine."

She let out a snort. "Of course I am. I feel wonderful."

"Well, at least she's sorted out how to work the morphine button." The doctor chuckled.

Lauren lifted her hand, a button held tightly in her grasp and pushed. There was a small whirring sound and a lazy smile crept over her face. "Yup," she muttered contently. "Got it sorted."

The doctor patted her leg again. "I'll be back in the morning to check on you. Any questions in the meantime, call the nurse." He picked up another button that was draped over Lauren's bed. "That's this button. Not that one."

Lauren gave him the thumbs up.

As soon as the doctor left, she turned to me. "You look worried," she said, a frown creasing her brow.

"I was. You gave me quite the scare."

Her frown deepened. "I didn't mean to." Looking over at Gabe, she flapped her hand at him. He pulled himself off the chair and stood at the other side of her bed. "Do you know where they keep the ice blocks?" she whispered.

Gabe grinned and looked over at me, shrugging his shoulders.

"You two have been playing nicely, haven't you?" Lauren asked, her eyes darting between us.

"Always," I said to her.

"Liar," she muttered. She started toying with my fingers, threading and unthreading hers through mine. "Did you tell him you asked me to marry you?" She blinked at me innocently.

"You what?" Gabe spluttered, taking a step back.

"Oh, don't worry." Lauren opened her eyes in a wide gaze. "I said no."

"It's the morphine," I growled at Gabe.

"You asked her to marry you?"

"But I said no," Lauren forcefully assured Gabe. She yawned, a giant yawn that overtook her face. "I'm going back to sleep now," she informed us as her eyelids drooped.

Gabe stepped away from her bed. "You fucking what?" he hissed at me.

"It was just something that came up, a spur of the moment thing."

"You don't do spur of the moment things, Tyler."

"Well, I do when it comes to her." I spat back at him. "There is no doubt in my mind that I want to be with her."

Gabe smirked, crossing his arms over his chest. "But she said no."

"It wasn't the time." Placing Lauren's hand down at her side, I walked over to him. All the promises I had made to myself about waiting, about giving her time flew out the window the moment of her crash. "But I'm going to ask her again. When she wakes up. Wakes up without her system being drowned in morphine."

"Don't," Gabe warned.

I stepped closer to him. "I just about lost her, Gabe. She could have died tonight. I won't risk that again. I want her. I need her to know how I feel about her."

"You're fucking relentless, you know that, right?"

"And that's a bad thing?"

Gabe stood taller. "In this case, yes."

"What would you know?" I muttered, glancing back at where Lauren was sleeping peacefully.

"What would I know?" Gabe walked back to the seat by the window and sat down, his elbows resting on his knees, his eyes lifted to mine. "Well, I know that I pretty much dated her for three months before she would even tell anyone. I know that you pursued her ever since I introduced her to you. Relentlessly." He emphasised the word. "To the point that she broke up with me after almost seven months of dating. Then, you didn't even wait two months before you fucked her. Literally. You wanted her to move to the city, so she did. She moved her life for you. And then, only months later, you humiliate her in front of friends and family. Now, days after you're back together, you take her to meet your mother and ask her to marry you. You need to let her breathe." He let out a long breath as though demonstrating. "Well, at least you didn't start pressuring her to talk about kids or something."

My wince must have been visible.

"Fuck, Tyler. What is wrong with you? Have you only got one speed when it comes to her? Lauren's had a shit storm thrown at her, thanks to you, to us. Just let her be. She loves you, Ty. It's clear for anyone to see."

My body was tense and tight, ready to fight, but after his words it all drained from me. I collapsed into the chair beside him. "Fuck. You're right. When did you get to be so wise?"

"I've always been wise," he said, sitting back and placing his hands behind his head with a wicked grin. "You just never listened."

Leaning forward, I covered my face with my hands. "I don't know what's happening to me. It's like I'm on a fucking emotional roller coaster."

"Give yourself a break. And count yourself lucky that you told me you were going to ask Lauren again and not her."

The door to Lauren's room burst open and Sadie appeared, hair in disarray, eyes darting around the room. "Why didn't you answer your phone?" she yelled at me as she darted over to Lauren's bed. "Is she okay?" She picked up her hand and held it tightly between both of hers. "Are you okay?" she whispered.

"She's fine," I told her. "Well, apart from a fractured pelvis and bruising and cuts all down her left side."

Tears sprung to Sadie's eyes. "Fuck," she said. Letting go of Lauren, she wiped her tears away and came over to wrap her arms around me. "Are you okay?"

"Not really," I replied, struggling to keep the tightness at the back of my throat at bay. "I thought I'd lost her."

"But you didn't." Sadie stroked my back reassuringly.

"But I could've." My words were muffled by her shoulder.

Gabe stood and stretched high into the air. "I might get going. Give me a call in the morning and let me know how she is. Let me know if there's anything I can do, yeah?"

I nodded and detangled myself from Sadie. "Thanks."

"And Ty?" I looked over at him. "You'd better call her family."

26

LAUREN

I woke from a painkiller-fueled sleep, wincing as I twisted in the bed, pain shooting up my left side. The events of the day before were foggy. The accident. The surgery. Afterwards. It was all there in the back of my mind, but I had to wade through mud and fog to bring it to the surface.

Reaching for the button hanging beside my bed, I pressed down, relishing the comfort the morphine brought, but it wore off too quickly. During the night, one of the nurses had adjusted the dosage and it no longer worked the same as it did before. As a result, my mind was clearer, but I cared about the pain a little more. Attempting to move my left side brought nothing but pain. My leg was limp. It refused to move despite the signals from my brain.

It was still the early hours of the morning. I could tell by the faintness of the light creeping in from around the slatted curtains. Tyler was sleeping in one of the chairs, head bent to his chest and hair falling over his eyes. Dark hair grazed his chin, and even in sleep, a frown pressed between his eyes. I wished I could touch him. I wished I could rub that little spot of flesh and take those lines away.

The memory of his proposal washed over me. For a moment, I thought it was a product of my drug-induced sleep. It was so unlike Tyler.

Tyler was controlled.

He was intensity and determination.

He did not blurt out proposals.

But even as my mind insisted it must be a figment of my imagination, I also knew it to be true. The burning panic of my refusal still haunted me. Part of me wished I had just said yes. I loved him. He loved me. It was meant to be simple. But I knew how quickly I became consumed by Tyler Thornton. I knew how quickly my mind and my body betrayed my rationale. There had to be a way to love him and still keep my head.

I just hoped he would understand.

Pushing the morphine button again, the machine beeped at me, warning that it was too soon. The noise woke Tyler. He stirred, stretched high, twisted from side to side and rolled his shoulders and neck, testing his sore muscles from being crammed into a chair for the night.

"Morning beautiful," he said when his eyes met mine. Getting to his feet, he walked the space between us and pressed a kiss to my forehead. "How are you feeling this morning?"

"A little sore." I wiggled in the bed and winced at the pain the movement brought. "What happened?"

I knew what happened. I knew about the accident and the surgery, but it was as though I needed to hear the words from Tyler's mouth to confirm it was true.

"You don't remember?" The lines between his brows deepened. "Maybe we should tell the doctor."

I adjusted myself in the bed again, trying to pull myself up, but gave up and flopped back when the pain got too much. "Everything is a little hazy and I had some crazy dreams. I just need you to tell me so I know what's true."

Dragging a chair over to beside my bed, Tyler took my hand between his, rubbing circles on the soft pad of flesh below my thumb. "You were driving back when another car crossed the centre line."

My eyes widened as my memory came back clearer. The flash of the headlights. The pain. Then nothing.

"The car crashed, causing a minor landslide of rocks to roll down and crush parts of the car. You were lucky to get away with the injuries you did. You did get quite the knock to your head, but they said that everything looked fine. Maybe I should get them to check again." Tyler started to rise to his feet, but I tugged on his hand.

"I'm fine, Tyler. A bit banged up, but fine."

He sat back down and smiled, but it wasn't his usual smile. It was one filled with sadness and worry. The pressure band around my upper arm inflated, relaying my blood pressure levels to the machine. It had done it repeatedly during the night. I wasn't sure if it was supposed to still be on, or if one of the nurses had simply forgotten to take it off.

"I'm sorry you had to miss out on watching Dante's game."

"I gave him a call last night but he must have already been asleep. I left a message though and explained what happened. I'll call him again later today." Tyler chewed on his lip, looking over at me hesitantly. "I was so worried, Lauren." His voice was soft and tender. "I've never been so scared in all my life. I never want to lose you. Never." The word caught in his throat and he shook his head a little as if to try and dislodge it. "You remember going over to meet Dante?"

I smiled. "Of course I do, it's just yesterday itself that's a little foggy."

Tyler cleared his throat and twisted his head from side to side as though stretching his neck. "So you remember the conversation we had the night before?"

I nodded. I was grateful I wasn't still attached to the heart rate monitor as I'm sure it would have spiked a little.

Taking a deep breath, he looked into my eyes. "I don't know why I blurted it out like that. I'm sorry. It wasn't fair to you. We've just got back together and you have no basis on which to take my word that I won't ever make you feel guilty for your past, or that my jealousy won't raise its head again." He shifted on the seat, his eyes glancing towards the door as a nurse walked past. "But I assure you it won't. I meant what I said, Lauren. I do want to marry you. But I want it to be when you're ready. When we're both ready. When there isn't a shadow of a doubt in your mind. I don't ever want you to feel pressured. I love you, Lauren Greer. With every part of me. Even if that means that you never want to get married or have children. None of that matters. All I want is your love. Nothing else. You are enough. You're more than enough. You're everything."

My throat grew tight. Tears formed in my eyes.

"Lauren?" Tyler said, his voice filled with concern. "Lauren, are you okay? Do I need to call a nurse?"

I shook my head, willing away the tears and tightness. "No," I managed to squeak out.

Tyler frowned deeply, a noise coming out of his throat almost like a growl. "I'm not a fan of that word at the moment."

I laughed at that, then clutched my side as the pain shot upwards.

"I swear I will make you want to marry me one day, Lauren Greer. You just wait and see. I will earn your yes. I will earn your trust and approval so you'll know how much you mean to me." He pulled his chair closer, resting his chin on the handle on the side of the bed. "But for now I am content. I'm content to just be yours and for you to be mine. I just thought you should know."

I was dangerously close to blurting out that I wanted him then and there. That I would do everything and anything he wanted if he would only keep looking at me like that. Like I was the only person that existed. Like I was made up of everything he could wish for. Like I was perfect. But I knew my emotions too well. I knew that I was too easily intoxicated by him. Instead, all I said was, "I love you."

And all he said was, "I know."

"Ah, you're awake!" The doctor strolled into the room, glancing between us when he noticed the tears in my eyes, and the look of adoration in Tyler's that was quickly replaced with annoyance.

"Should I come back?" he asked, waving a pen towards the doorway.

"Yes," Tyler replied at the same time as I said, "No."

The doctor looked between us again, then lifted his brows and rolled his eyes before stepping back out into the hallway and calling for a nurse.

"Right," he said, placing a clipboard on the foot of my bed. "How are you feeling today?" Without waiting for a response he pinched my big toe. "Can you feel that?"

I nodded, my lip caught between my teeth as tendrils of pain began to spread through my body.

"And what about this?" He tapped on my leg with his pen, and again, I nodded. "Good. Right." He placed his pen into his pocket and faced me. "How do you feel about attempting to stand?"

"Stand?" Tyler echoed.

The doctor winked at me. "Yes, that movement when you rest your weight on your feet and legs and lift yourself upright."

The muscles in Tyler's jaw pulsed as he controlled his annoyance. "She only had the surgery yesterday. She's still in pain."

The doctor winked at me again which only infuriated Tyler more. "Hmmm," the doctor mused, picking up the clipboard and studying the notes. "It appears you are correct, as noted by the surgeon here who just happens to be…" he screwed up his face as though pondering then broke into a smile of realisation, "me!"

Tyler twisted his head from side to side again, his jaw working back and forth. "I just thought it was a little early for her to be putting any weight on her leg."

The doctor clapped his hands, causing me to jump and then hiss in pain. "Right you are. That is exactly why she will not be putting any weight on that leg. Once she is safely in the wheelchair, perhaps you can take her for a walk around the corridors. It might be good for you to see some different walls. Maybe then, you will realise that in these parts, the doctors are the ones walking around with the name badges and the visitors, like you, aren't." He smiled brilliantly at Tyler and clapped his hands together again. "Shall we get started? The sooner you're up the sooner you can start your recovery. By tomorrow I expect you to be taking a few steps on the crutches and then you should be able to go home in a few days."

"A few days?" Tyler repeated.

The doctor looked up and blinked twice before saying, "Yes."

"Maybe you should head down to the café and get us something for breakfast?" I said, looking over at Tyler. His eyes narrowed and flicked to the doctor, but then he nodded and walked out.

The nurse walked in as he left and I couldn't help but notice the way she eyed him appreciatively. Her cheeks reddened when she looked back into the room and saw that I was watching her check Tyler out. I wanted to tell her it was okay. I still stared too.

"Right." The doctor clapped his hands together again and I wondered if it was the best habit for a surgeon to have during his post-surgery care. "I am going to leave you in the lovely hands of Maggie here, and she will assist you to stand." He walked out the door then popped his head back around the corner. "Don't push it too far this time. Just stand, stretch a little and then Maggie will help you lower yourself into the wheelchair."

The nurse with the red cheeks stood by the bed. "I'm just going to lower you down a little and then, if you can, move over to the edge of the bed."

The bed moved down robotically, startling me a little. I was a lot jumpier than usual and it wasn't exactly helping my pain levels. Lifting my injured leg was difficult. It wouldn't cooperate. In the end, I had to haul it over the edge with my hand and the nurse helped me lower it to the ground. Already my pain had increased dramatically, but I knew I had to do this. And with the way Tyler was acting, it was better that I did it while he was out of the room. Nurse Maggie pulled a walking frame over and help me stand. I was only allowed to rest one toe of my injured leg on the ground. Once I was fully standing, with my lip pressed between my teeth and a fine sheen of sweat covering my body, the nurse clapped enthusiastically. I was beginning to wonder if everyone that worked in the hospital had this habit.

"Perfect! You're standing."

And I was. But I did not feel well. It was almost as though I could feel the blood draining from my head and pooling in the pit of my stomach. The nurse must have noticed too as she very quickly brought over the wheelchair and lowered me into it.

Tyler still wasn't back from the café, so I took the opportunity to wheel myself into the small bathroom. The nurses had removed my catheter in the middle of the night and I had needed to use the bathroom for a while. The thought of standing was the only thing that stopped me. It took a few grunts of pain, but using the sink to steady me, I stood. Fumbling with the ties of the hospital gown, I undid the knots at my shoulders and sides and let the material fall to the ground. It was the first time I had seen myself since the accident. The left side of my face was covered in small cuts from the shattered glass and bruising had started to swell over my chin and cheekbone. Mascara left over from the day before shadowed the hollows beneath my eyes. My shoulder looked the worst, even though it felt fine. The bruising had already turned a deep purplish colour. Cuts littered my legs and the single bandage down the side of my leg was the only tell-tale sign I had had surgery. I sighed and ran my fingers over my side, testing for tenderness. I imagined the painkillers were dulling a lot of my senses and I was grateful.

A knock startled me. Again.

"Are you alright?" Tyler's voice drifted through the door.

I looked at the gown on the floor. I looked over at the toilet which I needed to somehow get myself to and everything overwhelmed me.

"Can you help me?" I asked, my voice quiet and resigned.

The door opened and Tyler took in my naked form. I watched him in the reflection of the mirror. "Lauren," he breathed, walking to stand behind me. His eyes met mine in the mirror as he feathered his hands over my shoulder, too scared to touch. "Are you… Is it…" He let his words fall.

My grip on the sink intensified. "I need you to help me get onto the toilet." A tear slipped down my cheek. Tyler stood on my good side, the side not covered in bruises and cuts, and I lifted my arm over his shoulder. Being as gentle as he could, he helped me manoeuvre my way over and sit down. Tyler walked out the door to give me privacy and came back when I called, helping me back into the gown and then into the wheelchair.

Wheeling me outside, we sat in the fresh air and nibbled on the muffins Tyler had bought and sipped on our coffees. Tyler kept looking at me, then turning away as though there was something he wanted to ask, but couldn't bring himself to.

"What?" I said finally.

"Would you consider staying with me while you recover?" He rotated the cup in his hand and took another sip. "You can go back to Sadie's whenever you feel like it, but just for the first couple of days, you know, until you can get around the place by yourself, you could stay with me so I could look after you."

"Well—" I started to say but Tyler cut me off.

"I just think I'd worry about you too much if you were alone. And we both know that Sadie will be busy with you off your feet."

"Won't you be busy too?" I asked, popping another piece of muffin into my mouth. It was blueberry and the purple stained my fingers.

"I can arrange things to suit. Work more at nights while you're sleeping. Work a little from home."

"Hmmm," I pondered, almost enjoying the way he was so eager to convince me.

"You can go back to Sadie's anytime you please. You can—"

"Yes."

"Yes?" he questioned.

"Yes," I repeated. "The thought of trying to get around that tiny house with the narrow hallway on crutches isn't exactly appealing. It's a good idea."

Tyler smiled and this time it wasn't one marred by sadness or worry. "I will wait on you hand and foot. I will be your loyal servant and fulfil all your wishes."

I looked over at him and smiled seductively. Or at least I hoped it was seductive. Goodness knows how it came off in my current state. "All my wishes?"

Tyler tilted his head to the side, grinning wickedly. "Maybe not all your wishes. You need time to heal. But everything else."

"Everything else?" I repeated, emphasising the 'everything'.

"Stop it," he warned, adjusting the placement of his hips on the seat. He gazed over the carpark. "Speak of the devil," he muttered.

"Morning!" Sadie called out. She was styled perfectly. Her hair was smooth and straight, falling like a blonde curtain down her back. She had on a dark suit, heels and just a flash of lace on her chest. She sat down beside Tyler. It amazed me how she always managed to look so put together and act such a mess. Reaching over, she plucked some of his muffin off and popped it into her mouth. "Sorry I'm late," she mumbled around the food.

"Late?" I asked.

"It's fine," Tyler replied.

"Late for what?"

Sadie chewed some more then swallowed. "Tyler has to pop into work for a bit today and get some things sorted. He asked me to get here by eleven but that meeting ran late. Got here as soon as I could."

I raised my eyebrows at Tyler.

"What?" he said, attempting to look innocent. "I just wanted to make sure someone was here to look after you in case you needed it."

"I'm pretty sure that's what all those nurses and doctors are here for. In fact, I'd almost say it was their job."

Reaching for Tyler's muffin again, Sadie took the whole thing and started to break off little pieces and pop them into her mouth. "Sorry," she said. "I'm starving." She hit Tyler's arm with the back of her hand causing crumbs to fall off the muffin and onto his leg. "Well, fuck off then."

Getting to his feet, Tyler stood behind me. "I'll just push her inside."

Sadie rolled her eyes and shoved the last of the muffin into her mouth and stood. Pushing Tyler aside, she grabbed the handles of the chair. "I told you to fuck off."

A smile danced around Tyler's mouth as he bent to kiss me. "I'm wondering if I made the right choice in calling her to stay with you."

"Argh." Sadie turned the wheelchair sharply, taking me away from Tyler. "You two are gross. She's injured for crying out loud. Take your mouth off her."

Once back inside, and cruising down the hallways at a speed that would make Tyler shudder, Sadie updated me on the meeting she had with some prospective clients. They were the owners of a small animal park outside the city.

"I feel pretty good about it all. I think they liked me."

"But most of the questions they had were about photography. How did you handle that?" I twisted to look behind me.

Sadie shrugged. "Fake it until you make it, baby."

"I should have been there."

"Yup," Sadie agreed. "It was really rather rude of you not to consider that when that car ploughed into you. You heard anything about the driver?"

"Only that he didn't have quite the same level of injuries that I have. The police are going to lay charges, Tyler said. It was someone used to driving on the other side of the road."

"Bloody tourists," she muttered.

27

LAUREN

It wasn't until four o'clock in the afternoon that Sadie left. I had told her to leave earlier, but she just rolled her eyes and insisted that Tyler would kill her. I reminded her that she didn't work for him anymore, that she didn't have to do what he told her, but she just shrugged and went back to watching the talk show on the extremely small screen that hung from the ceiling in the corner of the room.

Tyler had already called to tell me that he couldn't make it back for a few more hours. Even though he had organised to have the day off to attend Dante's game, the recent events had meant he was left trying to juggle things around for at least the rest of the week. I told him he didn't have to. I told him I would be fine, maybe a little bored, but fine, but he wouldn't listen.

And now that I was sitting here alone, I didn't mind the peace. My head was beginning to ache, and I was pretty sure that if I closed my eyes for a few minutes, I would fall asleep.

But Tyler obviously wasn't okay with my insistence that I would be fine because I had to force my eyes back open when there was a knock on the door.

"Hey you," Gabe said, his face breaking out into a side-splitting grin. "How you feeling today?"

Groaning, I struggled to sit up in the bed. I must have fallen asleep as somehow I'd lost almost two hours and I could hear the food trolleys rattling down the hall. "What are you doing here?"

"And it's good to see you too." Gabe laughed. "Tyler sent me."

"Argh," I moaned. "That man."

Dragging a chair over to my bed, Gabe sat down beside me, glancing up at the TV which was now mute, but images still flashed across the screen. "What are we watching?"

I shook my head, trying to dislodge the tendrils of sleep. "Are you sure he asked you to come?"

Gabe held up his hands as if declaring surrender. "I swear," he said. "Twice now he's asked me. Weird, huh? I think it's finally dawning on him that I didn't stand a chance."

"That's not—"

"You don't need to explain, Lauren. I know it's the truth. I was fooling myself by thinking differently. As much as it pains me, he loves you, Lauren. Like painfully, stupidly so. You turn him into a fucking idiot at times."

I blinked. "An idiot?"

"You know what I mean. The normal Tyler, the Tyler we all know and sometimes despise, is calculated and controlled. He plans out every stupid detail of his life. But Tyler with you is a different kettle of fish. I told him that too. He's reckless around you. Fuck me. Love me. Live with me. Marry me."

I struggled to contain my surprise. "He told you?"

Gabe grinned. "Yeah, but you did first."

"When?" I was horrified. There was nothing in my memory of telling Gabe about the proposal.

"You were still all hopped up on drugs and just sort of blurted it out. I made him tell me about it later, once you were asleep again."

"And," I swallowed a nervous knot that had suddenly appeared in the back of my throat, "are we good? You and me, I mean?"

Gabe's eyes dropped to the floor. "I love you, Lauren. There may be a part of me that always will. But I know we're not meant to be, you and me. I knew it that night at the club. And then later at Jake's fight. I knew there was no point fighting for you anymore. Not when you only wanted Tyler."

I reached for his hand, but he shied away from my touch. "Gabe, I'm so sorry. I never meant for any of this to happen."

His Adam's apple bobbed up and down as though fighting back emotion. "Did you ever love me?"

"My god, yes," I cried. "Yes, I did. Yes, I do, just not in the way you want. You were so good to me, Gabe. When Derek left, I was a mess. There was little confidence left in me. I felt discarded, unloved. Unwanted. And then you came along and changed everything. I will forever be grateful to you for that. There will always be a part of me that loves you."

Gabe rubbed his hands over his face and shook his head. "Good," he said, and attempted a grin. "I guess that's all I can ask for."

"You'll find someone, Gabe. You're much too gorgeous not to."

Gabe grinned. "I know. Not many women can resist this." He circled his face. "Problem is finding one I can't resist. One that isn't you." Gabe's words got caught in his throat and he kind of laughed-cried. "Ah, shit." He tried to laugh again. "I didn't come here planning on declaring my undying love for you. Tyler would kill me right now. He made me promise to keep my hands, eyes and mouth away from you."

"Well, you've kept that promise, so I'd say you're fine."

"Not because I want to." Gabe looked up and there was a glimmer in his eyes. One that pleaded. One that begged. He searched my face, hunting for the same response, and when he didn't find it, he rubbed his hands over his face again and muttered, "Sorry."

"Tyler never really told me much about what happened that night. Apparently, you beat him in some fight?"

That brought his smile back. "Fuck yeah, I did." He settled back in the chair. "It was glorious. Glorious I tell you. So we're at this sort of underground fight club, right?"

I leaned back into the pillow and listened to him retell the story. It was a lot more graphic than Tyler's version, complete with blow by blow details of how he beat him.

Things between Gabe and I were never going to be completely at ease. There was always going to be that underlying buzz of tension and awkwardness, but I was grateful for this moment between us. Grateful for his honesty. I only hoped he knew that what I said was true. As much as I loved Tyler, as much as I desired him, longed for him, Gabe had been there when Tyler wasn't. He was the one that helped put me back together. He was the one who held me to a mirror and told me I was beautiful. He would always hold a place in my heart, even if it wasn't the one he wanted.

"He told me that night that he wanted to spend the rest of his life with you," Gabe was saying.

"He did?"

"The night before, at the club, was when it truly dawned on me how you felt about him. You'd never snapped at me before but you did that night. I knew it was over. I knew I'd become a nuisance to you."

"Gabe…" I reached out to him again and this time he let me place my hand on his knee.

"But there at the fight, that was when I realised how much you meant to him. He was willing to swallow his pride and ask for my forgiveness. He was willing to beg me for you because he just wanted to make you happy, and he knew that wouldn't happen if we didn't get our shit together. He loves you, Lauren. And as much as I'd like to tell you there was some doubt to my statement, there is none. Tyler and I may never become good friends, but at least we understand each other now. There's a level of respect."

Tears threatened. Again. I wasn't sure if it was the events in my life, the amount of painkillers pumping through my system, or if I was due for that time of the month, but I was emotional. The last few days had been exhausting. "Just know that I never wanted to hurt you, Gabe. I never meant to fall for you and then Tyler. If I could go back and change things, I would in a heartbeat."

Gabe squinted up at me. "Yeah, if you could go back and change things I would have never had the chance to be with you. And even with the heartbreak you put me through, I still wouldn't give that up."

"You are almost too good, Gable Thornton."

He nodded, and slow and devious smile spreading over his face. "Yeah, I've heard that a lot."

I picked up the magazine beside my bed and whacked him across the head.

* * *

I spent a total of six days in hospital. By the time they let me out, I was desperate for the peace and quiet of Tyler's loft. There was no rattling trolley to deliver mediocre meals. There were no nurses popping into my room every hour or so during the night just to check I was okay. There were no alarms. No patients who insisted on having their TV at a volume level that could be heard throughout the hospital. There was just Tyler and me.

Peta called every day. Tyler had called her, as well as my family, once he knew what was happening as he didn't want them to worry needlessly. I told him to downplay the accident and my injuries. A fractured hip was all they needed to know. They didn't need to know about the surgery or the metal pins. Anything more and my mother would have been on her way up here to grace me with her presence. That was something I didn't need during my recovery.

My first trip out of the house was with Billie. She had insisted I go to a fancy dress shop with her to select costumes for a party Hamish and she were going to, but I knew it was simply to get me out and about. She rattled on about Hamish and his new lease on life which included only eating raw food and never consuming alcohol. Even though she didn't say it, I almost think she resented his sobriety, simply because it had shone a light on her lack of it. Still, she insisted, she was young. She didn't need to be trapped in the house all day with a baby and a husband who followed her around like a lost puppy.

For the entire first week, Tyler slept on the couch, certain that his presence in the bed would somehow hurt me, or disturb my sleep. The opposite was true. His bed without him was too large. My mind was constantly trapped on the other side of the wall.

But that was about to change.

I was going to insist on it.

28

LAUREN

Tyler was lying on the couch, laptop on his knees, glasses perched delightfully on his nose when I made my way out of the bedroom.

He jumped to his feet immediately. "Lauren, what are you doing out of bed? Are you alright? Can I get you something?"

"I'm fine." I used those words often. "I just want you to come to bed."

He frowned. "It's after midnight. You should be asleep."

Walking over to him with a crutch either side, I stood before him and balanced on one leg so I could put the crutches down and rest my hands on his chest. "I would be, if I could stop thinking of you out here, wondering what you're doing, wishing you weren't doing it."

Tyler smirked but replied, "You'll get a better sleep without me."

I spread my fingers, splaying them over his chest then dragging them over his shoulders and down his sides. "Come to bed?" I pleaded.

"Lauren," he warned, though his eyes had darkened. "Careful."

"Of what?" I teased.

"Of what you're doing." He removed my hands from his chest. "It hasn't even been two weeks since your accident."

"It will be tomorrow though." I tugged my hands out of his grasp and wrapped them around his waist, placing my cheek on his chest and inhaling his scent. It was a bad thing to do. Desire ached between my legs. Genuinely ached. Not like some tingle or a gentle quiver. This was painful. So physically painful I squeezed my legs together in an attempt to relieve the sensation.

Lifting my head, I looked up at Tyler and his hands hovered by my face. He was so gentle. His fingers felt like butterflies kissing my skin. Bending his head, he pressed his lips to mine softly. Gently. Just a tease. I moaned. Not quite a sound of longing, but some guttural cry of desperation. Tyler increased the pressure of his hands on the sides of my face. He increased the passion in his kiss. His mouth moved over mine, nipping at the fullness of my bottom lip. I wished I wasn't balanced so precariously, I wished I could lift into his arms and wrap my legs around his waist.

But then Tyler pulled away, careful to move his hands from my face to my side, always hovering, always close so I could lean on him.

Tilting his head, his lips brushed against my ear as he whispered, "I'm afraid of what I'll want to do if I sleep beside you."

"I'm afraid of what I'll do if you won't."

Cupping my face again, Tyler laughed. "Okay, you win." Bending down, he scooped me into his arms, carrying me back into the bedroom. "But you will not tempt me, Lauren Greer. We will not be having any sort of sex until we get the all clear from the doctor."

"Tyler!" I exclaimed. "The doctor isn't going to tell us when we can have sex again."

"Well, I'll ask him."

"Like hell you will."

He placed me on the bed gently and pulled the blankets to cover me.

"I feel fine," I insisted. Sure, I still got the odd twinge of pain and my muscles wouldn't cooperate like they were supposed to, but overall, I was feeling good. Awkward, but good.

"You can wait," he called over his shoulder as he walked away.

"Hey," I called after him. "You promised to sleep with me."

Walking back into the room, Tyler pulled his shoes off and paired them together beside the bed. "And I will. I was just powering down the laptop."

"Oh," I said, feeling slightly foolish.

Tyler hadn't changed since coming home from work. His tie was off, his shirt was loose and hanging out from his tailored pants. Waiting for him to undo the buttons and for his shirt to come off was torture. I wished I could rise to my knees and rip it from him. Press him to the bed, climb on top and devour him. But he took his time, placing his shirt and his pants neatly over the back of the chair before sliding into bed naked. Naked. It was like he was teasing me.

I wanted to turn to him but it still hurt to lie on my left side. I would have to content myself with conversation instead.

"What you thinking about?"

"Christmas," he replied. He placed his hands behind his head, his chest rising and falling. "Dad and Billie have invited us to their place for Christmas dinner. Your parents and sister too. Do you know what their plans are?"

Christmas was less than a week away and Mother had been calling repeatedly to ask my plans. It was tradition for me to spend it with them and I wanted to keep up that tradition, but I also wanted to spend it with Tyler. In the new year, I would return to my house where Sadie and Smudge were waiting. I would return to work. To normality. The Tyler bubble which I had promised myself not to get caught in again, would be burst.

"They want me to come home."

"Do you think they'd consider coming up here? I could call them. I'm sure I could convince old Clementine, but I wouldn't like to do that without checking with you first."

He was learning. "Actually, I think that would be good. And if you ask Mother, she's far less likely to insist I go down there for it."

"And what about Peta?"

"What about her? She'll have her own family to spend Christmas with."

"But what about afterwards? I was thinking that maybe I could use my influence to get them a night or two at the casino. They could come up for New Year. Have a break away from the kids."

"She would love that!" I squealed, genuinely excited by the thought. "I will call Mark tomorrow and see if we can organise it to be a surprise. I'll have to let Shrek in on the secret though. There is no way in hell we could organise it without his help. She's like a bloodhound, that one. Sniffs out a secret in seconds."

Tossing one of his pillows onto the chair beside his bed, Tyler leaned in for a quick kiss before turning off the light. I lay in the dark and listened to his breathing. Always a restless sleeper, I knew it would take a while before he fell asleep, so we lay in silence, the odd distant sound of traffic the only noise to break the stillness. I wondered if he was lying there, thinking about touching me as much as I was about touching him. To have him so close was almost as bad as having him in the next room. The memories of all the times he had taken me in this bed rose to mind. I couldn't help but imagine what he must look like beneath the sheets. He was lying on his back—that much I could tell. One arm would be bent at the elbow, his hand tucked behind his head. The other would probably be resting on his chest. His left knee was raised slightly, I could tell by the rise of the sheets, and the other was bent towards me. My thoughts drifted higher up his body, and I pondered whether he was soft or hard, or somewhere in-between. I wondered if our kiss had aroused him or if he was determined in his refusal not to touch me. I wonder if it would be slumped to the side, resting on his thigh, or if it would be stretched towards his stomach, pressed down by the weight of the covers.

I was desperate.

I couldn't lie on my side and turn towards him, so I crept my hand across the mattress until I touched the flesh of his side. He didn't react. His breathing remained the same. He stayed silent. But he also didn't stop me. Splaying my fingers, I moved them over his smooth skin, marvelling in the dips and swells of the muscles in his abdomen, then trailing them down further until I brushed the coarse hair that graced his pelvis.

He breathed in slowly and deeply. I heard the constriction of his throat as he swallowed. I ventured further, until I found him, hard and heavy. Wrapping my hand around him elicited a growl. A sudden exhale of air. A tightening of his muscles.

Still, he didn't stop me.

So I began to stroke, relishing the way he felt in my hand, the hardness of him, the thickness and the fullness. How I wished I could move more freely. I longed to take him in my mouth.

With a suddenness that surprised me, he turned, falling from my hand. The bed dipped as he rose to his knees and tossed the blankets away, leaving me lying in nothing but a t-shirt and soaked underwear. Without a word, he climbed over me, careful not to touch, careful not to cause me any discomfort. With his legs pressed either side of my body, he held himself above me, hands either side of my shoulders. The heat of him invaded my senses as he lowered himself, still not enough for his body to be pressed against mine, but close enough to dip his mouth and taste my lips. Close enough that his cock pressed against my belly. My kiss was feverish, lips fumbling against his in desperation. Reaching between our bodies, I grasped hold of him and he rewarded me with one of those groans that sent sharp spikes of desire into my deepest parts. Pushing my head back into the pillow, I arched, my body reaching for his. But instead of lowering himself to greet me, he roughly caught my bottom lip between his teeth. A warning I wasn't sure if I wanted to ignore or obey.

His body trembled with need. It vibrated through the mattress as he rested on one hand and reached between us, pulling my grasp from his cock. Tugging me, he pressed my arm into the bed, applying extra force with his fingers wrapped around my wrist.

"Stay," he ordered.

And then his hand was gone from mine, snaking between us again and taking hold of himself, guiding himself to rub over my wetness. He stroked himself back and forth, his weight still held above my body, touching only where he slid himself over me. Even his mouth hovered over mine without touching. More an exchange of breath than a kiss. My breathing quickened and I began to pant as the sensation of him sliding across me increased in tempo. He was pleasuring himself and pleasuring me with the same movement. Sheets curled beneath my fingers as I gripped them, needing something, anything to hold. My head rose off the pillow, pressing my forehead to his as I hungrily searched for his mouth, but he pulled away, leaving his head pressed against mine but my mouth untouched, save for the slightest whisper of breath.

When I came undone he swallowed my cry, finally bringing his mouth down onto mine as he jerked a final time and his seed spilt over me, hot and wet.

He still trembled when he lifted himself and climbed from the bed. Light spilt across the floor as he entered the bathroom and returned moments later with a damp washcloth.

"Did I hurt you?" His voice was dark and blunt as he wiped across the round of my stomach and down further, cleaning himself from me.

"Hurt me?" I repeated, still coming down from the dizzying high. "You barely touched me."

"Are you sure?"

I reached up, the shadow of his face visible in the dim light that stretched from the open door, and cupped his cheek with my hand. "I adore you, Tyler Thornton," I whispered into the night.

29

LAUREN

Christmas morning dawned and I woke to Tyler propped on his side, elbow pressed into the mattress, his head resting in his hand and staring at me.

"Morning, beautiful." He pressed his lips to my forehead as I stretched into the air. Cautiously, I turned on my side, wincing a little at the discomfort, but able to maintain the position.

"Merry Christmas." Tyler brushed my hair from my face and tucked it behind my ear.

"Merry Christmas," I replied, letting a smile overtake my face as I pressed both hands beneath my cheek. Tyler was naked again. He had made it a habit ever since that night when he rubbed himself against me until we both came. He was a tease though, as he hadn't touched me since. My eyes dropped to his chest. I blamed it on my inactivity, on boredom, how obsessed I had become with him. I couldn't stop imagining what it would be like when he finally had sex with me again.

"Hey," he chided, using his finger to lift my chin. "Eyes up here."

I laughed and rolled onto my back. "Are you going to change your stance on touching me?"

"Not until you're one hundred percent healed, no. I'm all or nothing. Restraint around you isn't possible."

I had attempted to recreate that night many times over the past week but Tyler had turned down every advance, stating that he was too afraid of hurting me.

"I don't think you understand how I'm feeling, Tyler Thornton," I teased. "I've been cooped up in this apartment for weeks now with nothing to stare at but your naked body and nothing to do but imagine all the things we could be doing. Do you want to hear about them?"

He groaned. "Fuck, Lauren. Now I'm hard. You need to stop it."

"But what if I don't want to?"

Tyler looked at me sideways, a frown creasing his beautiful face. "It's not going to happen. I told you how hard it was for me the other night not to press into you, not to lower myself and drive my—" He let out a low whistle of air, closing his eyes and shaking his head. "No." He opened his eyes again and gave me a warning glare. "I won't be tempted. When I do fuck you, and believe me I do intend on doing that, a lot, many times, it will be when we don't have to hold back. When I can take you and—" Another whistle of air. "Okay, now I'm the one who needs to stop. Subject change." Twisting over, Tyler reached beneath the bed. "Present time."

"Is it you?" I asked, attempting to give him my most seductive look. "Because right now that's all I want."

"Lauren," he growled again, and the sound of my name on his lips as a warning had me pressing my legs together. "Just open the damn present."

It was a thick envelope. White. My name scrawled across the front.

"What is it?" I asked turning it over in my hands. I did it only because I knew it would annoy him, and sure enough, he rolled his eyes.

"Just open it."

Turning the envelope upside down, I watched as the contents fell to the bed covers. It contained paperwork and a few flyers. And airline tickets to Fiji. My eyes widened and I looked over at Tyler who had a massive grin spread across his face.

"I thought we could do with a holiday," he said.

"To Fiji?" I studied the itinerary, frowning slightly when I saw the date. "It's months away."

Tyler pulled himself up in the bed. "You don't think I'd be booking a holiday with any chance you'd still be healing, do you? This way there will be no doubt, and I will be able to do all those naughty and dirty things you've been insisting that you've been thinking about."

Excitement rippled through me. A holiday with Tyler all to myself. "Thank you! I love it, Tyler." The package included rental of a beachfront property with its own secluded beach. It was near a resort, giving the option to dine out, but was also completely private. "It does make my present look rather small in comparison."

"You don't need to get me a thing. I have everything I need right here." He kissed me again. A chaste peck.

I let out a frustrated sigh as I pulled his present out of the bedside cabinet. "Merry Christmas," I said, giving it to him.

Tyler picked at the tape, removing it from the wrapping without causing much damage and slid his fingers along the seam. Immediately my mind went other places and I laughed under my breath at my desperation. Sadie had helped me with his present. I managed to find what I was looking for online but she had to be the one to go pick it up.

"I've been searching for this? Where did you find it?" Tyler turned the album over in his hand, his fingers running reverently over the images that graced it. The edges of the cover had been taped back together and there were some minor tears but Tyler didn't seem to mind. "It's a first press release too."

I shrugged and grinned. It had taken hours of scouring the net but I had managed to find a copy just outside the outskirts of the city. The man hadn't been keen on selling it at first, insisting that he only had listed it as a way to determine its value, but the more I upped my offer the more receptive he became.

"It's perfect. Thank you." He pressed another chaste kiss to my cheek. "I'm putting it on now." Tossing the covers aside, Tyler got out of the bed, his tight arse driving me insane as he walked into the lounge and placed the record on the player. The sultry sounds of jazz drifted through the doorway.

"Did Billie tell you what time she wants us there?" Tyler called out.

"Around one. Dinner's at two."

Tyler's head popped around the corner but the rest of him remained hidden. "Breakfast?"

"What's on offer?"

"Anything you want."

"Anything?"

"Lauren." There was that warning growl again.

"Fine. I'm good with whatever you feel like."

"Waffles it is then," he replied, his head disappearing again.

"Waffles?" I yelled out.

"A client sent me a waffle iron. I have no idea why," he called back. "Figured that now was as good a time as any to try it out." I could hear him rustling in the kitchen. Cupboards opening and closing. "Savoury or sweet?"

"Definitely sweet." I lay back in the bed contemplating whether to get up and join him or grab a little more shut-eye. The thought of a naked Tyler covered in nothing but an apron had me rising from the bed. I may not be able to touch, but I could still look.

* * *

"We're late," I said, glancing at the red glow of the clock in Tyler's car.

"Barely," he replied.

"Billie is going to kill us."

Tyler grinned. "I've already got three missed calls from her."

I fished around in my bag until I felt the familiar smooth surface of my phone and let out a groan when I turned it on. "I've got four."

I had forgotten that I'd never actually been to the main Thornton house. Any time I'd spent with them was at the holiday home and it was considerably less grandiose than this one. A long driveway led to a circle that wrapped around an immaculate garden in front of the house. Made entirely of red brick, the only other colour apart from the dark roof came in the form of cream pillars that framed the entrance. I let out a low whistle as I craned my head towards the window, attempting to take it all in.

"Impressive," I said to Tyler.

"Not really," he replied. "Billie made Dad move into this place after they got married. She said the old house was filled with too many memories of the other women who had lived there. Let's just say that Diana and Lynda had less garish taste than she does."

"Garish?"

Tyler grinned as he pulled to a stop outside the huge garaging beside the house. "You'll see."

Billie opened the door when we rang the bell. Her eyes were wide and her smile was tight as she greeted us. "You made it. Finally."

Tyler sighed, arms laden with Christmas presents. "We're half an hour late, Billie."

"Not according to Lauren's mother, you're not." She grinned at me through clenched teeth. "She insisted you told her to come at eleven."

As if raising the devil himself, Mother appeared behind her. "You did, Lauren. You told me eleven."

I smiled brightly and pushed past Billie, doing my best to ignore the glaring looks she was giving me. "Check your phone. I text the message to you and it said one o'clock."

"Nonsense," Mother scoffed. She pulled her phone from the handbag that she clutched to her side like a security blanket and glared at the screen. "I know how to read, Lauren, and it definitely said, oh." Her voice fell. "Better to be early than late." She raised her eyebrows in my direction.

"Is it, though?" Billie asked, shooting me another smile of wild desperation.

"Merry Christmas, Tyler," my mother cooed, reaching up to grab Tyler's face and press a kiss to his cheek. It was so unlike her. And it still annoyed me.

"Merry Christmas," he said back, throwing a wink my way. "Maybe some reading glasses should be on the Christmas list this year."

Mother laughed, actually laughed, and swatted Tyler's shoulder. If it were anyone else I would swear she was flirting.

"L!" a cry came as my sister entered the room. She hugged me, then held me at arm's length. "You look gorgeous!"

I let a frown pull my brows together. "Are you alright?"

"What do you mean?" she asked before flashing Tyler a grin and calling out, "Merry Christmas."

"You're all happy and peppy and stuff."

Morgan shook her head as though I was talking nonsense and called out to the next room. "Madi? Madi come say hello to your Aunty."

There was no reply.

"Don't bother her," I said. "We'll be in there soon. I'll say hello then. Anything you need help with, Billie?"

Billie now had a glass of wine in her hands and took a large gulp. "Come into the kitchen and see the dessert your mother brought. I had no idea she would bring anything." Her voice was shrill and tight and I couldn't help but stifle a laugh at the thought of someone else having to deal with my mother. It couldn't have happened to a better person.

"Oh my god," Billie said as soon as the kitchen door swung shut. "This is my third glass, Lauren. My third! If I keep going at this pace I'll be in bed by five o'clock, but she drove me to it. I wouldn't have survived without it. Hamish went and locked himself in the office, claiming he had some work to do. Your father and that husband of your sister's have been playing pool in the gaming lounge and that girl has just been sitting there with the gloomiest look on her face, staring at her phone. It's been horrible. Two and a half hours they have been here, Lauren. Two and a half." She took another gulp of wine. "I've been pretending to be busy in the kitchen since twelve, even though the caterers have done everything. Why didn't you answer your phone?" she wailed.

I shrugged, amused by Billie's outburst and reached over the counter to grab a grape off one of the platters. "It was turned off."

Mother must have walked into the kitchen because suddenly a smile stretched over Billie's face and she walked towards the fridge. "Come and look at this wonderful trifle your mother brought." She opened the door and pulled out the dessert. "Stunning, isn't it?"

There was nothing stunning about the trifle. In fact, compared to the other desserts that were stacked into the fridge it was boring and plain.

Billie's smile stretched wider. "I love sherry," she said.

"Oh, it hasn't got any sherry in it," Mother corrected her. "I don't believe in drinking alcohol."

"Really?" Billie's voice almost broke with the highness of her pitch. "Well, I hate to break it to you," Billie chuckled a weirdly deep chuckle, "but drinking alcohol exists whether you believe in it or not."

"What I meant was—"

Billie chuckled that weird sound again, cutting Mother off. "I know what you meant. I was just teasing you." She rolled her eyes in my direction and gave me another look that could only be a cry for help.

I merely grinned back at her. "Speaking of alcohol?" I lifted an eyebrow.

"Yes!" Billie clapped her hands together. "Of course, how rude of me not to offer. Right this way." And she took off out of the kitchen as quickly as her heels would allow.

As soon as we were alone, footsteps clipping across the entranceway, she turned to me. "I have no idea what I'm going to do with that trifle. It simply doesn't match the rest of the menu at all."

"You don't need to do anything other than put it out," I told her.

"But it's going to ruin the look of the table."

It was only as we walked into the main sitting room that I remembered Tyler's remarks on Billie's taste. The walls were white, the floor black. The window dressings were striped black and white and everything else was gold. Everything. Gold couches. Gold cushions on the couches. Gold paintings. Gold. Gold. Gold.

"Wow." I was unsure what else to say. "Everything is very . . . very decadent," I decided on.

"It's amazing, isn't it?"

I just smiled. Tyler's grandparents, Barrett and Annie were seated on the couch and I walked over to embrace them. I didn't visit every fortnight like Tyler did, but I still enjoyed going to see them every month or so, though Annie was beginning to lose her memory a little and sometimes struggled to remember who I was. Still, she was always pleased to see me regardless. Tyler had insisted his father get them out of the nursing home for the day. He also wanted them to be here for when his surprise visitor arrived.

"Aunty L!" Madi looked up from her phone. "When did you get here? Oh!" She looked around the room, her eyes lighting on Tyler. "Tyler's here too." Getting to her feet, she met me in the middle of the room for a hug.

"I told you that L was here, ages ago," Morgan huffed.

Madi plucked the wire hanging around her neck. "Headphones, Morgan."

"Mum," Morgan corrected.

"Leave the girl alone, Morgan," Alistair piped up from the corner. I looked up in surprise and a flush of colour crept over Morgan's cheeks.

"Whatever, Morgan." Madi rolled her eyes and looped her arm through mine. "Is Gabe coming?"

Tyler met my gaze across the room with amusement. He was standing next to my father, both had a bottle of beer in one hand and their other hands stuffed in their pockets.

"Both Gabe and Jake were told to be here at one. If they don't arrive soon, we will be eating without them. I won't have the food getting ruined."

Mother nodded enthusiastically. "Quite agree, Billie. That is your name, isn't it? Billie? I seem to remember you having a different name when you were younger. Didn't she have a different name, Lauren?"

"Yes, it's Billie," Billie replied once again, speaking through gritted teeth.

"Well, I quite agree with you, Billie. You've gone to all this effort to cook Christmas dinner and it shows ungratefulness if they can't even turn up on time."

Billie stretched another smile at my mother. "I must go find Hamish. He's being rude by working when we've got all these guests here. Won't be long."

The door slammed and Gabe walked in. "Merry Christmas!" he called out.

"Gabe!" Madi flew over and wrapped her arms around his shoulders in a tight hug. "Merry Christmas!"

He laughed and pushed her away. "Hey, Madi. Long time no see." He winked and Madi's eyes flew wide, shaking her head desperately, warning him not to say anything of her night out in front of Morgan.

Gabe walked around the room, giving me a quick embrace, shaking Tyler's and Dad's hands and nodding at my mother.

"Clementine," he said with a wicked glint to his eye. "So pleased you could make it. I've missed you."

Mother sort of blinked, unsure what to say, then muttered something about the kitchen and disappeared. When the doorbell rang, Tyler moved to the entrance. "I'll get it."

A small flutter started in my stomach. Tyler had talked with Claudia and organised for Dante to spend a few days with us. This was the first time he would be meeting the Thornton Family. And the first the Thornton's would know of him. I had questioned Tyler's decision, pondering if surprising them on Christmas Day was the best idea, but Tyler had wanted it that way. He wanted his father to have as much warning as he'd had.

Hamish and Billie walked back into the room at the same time Tyler and Dante did. Tyler's arm was slung over the boy's shoulder.

"Lauren!" Dante jerked his head upwards in greeting then walked over to embrace me. "You feeling better now?"

"Almost good as new." I smiled at Tyler over his shoulder and raised my eyebrows, challenging him.

"She's a lot better but not fully healed yet," Tyler corrected.

Hamish had frozen on the other side of the room, his eyes narrowing. There was no mistaking who Dante was. Even the way he walked mimicked Tyler.

"What the fuck?" Gabe had got to his feet and was glancing between Tyler and Dante.

Mother walked back into the room at that exact time and scolded Gabe's language.

"Everyone," Tyler's voice was deep and full of pride. "I'd like to introduce you to Dante, my son."

Billie squealed a little. Mother blinked. Dad shrugged his shoulders and took another mouthful of beer, earning a scowl from Mother. And Gabe strode over to Dante, arms wide.

"No fucking way!" He gripped Dante's shoulders, peering into his face then up at Tyler. "I'm an uncle?"

Hamish had gone pale. Billie was prattling beside him, spluttering questions. Sitting down on the couch, hands calmly grasped and hanging between his knees, Tyler told the story.

Hamish didn't say a word. His eyes locked on Tyler coldly. It was like he couldn't even bear to look at Dante.

"Well," my mother started, "I, for one, think this is a wonderful thing, especially considering that you..." she nodded my way, but Tyler glared at her in warning. Mother laughed nervously. "I think it's wonderful. Congratulations, Tyler."

"Thank you."

Hamish cleared his throat and walked over to place a hand on Tyler's shoulder. "A word." Then he walked out, expecting Tyler to follow.

Somewhere in the room, the baby monitor crackled and Billie jumped a little. "Ollie's up." She went to get him while Gabe and Madi peppered Dante with questions and Annie asked, "Has Gable dyed his hair?" in a loud voice and nodded in Dante's direction.

Barret simply patted her hand and smiled. "Yes."

I'm not sure what was discussed while Tyler and Hamish were out of the room, but when they walked back in, Hamish walked over to Dante and shook his hand stiffly. "Welcome to the family, son."

Tyler sat down beside me and leaned in close. "He was worried about the trust. The fucking family trust." Tyler shook his head.

Billie announced that dinner would be served at two thirty, giving up on Jake's appearance. But as soon as we sat down at the long table, decorated in black, white and gold, Jake entered and quietly took a seat.

"Pleased you could make it," Hamish said.

"Yeah," Jake grinned sheepishly. "Sorry I'm late."

"Where were you?" Billie asked.

Jake shrugged and reached for some ham. "Nowhere, just lost track of time."

"I think the right question would have been, who were you with?" Gabe grinned. He had Ollie in his arms, lifting him up and down and blowing raspberries on his belly.

"I smell gossip," Billie said leaning forward. "Spill."

"You really shouldn't be doing that at the table," my Mother barked at Gabe who poked his tongue out at her before burying his head in Ollie's squishy tummy again and making him chuckle with glee.

Jake muttered, "There's nothing to tell." It was only then that he glanced at the people around the table. A small look of confusion passed over him when his eyes rested on Dante. "Have I missed something?" he asked.

The entire table broke into laughter. Even Hamish. And then Tyler launched into the story once again. I sat back in my chair, food forgotten and looked at my family as they chatted around me, reaching across the table to help themselves to food and drink, Christmas Carols playing in the background.

This was my family. My strange, messed up family, but they were mine. Tyler caught my eye from across the table and smiled. And it was right there in that moment that I knew this was it.

I was his for life.

Epilogue

LAUREN

My eyes were closed.

The sun kissed my skin.

Waves crashed on the beach.

Life was perfect.

We had been on holiday for almost a week and it was heaven. We ate fresh tropical fruit, drank cocktails on the beach and spent a lot of time in bed. We had been attached to a harness and zip-lined down a mountain. We had snorkelled and watched colourful and curious fish. We had been on jet-skis and stand-up paddle boards.

Five months had passed since my accident. I had moved back into Sadie's house, much to Tyler's annoyance, but he didn't protest. We spent some nights squished together in my small bed and others lounging in the expanse of his. But either way, most nights we were together.

I was back at work. Slag had won a few decent contracts and we were going through the process of hiring a graphic designer and web developer to join our team rather than contracting out the work. My recovery had been aided with physio and my crutches had long been discarded.

Tyler had turned thirty-three and we had spent the evening at Maria's with Sadie and Gabe and Jake, laughing and drinking and eating food only Maria could prepare.

Dante had stayed with us many times over the holidays. He and his mother were in negotiations about whether he could board in the city to finish his high school years so he could be closer to Tyler. Tyler had wanted him to live with us, but Claudia was against the idea. Dante had been the one to suggest boarding school as a compromise.

Gabe and Jake had opened their gym and Jake had finally introduced us to a girl he was seeing.

Peta was still busy at the café. Mother and Father were exactly the same, although Mother's blunt manner was beginning to lessen. Madi was talking about coming to the city to go to university. Alistair and Morgan had this weird vibe going on where he had become more assertive, not putting up with her muttered criticisms, and strangely, Morgan always responded to him with heated cheeks and dark eyes. I wasn't sure what was going on. And I wasn't sure if I wanted to.

As I sat with my eyes closed, I realised the pages of Tyler's book had stopped turning. The deckchair he was spread on sighed in protest as he shifted his weight, adjusting his position.

I opened one eye to find him staring at me. He was restless. I had discovered during our holiday that Tyler's ability to relax had a time limit. He was content to sit in the sun but only if he had a book, and only for just over an hour before he dove into the water, took to the paddle board, or approached me with burning lust in his eyes.

He was unaware I was watching as his eyes roamed over my body. I was wearing a white bikini which stood out against my sun-drenched skin. It was small. It was skimpy. I had bought it the day before at one of the shops at the resort just a short stroll down the beach, and it was doing its job beautifully. Even as he was reading, his eyes would skim over me every so often and his tongue would dart out to trace over his lips. I think he was unaware that he was doing it, but I wasn't. My sunglasses gave the perfect disguise for me to be able to watch him.

"Keen for a swim?" he asked, getting to his feet.

I shook my head. "You go ahead though."

He was itching to take me with him, fool around as the waves crashed over us. I could tell by the way he held his hands near his hips, the way he shifted from foot to foot, unsettled, unsure. But there was a reason I said no. I could watch.

Tyler walked towards the ocean, white sand under his feet, blue sky and water glinting in the sun as his backdrop. After a few steps he dove under, then rose to the surface, powerful and muscled arms rising in strokes that took him deeper. I could have stayed like that forever. Just watching him.

But when he came out from the water, wet, glistening, muscled, and divine, it was hunger that pooled within me.

I loved this man.

And he was mine.

Once he was close, he shook his head. Droplets of water landed on me and I squealed with laughter. Lifting my legs from the deckchair, he slid beneath me, my legs now resting over his and wrapped around his waist. His eyes were dark. His intentions clear.

Leaning forward, he gripped a handful of hair in his hand and squeezed, letting the drips of water fall onto my breast, turning the white material translucent. My nipple, now hard and peaked, stood out prominently. "I think I like this one," he said, hooking under the strap on my shoulder, and running his finger down until he reached the soft flesh of my breast. Pushing the strap to the side a little, he groaned when my pale skin was exposed. He loved my tan lines. The little strips of white that ran over my shoulders. The perfect triangle patches that covered my nipples but not the full swell of my breasts. The thicker lines that graced my hips. And the slip of white over my bare sex. He had groaned the first time I stood bare for him. Groaned, and fell to his knees, grabbing the cheeks of my backside and dragging me close until his face was pressed against me.

"But as much as I like it, I think you should remove it." Tyler's voice was husky as he ran his finger up and down the strap of my bikini. Then both his hands reached behind me and tugged at the tied bow on my neck. The straps fell. Tyler grabbed one between his teeth, pulling it down until my breast was exposed.

"Fuck," he said slowly and with gravel in his tone. "Am I ever going to get used to the sight of you?"

Hooking his hand under my thigh, he slid me closer and lowered his head to my nipple. I expected to feel moisture. The velvety softness of his tongue against my skin, but instead, his teeth scraped over my nipple, pulling it into his mouth as he applied pressure. I hissed. Or moaned. Some sound fell out of my mouth, rising up from the depths of my being.

Removing the top of my bikini completely, Tyler took both my breasts in his hands, flesh spilling between his fingers. Through the thin material of his bathing shorts, his hardness pushed against me and I writhed, grinding into him as he had me open and pressed against him. Taking each nipple between his thumbs and forefingers, he twisted and pangs of pain and pleasure rippled through me.

"Open your eyes," Tyler commanded. "Look at me."

I opened them and looked into his eyes. Lust licked his irises. His mouth was held slightly open, chest rising and falling with need.

Lightning crackled in the distance. Thunder peeled across the sky. Tyler pinched again and my chest rose towards him. Pulling me closer, Tyler's mouth crushed against mine as I wrapped my legs tightly around his waist, pushing my pelvis into his, relishing the delicious steel of his hardness.

His hands were in my hair. Wrapped around my neck. Running feverishly over my back. Clutching the generosity of my breasts. Cupping my backside and digging painfully into my flesh.

His mouth trailed down my neck, sucking and pulling. My head fell back in ecstasy. The heavens opened and rain fell as a sheet around us. But Tyler barely noticed. He was too intent on devouring me, pulling every moan, every intake of breath, every seductive sound out of my body.

Lying me back onto the deckchair, he moved from under me and tore at the lower half of my bikini, tossing it aside. Then he released himself and stalked towards me, completely and utterly naked. My mouth watered with anticipation.

"Open," he said in that deep growl that weakened me.

Rain poured over him, over me. It danced over our skin, hot and cold at the same time. It ran in rivulets down his chest and tripped over the undulations of his body.

"What if someone sees?" I asked, my voiced hushed with desire.

"Then they will be very jealous. Now open," he said again, reaching down to grip my chin and pull my mouth open. "It's a private beach," he added, noting my hesitation. He licked his lips, then sucked his lower one between his teeth. A shudder of need trembled through me and I rose to my knees and took him in my mouth. Tyler let out a groan of pleasure and wrapped his hands into my hair, pulling it back from my face and gathering it in his hand.

I let out a gasp of surprise when he pushed to the back of my throat. Moisture slid down my legs. I was hungry for him. I needed him. Wanted him. Ached for him.

He rocked his hips back and forth as he pulled my hair tighter and tighter, until that lick of pain that sent shivers slicing through me danced across my scalp. He grew thicker in my mouth and I struggled to contain him, pulling back when I needed to breathe. His hands ran over my face and he dipped his thumb between my lips, breathing in sharply when I pressed it between my teeth.

"Lie back," he instructed.

I did as I was told and he stalked forward, lowering to his knees and taking his place between my thighs. He used his hands first, massaging my inner thigh, teasing me by rising higher and higher only to retreat when I wanted him the most. And then his mouth was on me. And again, instead of the smoothness of his tongue, it was his teeth that nipped gently at me. I panted. I squirmed. I dug my hands into his hair and pulled him closer.

I was lost in rapture. Rain poured over the parts of my body not covered by him, sending needles of pleasure across every inch. Tyler's mouth was desperation, kissing, licking, sucking and biting. Thunder rumbled again and I felt it in the very depths of my soul.

"I need to be inside you."

And then he was. Pushing against my entrance and slipping deep inside, Tyler let out a guttural moan of restraint as he held himself still, allowing me to feel the fullness of him. Then his hands gripped my thighs and he pulled out, only the tip of him pressed against me before plunging back in. Releasing his grasp on my thighs, he rose over me, eyes searching mine as he rocked back and forth. His hand reached behind my head and drew my mouth to his, ravenous.

My pants increased with his movement. His mouth was feverish. His hands needily dug into me. My orgasm rose quickly, exploding with such a force I cried out, letting both the rain and Tyler's cry of completion slip down my throat.

He slumped, still inside me, and I clung to him as our chests rose and fell in unison. "I love you," I whispered against his ear. His reply was to press his mouth against mine with lethargic satisfaction.

Untangling his body, Tyler got to his feet, his spent cock hanging between his legs, still slightly firm and heavy. He stretched high into the air and even though I was completely and utterly sated, my eyes still trailed over him, the word 'mine' whispering through my mind.

Holding his palms out to the pouring rain, Tyler's eyes searched the beach. "I guess we'd better head back inside." His eyes stopped on me. I was still naked, stretched out on the deck chair in lazy abandon. His head cocked to the side. "Unless…" He grinned wickedly.

I sat up quickly, Tyler's eyes glued to where my breasts swayed with the movement, and stretched to my tiptoes to kiss him, feeling the tenderness between my legs. "Later," I said, over my shoulder as I picked up my now soaked beach-dress and slipped it over my head.

As suddenly as the rain had started, it stopped. After covering himself with some shorts, Tyler gathered our belongings in one hand and took mine with the other. As we walked up the beach to the little track that led to the house, the clouds began to dissipate, revealing the amber glow of the sun as it spread over the water.

Everything was perfect. Well, almost.

I glanced up at Tyler, nervous butterflies in my stomach and took a deep breath. "You know that question you asked me when we met Dante for the first time?"

Tension seeped into Tyler's movements and he looked at me sideways. "Yes?" he said with a question framing his expression.

"I think you should ask it again."

About the Author

Sabre Rose writes about love and lust. Flawed people in messy relationships. Happiness and heartbreak. Loyalty and betrayal.

With stories as unpredictable as they are steamy and intense, Sabre draws you into the lives of her characters and their complicated families.

The ideas floating around her head range from delightful to dark, so sign up to her newsletter at
www.subscribepage.com/sabrerose
to keep up to date with her latest news and releases.

Social Media:
www.facebook.com/sabreroseauthor
www.twitter.com/sabreroseauthor

Website:
www.sabreroseauthor.com

Email:
sabreroseauthor@gmail.com

Other books in the Series

Touched (Thornton Brothers 1)

Tempted (Thornton Brothers 2)

Taken (Thornton Brothers 3)

Printed in Great Britain
by Amazon